Sometimes love strikes when you least expect it. . . .

Welcome Venable was having a blast. To the bittersweet rhythm of the music, she moved and dipped and stamped and yipped until she felt she would weep with the joy of the dance. Losing herself in the emotion of the movement, she became one with the moment, the motion, and the friends who surrounded her. She danced on until she thought her heart would burst.

"Man! Did you see that woman?" Shark asked.

"See her? Hell, I feel like I've been run over by a Peterbilt truck loaded with bananas."

That was an understatement. The minute Wade had spotted her, something had come over him, a feeling of such intensity that for a minute he was sure he was having a heart attack. He'd never felt anything like it. And the more he watched the redhead dance, the more powerful the feeling became. His guts were turned inside out, and he wanted her—in fact, he was horny as hell. But his reaction hadn't been just a case of raging testosterone; his testosterone had been raging since he was fourteen. This was something different. Something—hell, he didn't know—something . . . profound.

"Man, what's the matter with you? You look like you been hit up beside the head with an axe handle."

Wade blew out a breath and nodded toward the woman dancing. "She's the matter with me. The redhead."

Shark grinned. "Fine-looking woman. You planning on gettin' you a piece of that?"

"Watch your mouth, my friend. That's the woman I'm gonna marry." Wade's gut tightened. "I've been waiting for her."

Shark took another swig of

"Believe it. That lady is m

Shark let out a low whistl

ing."

Wade smiled. "She will be

FOR THE VERY BEST IN ROMANCE—
DENISE LITTLE PRESENTS!

AMBER, SING SOFTLY   (0038, $4.99)
by Joan Elliott Pickart
Astonished to find a wounded gun-slinger on her doorstep, Amber
Prescott can't decide whether to take him in or put him out of his misery.
Since this lonely frontierswoman can't deny her longing to have a man
of her own, she nurses him back to health, while savoring the glorious
possibilities of the situation. But what Amber doesn't realize is that this
strong, handsome man is full of surprises!

A DEEPER MAGIC   (0039, $4.99)
by Jillian Hunter
From the moment wealthy Margaret Rose and struggling physician Ian
MacNeill meet, they are swept away in an adventure that takes them
from the haunted land of Aberdeen to a primitive, faraway island—and
into a world of danger and irresistible desire. Amid the clash of ancient
magic and new science Margaret and Ian find themselves falling help-
lessly in love.

SWEET AMY JANE   (0050, $4.99)
by Anna Eberhardt
Her horoscope warned her she'd be dealing with the wrong sort of man.
And private eye Amy Jane Chadwick was used to dealing with the wrong
kind of man, due to her profession. But nothing prepared her for the
gorgeously handsome Max, a former professional athlete who is being
stalked by an obsessive fan. And from the moment they meet, sparks
fly and danger follows!

MORE THAN MAGIC   (0049, $4.99)
by Olga Bicos
This classic romance is a thrilling tale of two adventurers who set out
for the wilds of the Arizona territory in the year 1878. Seeking treasure,
an archaeologist and an astronomer find the greatest prize of all—love.

*Available wherever paperbacks are sold, or order direct from the
Publisher. Send cover price plus 50¢ per copy for mailing and
handling Penguin USA, P.O. Box 999, c/o Dept. 17109,
Bergenfield, NJ 07621. Residents of New York and Tennessee
must include sales tax. DO NOT SEND CASH.*

ANGEL HOURS

Jan Hudson

PINNACLE BOOKS
KENSINGTON PUBLISHING CORP.

PINNACLE BOOKS are published by

Kensington Publishing Corp.
850 Third Avenue
New York, NY 10022

Pinnacle and the P logo Reg. U.S. Pat. & TM Off.

First Printing: October, 1996

Printed in the United States of America
10 9 8 7 6 5 4 3 2 1

For Denise Little, editor and angel extraordinaire,
for all those other angels who, through the ages, have
given me love, support, advice, and laughter:
From Alex, Anice, and Arnette
to Zelda,
and for the "naughty Grecian girls" who
became Elsie's pearls.
Efharistó, paréa.

I have found power in the mysteries of thought,
exaltation in the chanting of the Muses;
I have been versed in the reasonings of men;
but Fate is stronger than anything I have known.

Euripides
c. 485-406 B.C.

Prologue

But the bravest are surely those who have the clearest vision of what is before them, glory and danger alike, and yet notwithstanding go out to meet it.

Thucydides
c. 460-400 B.C.

Los Angeles, late January

Juiced on adrenaline, Wade Morgan struggled to block out the roar of the crowd and concentrate totally on the most important play of his career.

Third and goal. This was it. Only eight yards stood between the L.A. Vulcans and a Super Bowl victory. They were down by four points with eleven seconds to go.

Wade had to make it. He had to. He was thirty-seven years old and had been plagued with injuries all year. Olmstead, that hot-shot fancy dancer who'd been the Vulcan's first round draft pick, was nipping at his heels for the starting position. Be damned if he was going to let that happen. He had another good year or two in him.

Poised behind the center, his hands ready for the snap, Wade ground his teeth, took a deep breath, and began to bark the cadence.

Driver snapped the ball into Wade's hands. He turned left to hand off to Frederick.

Sonofabitch! Frederick wasn't there.

Before he could react, a feminine voice whispered in his ear, "Sweetie, roll out to your right," and, hell, that was as good an option as any. He rolled out right.

There wasn't a receiver in sight, but oddly enough, a hole the size of his swimming pool opened up immediately in front of him. Tasting victory and a hero's acclaim, he tucked the ball against his side and charged through the gap in the line.

Suddenly, Spoiler Swenceski, beefy arms outstretched, materialized in his path, and Wade felt his hopes sucked into a black void. Then as the time clock clicked to zero, everything seemed to decelerate into slow motion. Swenceski tripped over his own feet, and all two hundred and ninety pounds of him went sprawling onto the turf. Wade hurdled over the tackle's prone body into the end zone.

"Yes!" he shouted as he thrust the ball aloft.

The crowd went wild. Pandemonium erupted in the stands and on the field.

Yelling and laughing wildly, the Vulcans hugged and slapped and jumped and jostled. Drunk with victory, Wade's teammates hoisted him onto their shoulders and carried him to the sideline.

Later in the locker room, champagne flowing and men whooping and hollering, Robb, a battle-scarred veteran, grinned and gave Wade a high five. "Man, you're one lucky son of a bitch. I've never seen anything like that. Looked like Spoiler took a dive. What happened?"

Wade shot him a cocky grin in return and shrugged. "Damned if I know. Must've been my guardian angel hanging tough."

One

Zeus does not bring all men's plans to fulfillment.

Homer, *The Iliad*
c. 700 B.C.

Paris, April

"Hi there, sugar plum."

The maître d's eyebrows shot up and his lips pursed. But when he turned and recognized the patron, a smile escaped from his deep-freeze mouth and a twinkle came into his eyes. *"Bonjour,* Mademoiselle Welcome," he said, bowing slightly.

"Bonjour, yourself, Henri," Welcome Venable said, deliberately exaggerating her Texas drawl and flashing him a broad grin. She snapped a yellow rose from the armful she carried and fitted the bud into his lapel. "Isn't it a glorious day? How's that new granddaughter of yours? Growing like a weed, I'll bet, and absolutely gorgeous."

His chest swelling noticeably, he beamed and kissed his fingertips. Ordinarily Henri was a reserved man, as was befitting to his position, but he fell under Welcome's spell as other men invariably did. "Monsieur Moreau had already arrived and is seated. This way, Mademoiselle Welcome."

Welcome and Eduard Moreau frequently lunched atop the Théâtre des Champs-Elysées or at the nearby Plaza since both places were convenient to her offices. But even if she hadn't been well known as a patron, in all likelihood she would have been recognized as "somebody" anyway. As she crossed the expanse of the rooftop restaurant in the heart of the Golden Triangle, the luxury-shop-laden neighborhood which was home to most of Paris's couturiers, heads turned to watch her.

A stunning woman with long, flawless legs and a riot of rich red hair that tumbled over her shoulders in lively disarray, she had graced the runways of the best couturiers and the covers of the world's most prestigious fashion magazines for the past ten years. Even blasé Parisians couldn't resist the magnetic lure of her presence when she entered a room. She had that certain something that was difficult to define and impossible to cultivate, an innate charisma.

Welcome knew the effect she had on people; she capitalized on it, milked it dry. Hell, even though it had gotten damned old lately, it had been her bread and butter. For the past several years, she'd had a ball and made a shit-pot full of money off of being an exhibitionist—and socked away the biggest part of it. She had enough money now that she never had to work another day in her life if she didn't want to.

She'd come a long way since she'd been left on that doorstep in Athens, Texas.

But today there was an extra spring to her step, a more dazzling radiance to her smile. Her effervescence seemed contagious as she exuberantly distributed yellow roses to various people who sat at tables along her path. For those who were startled by her behavior, she added a wink or a sultry chuckle. To several acquaintances in the room, she wiggled her fingers and called out, "Hi there, sugar. How ya doing?"

By the time she reached her destination, the entire room had caught her mood. Diners smiled indulgently, and the atmosphere buzzed with a new energy and excitement.

This was *Welcome*. She needed only one name.

Eduard Moreau stood waiting for her. He too smiled indulgently. Tall and slender, impeccably dressed in business attire, Eduard was a handsome man, the epitome of generations of superb French breeding. He had the fine manners, easy grace, and quiet confidence that come with old family and old money. He was darned near perfect. In the five or more years that she'd known him, Welcome couldn't recall even hearing him belch. Sometimes she wondered if he ever did.

And, try as she might, she couldn't imagine Eduard eating juicy barbecued ribs with his hands and licking the sauce off his fingers. The truth was: for all his perfection, Eduard was . . . well, he was downright stuffy. And measured by the good ole boys she had grown up with, sort of a wimp. While she was very fond of him, she'd never managed to fall in love with him, which was just as well as things were now.

"This is for you, sugarplum." She tapped his nose with a rose, then handed it to him. "The last one's for me."

He chuckled and reached across to kiss her cheek. "Ah, *chérie*, you never cease to amaze and delight me. You captivate us all."

She shot him a cocky grin. "That's the name of the game, sweetie. The secret is to remember that it *is* a game and not get too carried away with yourself. Fame is fleeting, especially in my business and when you're on the downhill side of thirty."

"*Chére amie,* you'll be forever young. You grow more beautiful every year."

She laughed. "Spoken like a true Frenchman. Lord a'mercy, you're good for my ego."

After they were seated and wine was poured for Welcome, Eduard said, "You seem especially cheerful today. Did the roses make you so happy? Who sent them?"

Even though his questions seemed casual, she heard the slight edge of jealousy in his tone. This wasn't going to be easy. "The roses are from Margot. She knows how I love them."

"From your assistant?" He raised his brows slightly. "Is there some special occasion that I've missed?"

"We'll discuss it later." She picked up her menu. "Right now I'm starving. Let's order."

"What would you like?"

"What I would *like,*" she said twirling her rose against her chin, "is a humongous chicken-fried steak and a big bowl of cream gravy thick enough to stand a spoon in."

Looking amused, Eduard glanced at her over his menu. "I doubt that chicken-fried steak is in the chef's repertoire."

"I'd bet my last tube of lipstick on it. Reckon I'll settle for the lamb."

While Eduard ordered, she stared out the window at the landmarks of the city that had captivated her all those years ago. Paris wasn't nearly as exciting as it used to be. Now she wished that the river below was the Trinity instead of the Seine and that the Eiffel Tower was a Texas oil derrick.

The world of high fashion had totally lost its appeal. She had grown tired of being a celebrity, of living in a fishbowl. She wanted to go home and lead a normal life. She wanted . . . well, she wasn't exactly sure what she wanted, but it wasn't continuing this superficial existence among strangers.

Nor was it Eduard.

Something tugged at her insides, urging her to get on with life instead of merely frittering away her days with shallow, though lucrative, projects.

"And now," Eduard said when the waiter was gone, "tell me the reason for your gaiety."

"I'm retiring my false eyelashes and hot rollers and getting out of the business. I've even sold Bienvenue les Femmes. I signed the papers only an hour ago."

"You've sold your model agency? I must say that surprises me. But I'm delighted. You've always worked much too hard." He reached across the table and laid his hand over hers. "Does this mean that you might at last consider my proposal? You've always said that you were too involved in business to pay proper attention to a husband and family."

Welcome had known this was coming. Trying to find a way to let him down gently, she'd practiced dozens of answers. None of them were quite right. She took a deep breath and patted his hand. "Sweetie, I'm homesick. I'm going back to Texas."

"I suppose I could learn to like Texas, at least for a part of the year."

She shook her head. "I don't think you'd fit in where I'm going. It's . . . very provincial."

A painfully long pause hung in the air. A slight ripple of jaw muscle was the only indication that Eduard was affected by her announcement. Finally he said quietly, "I take it that your plans don't include me."

"No."

"I see. Then you won't consider marriage to me under any circumstance?"

"No, Eduard. I'm sorry." She patted his hand again. "You know that I'm very fond of you, but I don't think a marriage between us would work out. I've always told you that."

"Is there nothing I can say to change your mind?" When she shook her head, he asked, "When are you leaving Paris?"

"Tomorrow."

His forehead wrinkled. "So soon?"

"Yes. But I plan to spend a couple of weeks in Greece before I fly back to the States. I've never been there, you know. I can't imagine how I've missed it, and I've always wanted to visit."

"I know the country well. I could come along to act as guide."

Welcome shook her head again. "Sorry, sugarplum, but my friend Meri Gabrey is meeting me there on business. Her husband is opening a posh new hotel in Athens, and we're shooting the photos for the brochure. It will be my last professional job."

"Ah . . . I see. Well . . ." He averted his eyes and smoothed the napkin in his lap. "Ah, here is our lunch."

Despite their best efforts, the rest of the meal was awkward. When they had finished, Eduard escorted her from the restaurant.

"May I drop you somewhere?" he asked.

"Thanks, but it's such a lovely day, I think I'll walk home."

"May I see you tonight?"

She brushed an imaginary speck from his lapel. "I have to pack."

"So this is all I receive? An *au revoir* on the street?"

"Eduard, sweetie, I've told you a dozen times that I'm not cut out to be the sort of wife that you want, that our relationship was temporary with no strings. You said that you accepted those terms. We'll always be friends."

His demeanor remained pleasant except for his eyes. They went hard. "Is there someone else?"

"No. No one else." She kissed his cheek. *"Au revoir, mon ami.* I'll be in touch." She turned and strode away.

Feeling like a dirty dog, Welcome walked the blocks to her apartment quickly, failing to enjoy the sunny day or the blossoming trees. Guilt clung to her shoulders and dragged down her mood. Was there a way to have broken the news to Eduard more gently? No, she decided. He had no reason to expect more of her. She'd told him time and time again that there would be no marriage, no lasting commitment between them.

Hells bells! Why was she feeling so damned guilty?

For all his politeness and gentle manners, Eduard Moreau was a manipulative devil. She would have respected him more if he'd raised hell, yelled and cussed a little—shown some honest emotion—instead of being so damned *civilized.* God, she was so sick of these mincing, slick continental types. Give her a straight-up, in-your-face American male any day of the week. She wanted a man with more balls than she had—if there was one—a man who wasn't too prissy to scratch when he itched.

Just as she rounded the corner at her street, someone called out her name from the sidewalk cafe across from her building. She turned and spotted a tall, blond man waving to her.

Philip Van Horn.

She waved back and crossed the street to join him. "What are *you* doing back in Paris, Philip? I thought you'd been reassigned to Cairo."

"I've come to see you, my love," he said, catching her hands in his and kissing her cheek. "Let's run away together."

Welcome rolled her eyes. "Yeah. Sure." Besides being *very* married, Philip worked for the U.S. govern-

ment. He hung out at the American embassy and had
one of those titles that sounded like a CIA cover—
which, in fact it was. Although he would never admit
it, Welcome knew that he was an agent, and he knew
that she knew. She had, from time to time, done small
favors for him. She wondered what he wanted now.

"Join me for coffee?" he asked, signaling for the
waiter before she had time to answer.

They chatted until their coffee was served. When
they were alone again, Welcome said, "Now tell me
why you're really here."

He smiled. "I understand that you're leaving tomorrow for Athens."

"And exactly how did you know that?" She quickly
held up a hand, palm out. "Disregard that. I forgot
that you have a crystal ball down at the embassy."

"Clever lady." His smile broadened. "What are your
plans?"

"I plan to veg out for a few days, maybe do some
sightseeing, then Meri Gabrey is meeting me, and
we're going to do a shoot for one of her husband
Ram's new hotels. This will be my swan song as a
model."

"You're giving it up?"

"Yep. I'm going to mosey on back to my ranch down
in Texas and punch some cows."

Philip burst into laughter. "Punch some cows? You?"

"Yes, me. What's so funny about that? I grew up on
the ranch. I can ride and shoot and spit with the best
of them. Don't get on my bad side, sweetie, or I might
not run your little errand."

"What errand?"

"The one you've come to ask me to do." She leaned
forward and whispered, "You're really a lousy spy,
Philip. I can read you like a book."

"A spy? Me? Where did you get such a ridiculous

idea? But speaking of errands, since you're going to be in the neighborhood, I was hoping that you could make a small delivery to a friend in Athens. It shouldn't take more than half an hour of your time." He pulled a box from his pocket. Wrapped in silver paper and tied with gold cord, the package was about the size of a small paperback book.

"What's inside? Won't I need to declare the package with customs?"

"Inside is a gold coin bracelet. I think you'll find it very attractive. Wear it on your trip along with a few other bangles. I don't think you'll need to declare it. At noon on the day after you arrive in Athens, go to a shop in Plaka—the old part of the city—and tell the proprietor that you would like to speak with Miklos about some glassware. When you are directed to Miklos, he will tell you that he deals only in antiquities, then give him the bracelet, and that's it."

"Sounds simple enough. Exactly where is the shop?"

"Not far from the Acropolis. Plaka is an old district in Athens, reminiscent of the Left Bank here or the French Quarter in New Orleans. The name of the shop and its address are inside the package."

"Is the bracelet valuable?"

"It's worth a tidy sum, and it isn't insured. Don't lose it."

"Who is Miklos?"

Philip looked amused. "You know better than to ask that. Let's just say that he's a very good friend of my Uncle Samuel."

She picked up the yellow rosebud lying beside her cup and sniffed the fragrant petals. "And what do I get out of this?"

One corner of his mouth lifted in a wry expression. "The same thing you always do—a buzz."

Welcome chuckled. "You know me too well." She

tapped his nose with the rosebud as she added, "But don't forget the flowers." Philip always sent a mammoth bouquet after she did him a favor. She tucked the package into her handbag, stood, and prepared to leave.

"Where will you be staying?" Philip asked.

"At the Grande Bretagne on Syntagma Square."

"Ah, the GB, my favorite hotel in Athens. It is superb, one of *the* grand hotels in Europe. Insist on a suite on the sixth floor facing the square—they're prime. I envy you. I wish I were going along."

"Then why don't you go and deliver the bracelet to Miklos yourself?"

"Because—let us say that my face is too well known."

Amused, Welcome said, "And mine's not?"

He gave her a broad wink and pressed a kiss into her palm. "We are known for different things."

"No doubt. Well, don't worry about your little trinket. I'll take care of it for you." She kissed his cheek and told him good-bye.

Welcome started across the street to her building, her mind on the tons of details she had to tend to before she left Paris.

"Dammit, woman!" a deep voice bellowed. "Watch out!"

A strong arm hooked her around the middle and flung her backward a millisecond before a speeding car roared past, a car that would have struck her.

Too stunned to cry out, she landed on her butt against a door, and conked the back of her head on the hard wood. Her vision blurred, and speckles danced before her eyes. She could see only the faint image of a broad-shouldered, fair-haired man, but she heard him clearly as he shouted in her face, "Dammit, don't you know you could have been buzzard bait?"

Philip helped her to her feet. "Are you all right?" He picked up her purse and handed it to her.

Welcome blinked her eyes, and her vision cleared. She rubbed the back of her head and her bottom, then twisted her shoulders, testing for injury. "Other than having the bejesus scared out of me, I think so. Just shaken up. Thanks for jerking me out of the way. In another second I really would have been road kill."

"I didn't jerk you out of the way," Philip said.

"You didn't?" She frowned and looked around. "Then where's the man who did?" No one else was near. She saw nothing except the yellow rose smashed flat in the middle of the street.

"I didn't see anybody. You just sort of zipped backward and fell."

"But I heard—"

"You heard?"

"Never mind," Welcome said, waving off the subject. "You wouldn't believe it if I told you."

Los Angeles

Wade Morgan bolted upright, his heart beating wildly. The room was dark and it took a minute for him to realize where he was—in his own bed at home.

A dream. He'd had a dream. He couldn't remember what it had been about, but a sense of danger lingered in the edge of his consciousness. He shook his head and swiped his face with his hand.

Glancing at his bedside clock, he saw from the red digital numbers that it wasn't yet six A.M. He groaned and flopped back on his pillow. After the late night he'd had, no way was he getting up at that hour.

He rolled over and drifted back to sleep.

Two

The moon had set, and the Pleiades; it is midnight, and time passes, and I sleep alone.

Sappho
c. 612 B.C.

Paris

The telephone was ringing as Welcome unlocked the door to her apartment. "Just step over the boxes," she told Philip as she hurried inside. "Let me get that call." She barked her shin on a packing crate and yelped as she snatched up the phone. "Hello. Hello."

"Where is the alcohol?" Philip asked. "The bathroom?"

"Off my bedroom, on the right. Hello. Hello." Damn, she'd missed the call. She dropped the receiver back into the cradle and followed Philip, kicking off her shoes as she went. "I think you're making too much of a little bump and a scratch."

"Humor me, my dear. If you won't go to the hospital, at least let me do a little first aid. Sit down here at your dressing table. Did I ever tell you that I almost became a doctor? To my mother's great sorrow, I left med school after one year. All those cadavers unhinged me. Bend your head over."

"Ouch, that stings."

The telephone began to ring again, and Welcome started to rise to answer it. Philip stayed her with a hand to her shoulder.

"Hold that pad against your head," he said. "I'll get the phone." He strode to the bedside table. "Hello. Hello." He frowned and spoke more loudly. "Hello." He shrugged and hung up. "Nobody there." Before he'd taken two steps, it rang again. He answered. After a moment he laughed. "Meri, this is Philip Van Horn. I haven't seen you or Ram for a while. How are you?"

Welcome rose and moved to the side of her bed. After a few pleasantries with Meri, Philip handed her the receiver. "Meri Gabrey calling from Cairo. It's a poor connection."

"Hi, sweetie."

"Hi, yourself. I've had the very devil trying to get hold of you."

"Well, you've got me now. What's up?"

"I've got good news and bad news."

"What's the good news?" Static fried and crackled on the line, drowning out Meri's reply. "Say again, sweetie. I didn't hear you."

"I'm pregnant!"

Welcome let out a whoop. "Fantastic! Does this mean I get to be a godmother?"

"Looks that way. But now I won't be able to meet you in Athens to do the brochure. Are you going to kill me? I wanted to see you and do the shoot, but you know how overprotective Ram is, and he went totally wild at the notion of my traveling right now."

Welcome laughed. "I can imagine. He's going to be a basket case until this baby is born, but he's right about your going to Greece at this stage. I'd never forgive myself if anything went wrong. I'm sure that Ram feels the same way."

"How do you want to handle the job? I suppose that

we can subcontract it to another agency, but I'd really like to keep control and for you to be the model. I'm sorry for the mess."

"Don't worry about it, Meri. The important thing is for you to take care of yourself and my godchild. I know several photographers who will jump at the chance to do this. I'll find someone and tend to everything. Don't worry yourself one little bit. And if you feel like putting me up, I'll plan to detour for a visit on my way back to the States."

"We'd love to have you. I was looking forward to spending time with you in Athens. Are you sure you don't mind my leaving you holding the bag with the brochure?"

"Under the circumstances, not a bit," Welcome said. "I'll have whichever photographer I can arrange give you a call about details. Is that okay?"

"Whatever I can do to help. I feel so guilty about this."

"Come on, sweetie. A few pictures can't compare to a baby."

The static began spitting again, and the connection broke entirely. Familiar with the vagaries of the Egyptian phone system, Welcome made a disgusted noise and hung up. "Oh, heck," she said to Philip, "Greece won't be nearly as exciting without Meri along."

Los Angeles

Wade Morgan grunted, slapped off the alarm, and rolled out of bed. He stretched, yawned, and scratched his chest where the tawny-colored hair was beginning to gray. Hobbling until he could work the kinks out of his stiff knees, he headed for the bathroom.

He flipped on the light switch, said, "Mornin', Red,"

and patted the bottom of the bikini-clad redhead in the picture hanging beside the switch. It was a ten-year-old ritual, almost as automatic as breathing. He didn't know the model in the picture—a page torn from a swimsuit edition of *Sports Illustrated*—but she was his lucky charm. And damned gorgeous. The first time he'd seen that photograph, something funny clicked inside him. He'd been in a hot and heavy relationship with a starlet named Bambi at the time, so he stuck the magazine under his socks.

When he and Bambi fizzled, he'd had the picture framed. A time or two he'd thought about trying to find out the redhead's name and look her up, then reneged. Better to keep the fantasy than to find out that she had a Brooklyn accent, a horse laugh, and the I.Q. of a boll weevil.

As he finger-combed his thick mane, he frowned into the mirror. Those weren't sun-streaks he saw in his hair. Those were silver threads among the gold. And the crow's feet at the corner of his eyes seemed to get deeper by the day. He wasn't a vain person, but Wade knew that his age was beginning to show. And football was a young man's game.

A few minutes later, he'd pulled on sweats and was tying his shoestrings when Shark stuck his head in the door. "You up?" Shark's broad, familiar smile wrinkled his ebony face.

"Up to no good," Wade answered. Their exchange was another ritual, one older than the picture. He and Shark went way back. They'd grown up together, dirt poor, in Athens, Georgia. They'd played football together in junior high and in high school, then gone on to Georgia Tech together with Shark as center and Wade as quarterback. Shark hadn't made it into the pros. In fact, he hadn't made it out of Georgia Tech. Shark had been through some really bad times before he and Wade hooked up again. Now he lived in an apartment by the pool and was Wade's bodyguard, personal trainer, and cook—when he could get around Corazon, who insisted that the kitchen was part of her domain.

"Let's move it," Shark said, clapping his hands. "We're gonna do five miles this morning before we do an hour on the weights."

Wade groaned. Sometimes Shark took his job too seriously.

Wade and Shark sat in the spa with jets of steamy water massaging tired muscles and turning them lazy.

"Why does it seem to get harder every spring?" Wade asked.

" 'Cause it *is* harder," Shark said. "You and me ain't kids anymore. You thinking any about hanging it up?"

"Not on your life. I'm a long way from ready to retire. Barney's nearly got a new three-year contract sewed up with the front office—and with a hefty increase." Wade laced his fingers behind his head and leaned back. "Me retire? And do what? Raise peanuts on some Georgia farm? No way. I want to be the Vulcan's quarterback, and I want to win another Super Bowl ring. Hell, I'll admit that I like being somebody and living high on the hog."

Shark's grin flashed. "And you like the women."

One corner of Wade's mouth lifted. "That, too."

They sat in silence for a several minutes, half dozing, letting the jets loosen the kinks.

"Shark?"

"Huh?"

"You ever been to Athens?"

"Hell, man, you and me was born there."

"I don't mean Athens, Georgia. I mean Athens, Greece."

"Nope. Never been. Why you asking?"

"I've been thinking about it all morning. It's the funniest thing. I can't get it out of my mind."

Shark lifted his head from the rim of the spa and frowned. "Can't get what out of your mind?"

"Athens, Greece. Craziest thing. I've got a powerful urge to pack up and go there. Right now. A powerful urge pulling at my insides. Does that sound peculiar to you?"

"Some." Shark laid his head back. After a few minutes silence he said, "When we going?"

"How about tomorrow?"

"You take off to Greece in the middle of contract negotiations, Barney's gonna have a fit."

"You're right," Wade said. "It was a stupid idea."

Three

O bright and violet-crowned and famed in song, bul-wark of Greece, famous Athens, divine city!

Pindar
518-438 B.C.

Athens

Feeling giddy with anticipation and dressed for spying, Welcome slipped the Athens travel guide, along with the directions from the concierge, into the pocket of her trench coat, snapped down the brim of the fedora that hid her hair, and crossed the monumental marble lobby of the GB, heading for the front door of the hotel. In truth, her outfit—including sweatshirt and jeans—was more a concession to the cool mistiness of the morning rather than to her mission, but the tan trench coat, oversized sunglasses, and hat did seem a great joke.

Too, the disguise would help her elude the ever-present paparazzi or star-struck teenaged girls giggling and begging for her autograph or for tips on getting into the business. That part of her life was over, thank God. She would be glad to trade prominence for privacy.

As she hurried down the steps and across Constitution Square, a flurry of pigeons made a wake ahead of her.

Although she had a couple of hours until her noon appointment, Welcome had started out early to allow herself time to locate the shop in Plaka, then do some browsing in the colorful area at the base of the Acropolis.

The Acropolis.

Her step faltered, and she turned to look up toward the hill and the columned ruins atop it. An odd sensation squeezed at her heart and made her breath catch. The hill and the temple seemed so familiar.

Hauntingly familiar. Yet totally strange.

If she squinted her eyes slightly, it almost seemed as if she could picture the temple in its original glory: gleaming white columns instead of pitted ones, a wooden ceiling with gilded and brightly painted panels and topped with a sloping tile roof rather than a gaping hole. She could have sworn that she saw the sun flash off the huge bronze figure of Athena that once stood on the summit. For the space of half a heartbeat, glorious statues with ivory-smooth skin graced the empty niches, then disappeared.

The feeling was eerie. Creepy.

She shook it off. Why shouldn't the sight of the Parthenon be familiar? Lord a' mercy, she, along with most of the students in the world, had seen dozens of pictures of the place in textbooks.

Odd that in all her years in Europe, she'd never been to Greece. She'd been in Italy many times, and even once or twice to Turkey, but never to Greece. The timing never seemed right. In fact, even now she felt ambivalent about being here. Something about the country intrigued her but at the same time repulsed her.

Maybe it was the pollution that turned her off Athens. Now the fumes weren't so bad, but friends had told her that summer in the city had become almost unbearable with cars and manufacturing plants belching out noxious vapors. But the damp April day was fairly pleasant, the smells no worse than Paris or New York.

Athens struck her as a jaw-jutted center of loosely organized chaos, noisy, busy. Pedestrians rushed by, going in various directions and carrying odd things—a birdcage, a crystal chandelier, a stack of dented hubcaps, a toilet seat.

Following the instructions of the concierge, she walked the few blocks to the old city, the heart of Athens. The streets became narrow lanes, and long rows of steps joined the various levels of sloping terrain and tightly packed one- and two-storied buildings. Many were houses, restored or in the process of being refurbished in startlingly bright colors; others were shops of all sorts or tavernas with gay awnings and tantalizing menus displayed by the front doors.

Merchants and shoppers were already about, a general mood of unruly aggressiveness prevailing. A feather-duster peddler, with a penetrating call like a peacock, hawked his wares while fracturing lines of epic verse. A middle-aged Greek man turned a graffiti-bedecked section of stone wall into a soapbox, declaiming passionately and gesticulating wildly. Not understanding the language, Welcome had no idea whether he was ranting about the price of fish or the morals of a political foe, but she admired his fervor. Only one or two passersby stopped to listen; most ignored him.

Welcome found the shop easily, but rather than go in before the appointed time, she continued down the street and went inside a silversmith's shop to browse, then spent a half hour in a small museum she found tucked away on a side street.

When she exited the museum, the misty coolness had burned off and the trench coat and fedora felt oppressive in the bright sunlight. She made her way back to a small outdoor café across the street from the Metaxas Art and Souvenir Shop and ordered orange juice and bottled water. She slipped off the coat and fanned herself with the hat, the coins on the bracelet jingling with each movement of her wrist.

Even though she was still twenty minutes early, she was suddenly extremely anxious to be rid of the bracelet. She finished her drink, paid her check, and crossed the street to the shop. A bell sounded as she stepped inside. Smells of strong coffee and wool hung heavily in the close surroundings. A middle-aged man, the only attendant in sight, was showing wares to a very pregnant young woman.

The short, sturdy man sported a marvelous shock of steel gray hair, and the friendly smile that he flashed Welcome sparkled with a profusion of gold. "I'll be with you in one moment."

"No hurry," she replied. "I'll browse."

The shop was crammed with an abundance of merchandise—everything from jewelry to souvenirs to clothing to excellent flokati rugs. Welcome's attention gravitated to the wonderful shaggy wool rugs, several of which she saw displayed on the mezzanine above.

Thinking that a couple of these would be great at the ranch, she climbed the stairs and weaved her way through shelves full of pottery, high stacks of T-shirts, and hangers of caftans.

More rugs were rolled and stored in bins along the back wall of the dimly lit area. She'd dumped her coat and hat on a stool and was on her knees pulling out a shaggy rust-colored flokati when she heard the bell on the door tinkle. Either the pregnant woman had left or someone else had come in. Before she could push herself to her feet, the bell sounded again.

She rose and retraced her path through the merchandise to the stairs. Her sneaker was about to reach for the first step when she heard a commotion and men's angry words. Although she didn't understand the language spoken, she clearly grasped the menacing tone. Trying to see what was going on, she glanced at a mirror near the door that captured the men's reflections.

Welcome went dead still.

A burly, dark-haired stranger had grabbed a handful of the clerk's hair and dragged him halfway across the counter. He pressed a wicked-looking knife against the older man's throat.

Bile scalded her esophagus. She clamped her teeth together to keep from shouting.

More angry words.

The clerk's eyes bugged to owl-sized. His tone pleaded for mercy.

The stranger spat out a single guttural word. His knife flashed, slashing fast and deep.

Blood.

Oh, God. So much blood.

Horrified, Welcome opened her mouth to scream.

A hand clamped her mouth shut. An arm snaked around her waist and lifted her from the floor. Terrified, she began kicking and bucking and elbowing.

"Dammit," a voice whispered against her ear, "be quiet. I'm trying to help you. We've got to get back, get down, hide. Okay?"

Her heart slamming against her chest, Welcome nodded her head rapidly to show that she understood.

The man made a few steps back, then set her on her feet, and removed his hand from her mouth.

"Who are you?" she whispered.

He touched his finger to his lips and pulled her to the back of the mezzanine. When they were squatting among the souvenirs, he said softly, "We have to get out of here. Now."

"Can't we just hide and wait?" No matter how hard she tried to control it, her chin trembled with terror, and her whole body quivered like a plucked duck in a blue norther. The gruesome horror of what she'd witnessed continued to consume her mind. Dear Lord, she'd never seen so much blood.

The man shook his head. "He's locked the front door, and he'll be up here in a couple of minutes."

Welcome glanced to the front of the store. The mirror by the front door was out of her line of vision. She couldn't see anything that indicated what was going on downstairs. "How do you know what he's doing?"

"I know. Trust me. We have to find a rear entrance. Quick."

They crept to the back of the mezzanine, and he very carefully opened the only door there. It led to a large storage room with a dingy window at the far end—and another door. He yanked her inside.

While the man barricaded the entrance behind them with crates, Welcome ran to the exit door and frantically twisted the knob. Locked! "Dammit, wouldn't you know!" she muttered. She tried the window, pulled at the damned thing until she almost got a hernia from the effort.

It wouldn't budge.

"Here, let me," the man said.

The muscles of his arms bulged, those of his back rippled and strained.

A crackling sound, then slowly the window inched up. He strained harder. The opening grew larger. He stuck his head out and looked around. "There are steps down there. If I hold onto your hands and lower you, you can reach them. The minute your feet touch, run like hell away from here."

"What about you?"

"I'll be right behind you." He slapped her jean-clad bottom. "Go!"

Welcome swung a leg over the sill and eased through. The man held on to her hands and carefully lowered her down the side of the building. As she dangled there, her heart in her throat and hysteria flitting around trying to escape from between her clenched teeth, she looked up into his face.

"Trust me," he said.

His eyes captured hers. Strength and courage radiated from their gray-green depths. Her panic dissipated. At that moment she would have followed him through Hades.

A crashing sound came from above, and Welcome bit back a scream. The man holding her glanced quickly over his shoulder, then leaned further out the window until her toes touched the step. "Run like hell!" he told her.

She ran.

Twisting and turning through the narrow streets and alleys of Plaka, she ran until her chest heaved with great gasps and her side seized with stitches. Unable to go another step, she stopped, plastered herself against a wall in a shadowy recess, and tried to catch her breath.

"You okay?"

Welcome startled and yelped at the sudden sound of a male voice beside her. When she saw that it was her rescuer, her hand slapped her chest to hold her heart in. "Lord, you nearly scared the pee-doodle out of me. I didn't even hear you coming." She leaned her head against the wall and sucked in deep breaths of air. Drops of sweat dripped off her nose and others trickled down her neck. She swiped at her forehead with her shirt sleeve.

"Here," the man said, handing her his handkerchief.

"Thanks." She blotted her face and clutched the damp cloth in her shaking fingers. "Thanks for the handkerchief and for saving my ass. How did you happen to come along? Did Philip send you?"

The man shook his head. "Are you okay?"

"No, I'm not okay. I just witnessed a very bloody murder and got the bejesus scared out of me and my knees feel like dumpling dough. Are you sure Philip didn't send you?"

He shook his head.

She frowned at him and peered into his eyes. It was like free falling into an endless abyss. "God, your eyes are gorgeous. You're not with the CIA?"

He grinned. "The *CIA*? Me?"

She let out an exasperated sigh and leaned her head back against the wall. "Of course you are, but you wouldn't admit it in a million years. I don't know why I even asked. Shouldn't we call the police or somebody?"

"Oh, I don't think that would be a very good idea."

"Why ever not? Good Lord, we just witnessed a brutal murder in broad daylight."

"Well, uh, certain circumstances might be . . . difficult to explain."

"Ohhh," she said, the light dawning. She jiggled the coin bracelet on her arm. "Like having to explain this. I guess you're right, but maybe we should at least report it anonymously.

"Let me take care of it. We need to get you back to your hotel. You look wrung out."

"I am, but right now I'd sell my soul for a glass of water and a slug of brandy."

He smiled. "I think we can accommodate you a lot cheaper than that. Can you hold off for a couple of minutes? Let's get back to Constitution Square first. It's safer."

Welcome nodded and they started walking in the direction of Syntagma, Constitution Square. He slipped his arm around her waist, and she leaned against him, grateful for his big, comforting body and the power that emanated from his rock-hard form. He reminded her of one of those marvelous Greek statues, dressed in jeans and come to life. As they walked together, she grew calm, as if drawing strength from his presence.

"I can't begin to tell you how thankful I am that you came along— I don't even know your name," she said.

He chuckled. "But I know yours."

"Of course you do. Philip told you."

"Ah, this looks like a good place to stop." He led her to an outside table at a cafe on the square. Only a few patrons were scattered among the several vacant tables.

A waiter caught sight of them and approached. As Welcome's companion held a chair for her, the waiter smiled affably and asked, "May I take your order, please?"

After she was seated, her rescuer bent and whispered against her ear, "Order your drink, and I'll make that phone call." He kissed the side of her neck.

"I'll have bottled water and a brandy," she told the waiter. "And the gentleman . . ." She glanced over her shoulder. He was gone. "I don't know what the gentleman will have."

"What gentleman, miss?"

"The gentleman who was just here. Tall, dark blond hair, broad shoulders. He was wearing jeans and a red shirt. You couldn't miss him."

The waiter frowned and looked around. "I didn't see anyone with you. You came alone."

"But—"

A prickle rushed across the nape of her neck, and Welcome fell silent.

Four

*How dreadful knowledge of the truth can be
When there's no help in truth!*

Sophocles
c. 495-405 B.C.

Palm Springs

Wade cried out and jerked awake, his fists clenched, his heart racing like an Indy contender.

"Man, what's wrong?" Shark asked, shaking him again.

Wade tried to clear his head, squinted at his unfamiliar surroundings, and fought back the godawful feelings that churned in his gut. "Shark?"

"Yeah, man, it's me. What's going on with you?"

"Don't know. Nothing. Why?"

"Sounded like you was mixing it with a gang of home boys in a back alley. Never heard such takin' on."

"Don't remember. Must've had a bad dream."

"Some dream. You looked like you were ready to go a few rounds with Tyson when I finally got you awake. Something must have given you the heebie-jeebies. You been making more noise for the last hour or two than a peanut thrasher, flailing around and moaning something awful. I could hear you from my room. Thought first you had the TV on."

Wade sat up on the side of the bed and rubbed his face. "I don't remember anything. Must have been something I ate."

"We ate the same thing, and it didn't bother me none."

"Hell, you could eat stewed Firestone radials, and it wouldn't bother you. Some of us are more the sensitive types." Wade laughed and gave his friend a playful poke.

"Sensitive?" Shark snorted. "You got a stomach like a wood stove. Chasing that dumb little white ball all day yesterday probably got your head messed up."

"Could be."

Shark thought that golf was a sissy game, mostly because he could never get the hang of it. Not that Wade was all that good himself, but he'd agreed at the last minute to play in the celebrity tournament for a children's charity. Steve Young had been scheduled, but he'd come down with something.

Wade's team had lost, and he never had taken losing too well.

"What say we grab our stuff and head home?" Wade asked.

"At four o'clock in the morning?"

"I can't go back to sleep, and we were going to leave in a few hours anyway." Wade couldn't explain to Shark the terrible feeling of foreboding that lingered in his brain like a flock of buzzards perched on a dead tree. Hell, he didn't understand it himself.

"That cloud of dust you see is me leaving. We been here way too long already."

"But we've only been here one day."

"That's too long for me. I don't like this place."

They packed and hit the road. On the way out of

town, they pulled into a truck stop for breakfast. One of the truckers recognized Wade and poked his seat-mate at the counter. Before long most of the dozen or so people in the restaurant were gawking. A few called out to him; one guy got his autograph. Used to it, Wade handled it good-naturedly.

The waitress who came to their booth practically rubbed her boobs in Wade's face as she poured his coffee. Used to that, too, he ignored her overture, es-pecially since she was carrying an extra twenty-five pounds on her hips and needed some serious dental work on her front teeth. They both ordered the num-ber two specials, and the waitress left.

Wade took a swallow from his mug. "Man, that's good." He took another swallow. The uneasiness that he'd felt earlier hadn't let up. If he'd been the type who was prone to anxiety, he'd have said that he was anxious. Extremely anxious. But there was no reason for it. "Say, Shark?"

"Yeah?"

"How about when we get back to L.A., we hop a flight to Athens?"

"Athens, Georgia, or Athens, Greece?"

"Greece."

"Are you on that tune again? Man, what is it with you? Barney'll have a shit fit if you take off to Greece right now."

"Yeah, you're right. Forget it."

Athens

As Welcome let herself into her hotel room, she was still shaken. The horrifying scene from the shop re-played over and over in her head. The brandy hadn't helped much. Neither had her rescuer's failure to return. The waiter had reassured her twice that she had come to the café alone. While she knew very well that she hadn't, it was odd that the man moved around like Lamont Cranston. She'd waited for almost an hour before she'd finally given up.

Although she was sure that there was a logical explanation for his shadowy appearance and disappearance, the incident was creepy. Definitely creepy. They didn't call those CIA types "spooks" for nothing.

A shrill jangle pierced the quiet; Welcome startled and yelped. Her keys flew from her hand.

"Dear God." She slapped her chest and caught her breath, relieved when she realized that it was only the telephone. Snatching it up, she shouted, "Hello. Hello."

Silence.

"Hello. Hello. Is anyone there?"

More silence.

She slammed down the receiver. A wrong number? A bad connection? A heavy breather?

The murderer after her?

"Get a grip, girl," she muttered to herself. She fell back on to the bed and stared at the ceiling. There was no way that the murderer could have seen her, much less know her identity or how to locate her.

But she'd gotten a good look at him. A very good look. Again she wondered if she should call the police. Her rescuer had said that he would take care of all the particulars, but after his vanishing act, she was beginning to have second thoughts.

Yet, if she contacted the police, what would she tell them? She certainly couldn't explain her reason for being in the shop. Holy Hannah, what a horror.

She paced. And she stewed. And she paced some more.

When she raised her hand to brush an errant strand of hair from her forehead, the bracelet jingled.

The bracelet!

Dear God, she'd forgotten the bracelet. She had to deliver it to Miklos. Or was it Miklos who was lying across his counter with his throat slashed?

She could think of only one way to find out: return to Plaka, the scene of the crime. Undoubtedly some of the neighboring shopkeepers would know. The area was sure to be abuzz with the grisly incident. She had only to put on her spy outfit and do a little covert reconnoitering—

Oh shit!

She'd left her coat and hat in the shop.

Near the flokati rugs.

Frantically, she tried to remember if there was anything about either item that would identify her.

Certainly not the hat. Purchased years ago at some inexpensive shop or other on the Left Bank, the brown fedora was like thousands of others. The trench coat, which wasn't new, sported a designer label but not her name. The only thing she could remember being in the pockets was an Athens travel guide, which wouldn't differentiate her from a horde of tourists.

Her wallet, along with identification papers and cash, was in her waist pack. No way could the murderer know who she was.

But he'd known that *someone* else had been in the shop, and realizing that he would be concerned with locating any witness, she shuddered.

Maybe she should just forget about going back to Plaka. Maybe she should phone Philip and tell him to forget about her delivering anything, anywhere, to anybody.

A premium idea.

She quickly put in a call to Philip at the special number he'd given her in case of emergency. Not to worry, he'd said. The switchboard could patch her through to him wherever he was at any time, day or night.

A woman answered. "Mr. Jones" was unavailable. Could she speak with someone else or leave her number?

Welcome left her number, then slammed down the phone. Great. Just frigging great. So much for immediate emergency access to Philip. He was probably out playing tennis.

Now what was she supposed to do?

She paced some more and tried to think.

Go back to Plaka. Yes, that was it. She could at least pick up some information before she decided.

Quickly, she pinned up her hair, covered it with a scarf, and grabbed a jacket.

Just as she closed the door behind her and the lock clicked, the telephone rang. Damnation! It was probably Philip. She fumbled through her waist pack for the key, then dropped it. The phone rang again.

"I'm coming!" she yelled as she searched the floor for her key. Finding the errant culprit, she shoved it in the lock as the phone rang again.

As soon as the door was open, she bounded for the phone and snatched it up in mid-ring. "Hello. Hello. I'm here."

Silence. She'd missed the call.

"Well, shit fire and save matches!" Welcome slammed down the receiver and stalked from the room.

She walked the few blocks to the shop in Plaka. Other than a CLOSED sign on the door, things looked normal. No throngs of curiosity seekers huddled around whispering and pointing at the shop. No police guarded the door; no TV cameras rolled. The only interested passerby was a small dog. He sniffed around a potted plant by the shop's entrance, then lifted his leg and doused the pink geranium.

Pretending to window shop, she tried to peer inside, but with all the merchandise crowding the place, she couldn't see much, but she could see enough to tell that the counter didn't still have a body draped over it.

Of course the killer would have moved it out of sight. Or even to another location. Though surely not in broad daylight. She shivered when she thought of the killer dragging a carpet-wrapped body out the back door. If it hadn't been for the guy who helped her out of the shop, there might have been two carpet-wrapped bodies.

Swallowing back the sour lump rising in her throat, she fought the urge to hightail it back to the hotel and hide under her bed. Just to be sure, she rattled the doorknob, but the place was locked tight.

She casually strolled to the sidewalk cafe across from the shop and sat down. The same waiter who had served her earlier approached.

In his early twenties and darkly handsome in the way so many Greek men were, he flashed her a narcissistic smile. "Ah, *yá sas*" he said in greeting. "You come again to my table." As he presented the menu, his expression said that he believed that his profile was the drawing card for her return.

She opened her mouth to whittle the cocky kid's ego down to a more manageable size, then paused. Welcome had learned at her mama's knee that you can catch more flies with honey than with vinegar.

Instead of handing him a putdown, she removed her sunglasses and bestowed her famous sultry smile on him—the one that had sold a ton of La Belle lipstick and earned her beaucoup de francs.

The waiter's chest swelled noticeably.

She fluttered her lashes, then dropped her gaze downward and slowly swept up the length of him. By the time her blatant perusal reached his face, the kid was practically pawing the dirt, and too green to know that he was out of his league.

"Well, hello there, sugar," she drawled. "Aren't you a cutie pie?"

His open, beaming smile revealed his youth, and Welcome had to adjust his age downward. About eighteen, she suspected.

He bowed slightly. "I am Takis. How may I be of service?"

"I'm famished," she said, suddenly aware that she was indeed hungry. Stress always made her hungry. "Could I get some soup?"

"Only soup?" He looked affronted. "You must have more than soup. Forget the menu." He snatched the folder from her. "Tell me your heart's desire, and I will have it made especially for you."

"You wouldn't happen to have chicken-fried steak, would you?"

He frowned. "Fried chicken and steak?"

She smiled. "No. Chicken-fried steak, but never mind. What would you suggest?"

"You like an appetizer? I bring bread and *tzaziki*. *Tzaziki* is like a dip with yogurt and cucumbers. Very good. Then maybe some *avgolémono*—that's chicken soup with egg and lemon—and *moussaka*. You like *moussaka*? My grandfather says the *aubergine* is very good today. And the fish—"

"Stop, Takis." She held up a hand. "If I ate all that, I'd be fat as a pig."

"You?" He made a big production of looking shocked. "Never."

She couldn't help but smile as his theatrics. "Still, I'll have just soup. And maybe a small portion of *tzaz-*

iki," she added, then glanced at the door across the street. "I was hoping to pick up a rug I admired earlier at that shop, but I see that it's closed. I wonder why."

Takis shrugged. "Maybe the owner is out."

"When do you think he might return?"

Takis shrugged again. "Who knows? He comes; he goes. If you want a rug, I know a place where you can get the best and for much less money than you would pay there." He gestured toward the shop door with his head, then glanced at his watch. "In one hour, my work here will be finished, and I'll take you to the place I know."

"I'm really interested in the rug at this particular shop. Is the owner named Miklos?"

Another shrug. Takis wasn't interested in the shop across the way. "My grandfather might know. The place where the rugs are is only a short drive. You have a car?"

"No. Where is your grandfather?"

"Inside. If you're a stranger here, you'll need a guide. I can show you all the best bargains and the most beautiful sights in Athens. We can take a ship to Poros, Aegina, and Hydra, or we can drive up to Delphi. If you don't have a car, we can go shopping on my motor scooter, but for Delphi, you must rent a car."

Welcome shook her head at his fast hustle. "Whoa, pardner. All I want is my lunch."

Takis looked sheepish, then grinned and bowed. "Right away."

"And please ask your grandfather about the shop's owner."

"And I'll ask too about the fried chicken and steak."

She chuckled. "That's chicken-fried steak, and never mind about that."

Welcome had underestimated the Greek obsession with food. In two minutes Takis was back, accompanied by an older man with gray hair, piercing black eyes, and a barrel chest. An apron was tied around his middle.

"Excuse my grandson," he boomed. "He is starstruck to meet you, and he don't get your order right. I am Spyros Katrakis. Welcome to my taverna. What you want to eat? Chicken? Steak?"

Rarely intimidated by anyone, Welcome was momentarily taken aback by the old man's demeanor. "I—I just wanted some soup."

"Soup? Paah! You must have more than soup. I cannot allow a famous lady like yourself to leave Spyros Katrakis's taverna hungry. *Ella, ella!* Come, come. We go to my kitchen, and you show me the chicken or steak you want. You want it fried. I fry. *Ella, ella!*"

Before she could refuse, Spyros swept her up with the whirlwind of his personality and an arm linked with hers and propelled her inside the cafe. Welcome cast a questioning look over her shoulder at Takis who trotted along behind them. The boy merely rolled his eyes and shrugged.

"Mama! Mama!" the grandfather called to an older woman stirring a huge pot. "Look who I have found sitting at one of our tables: the famous lady from Niki's magazines." To Welcome he said, "Our granddaughter has pictures of you all over her bedroom. She wants to make her hair red like yours, but I put my foot down." He slapped his forehead. "Such an old fool I am. I know your pictures, but I don't know your name."

"My name is Welcome. Welcome Venable."

"Ah, welcome, Welcome." He gave a belly-shaking laugh and patted her hand. "I make a joke. *Ella,* come, meet my wife and family."

After he had effusively introduced her to myriad relatives who were busy in the kitchen, he ushered her to an area where various meats were in a refrigerated case. "Look, here are plenty chickens. And here are beefsteaks. Filet mignon, the best." He kissed his fingers. "The beefsteaks I mostly grill, but if you want fried, I fry."

"Mr. Katrakis, your hospitality overwhelms me, but, really, I want only a small meal. Some *tzaziki* and some soup."

"No Mr. Katrakis. You call me Spyros. I call you Welcome. And I serve you anything you want to eat, but Takis said that you wanted fried chicken and steak."

"Not exactly. I asked if you had chicken-fried steak."

Spyros's shaggy gray eyebrows came together in a frown. "What is this chicken-fried steak?"

Welcome laughed. "It's a dish that Texans make from roundsteak."

"Oh, Texas. You from Texas? With the cowboys and the six-shooters?"

"I'm from Texas. And we have a few cowboys, but not so many six-shooters."

"We don't have the round steak," Spyros said, "but I will send Takis to the market. You wait and tell me exactly how to make this chicken-fried steak."

"No, Spyros, please. You have too many customers now. Tomorrow I'll return when you're not so busy, and we'll make it. I'll give you a list of ingredients." When he looked as if he might argue, she laid her hand on his arm and said, "Please. Tomorrow."

He shrugged. "Very well. Come. Sit at my best table, and we'll have wine while your food is being prepared. Takis! A bottle of my special wine and glasses." He escorted Welcome to a table in an alcove and seated her with a flourish.

In the midst of wine, more food than she could ever eat, and being tended like an honored guest, Welcome did discover from Spyros that the owner of Metaxas

was Pandelis Metaxas. From his description, she surmised that he was the person who was killed.

"I tried the door a few minutes ago," Welcome said,
"but the shop was closed. I wonder where he is."

"Who knows about that one?" Spyros made a dis-
missing gesture with his hand. "He comes, he goes. If
you ask me, he doesn't spend enough time with his
business. He doesn't care if he has customers or not.
When Grigoris Vasilenas owned that place, he worked
long hours. He had fine merchandise and many customers. Now—" he made a derisive, dismissive noise
"—now is nothing. You don't want nothing from that
place. Takis will show you better shops."

"Does Mr. Metaxas have someone who works for him
named Miklos?"

Spyros shrugged. "Who knows? Sometimes he has a
clerk for a few days, then *poof,* he is gone. I never even
know their names. That Pandelis Metaxas is a crazy
one. You better stay away from him."

No amount of gentle prodding brought her any
more information. Nothing unusual or exciting had
happened in the neighborhood that day. Obviously
Spyros and his family weren't aware of the murder that
had occurred only a few feet from their entrance.

Which meant that the body hadn't been found.

Which meant that the police hadn't been called.

Which meant that her rescuer had lied to her.

Damnation!

Now *she* would have to call the authorities. Her con-
science wouldn't just let a dead body stay locked up
in that shop.

Welcome quickly hung up the public phone, then
hurried back to the curb where Takis sat on his scooter
and climbed on behind him.

"The museum, James," she said imperiously.

"James? My name is Takis."

She laughed. "I know, sweetie. Let's roll."

It was after midnight when Welcome slipped her key into the lock of her hotel room. She was pooped, and the notion of a warm bath and cool sheets sounded marvelous to her aching body. Keeping up with Takis, and later his sister Niki, as they showed her the sights of Athens reminded her painfully that she would never see thirty again. She simply didn't have the energy of a pair of teenagers, even if she was in excellent shape.

The phone rang just as the door swung open, and she ran for it.

"Hello."

Silence.

"Hello, hello."

More silence.

Damnation! She slammed down the receiver. The call probably had been from Philip. And she'd missed it by a hair. She was having the world's worst luck with phone calls.

When she pitched the key on the dresser, she noticed the flowers. Two dozen yellow roses. She leaned close and drew in a breath of their scent.

"Ah, Philip, you've come through again, you dirty dog. But I haven't kept my part of the bargain yet."

A movement in the mirror caught her eye. She whirled around just in time to see the door to the hall close very slowly and hear the snick of the latch.

Five

He harms himself who does harm to another, and the evil plan is most harmful to the planner.

Hesiod
c. 700 B.C.

Athens

The phone rang. Welcome sat up in bed, scraped her hair from her face, and peered at the clock. 4:30 A.M. Who would be calling at this ungodly hour?

"Hello."

Silence.

This wasn't a bad connection or a missed call. She could hear breathing. "Hello."

Still silence.

"Listen to me, you sick son-of-a-bitch, if you've got something to say, spit it out, but quit calling me and playing mummy!" She slammed down the phone and yanked the plug from the wall.

She got up and went to the bathroom, then checked the door of her room to make sure that it was locked and dead-bolted. For extra measure, she dragged a heavy chair in front of the door as well. Although she had tried to put what she had seen in Metaxas's shop from her mind—and spending time with Takis and Niki had helped—the horror hovered there constantly.

Now the scene replayed again. She could see the blood.

And she could see the killer's face.

Was he the man on the phone? Had he somehow discovered her identity?

Get a grip, girl. Hell, a killer like the one she'd seen wouldn't make crank calls. Crank calls were the vehicles of the meek, of cowards. Men like the one she'd seen in the shop would just grab you and slit your throat before you knew what happened.

Oh, God.

But there was no way he could know who she was. No way.

Philip, where in the blue blazes are you? I'm going to strangle you for getting me into this mess. Why don't you call?

Then she remembered the disconnected phone and quickly replugged it. She got in bed and tried to go back to sleep, but her thoughts were going ninety miles an hour. She lay there and stared at the ceiling until dawn peeked through the slits in the draperies.

"Dammit, Philip Van Horn, if I can't sleep, you're not going to either." She snatched up the receiver and dialed the special number.

"Mr. Jones" wasn't available, she was told. "Well, he'd better damned well become available in a hurry," she informed the tight-assed woman she spoke with. "I've got problems."

Promising to have Mr. Jones get back with her right away, the voice on the phone took her number. Again.

Welcome laid in bed with the covers pulled to her nose, and told herself not to be such a wimp. It wasn't the killer calling her; it was some infatuated fan—a bellboy or somebody like that who had seen her and knew her room number. She'd had crank calls before from men who declared that they were in love with her. Once or twice it had taken several tries before the guy got up nerve enough to speak to her.

Relax, she told herself. Think of warm beaches and gentle waves.

She was just dozing off when the phone rang.

She grabbed it and said, "You'd better talk to me this time, you bastard!"

"Well, well, well. Testy this morning aren't we?"

"Damn you, Philip! Where have you been? I've got problems!"

"Sorry, love. I had a run-in with a Mercedes. It hit me as I was crossing the street, gathering wool instead of paying attention to where I was going. Gave me a concussion and broke my leg in two places. I'm in the hospital now sporting some new stainless steel pins and a cast up to my—" He cleared his throat. "My cellular phone got banged worse than my leg, and I just now got a replacement. Plus I've been pretty well out of it."

"Oh, Philip, I'm sorry. When did this happen?"

"Shortly after I left your place the other day. My watch got smashed all to hell, too. Hated that. I loved that watch. Janine gave it to me last Christmas. Cost the earth." Janine was Philip's wife. "What sort of problems are you having? Didn't you like the fellow I fixed you up with for dinner?"

Knowing that his cryptic question was prompted by their being on unsecured telephone lines, she answered in kind. "I don't know if I like him or not. I went to meet him, but I got stood up."

"Sorry about that. Maybe you can get together again."

"Not likely. I understand that there was a *death* in the family, a serious tragedy, and he's unavailable. I feel wretched about the situation, *really* wretched. You can't imagine *how* wretched. What shall I do with your gift?''

"Hmmmm. Why don't you stash it for now, and I'll get back to you in a few days. How long do you plan to be in Athens?''

"I'm not sure. Several days at least. It depends on my photographer's schedule. I'm waiting to hear when we can begin shooting. Philip, I'm really distressed about your injuries. Are you going to be okay?''

"Eventually. Don't concern yourself with me or my rude friend. Just have a good time. I'll be in touch in a day or two. Bye, love.''

"Bye, Philip.''

After she hung up, Welcome tried to go back to sleep, but it was impossible. She called room service for coffee, juice, and rolls, then headed for the shower.

Perhaps it was simply a reflection of reckless Parisian driving habits these days, but she thought it seemed odd that Philip should be hit by a car so soon after one almost creamed her. Was it merely a coincidence?

Surely it was. The only recent connection between Philip and Welcome was the bracelet. And she hardly saw how anyone could react so quickly to her involvement in the delivery. No she'd just been preoccupied and hadn't been alert to traffic; Philip had probably been the same. Parisians drove like bats out of hell, and to step off a curb without looking was suicidal.

Who was driving the car that hit Philip? She'd have to remember to ask him.

Wade paid the driver and climbed out of the cab after Shark.

"Man, I can't believe I let you talk me into this," Shark said. "I thought you said it was a stupid idea."

"I changed my mind, but I'm beginning to regret it. You feel as bad as I do?"

"Don't know, but if you feel like you got a head full of hornets, eyes full of wood ashes, and cleat marks on your rump from the whole Steeler line running over it, I'd say we're about even."

Wade chuckled. "That about covers it."

"Man, it's a *long* way from L.A. to here. A *long* way."

The two of them followed the uniformed attendant who had taken charge of their bags and whisked open the door.

Inside the lobby, Shark stopped dead still. "My Gawd," he said, gaping at the grandeur. "I ain't seen this much marble since Mama and me went shopping for her aunt Gracie's tombstone. Is this a museum or something?"

"Hell, I hope it's a hotel. My ass is dragging. All I can think of is some decent food, a hot bath, and a bed."

"With a few vestal virgins thrown in?"

"Not me, pal. I'm too tired. I told you that I was getting too old for that stuff."

Shark hooted with laughter as they walked to the registration desk. "That'll be the day."

After Welcome stashed the coin bracelet in the hotel safe, she felt considerably relieved. As she started for the door, she noticed two very large men at the reservation desk. Probably American, she surmised from the cut of their clothes. Even though she couldn't see the light-haired man's face, for a moment she thought that she recognized him. She could have sworn—

Naw, she told herself, shrugging off the notion, it was the cute butt that had attracted her attention. She was a sucker for broad shoulders and a nice set of buns.

Reminding herself that now was not the time for distractions, she briskly exited the hotel, planning to do some sightseeing.

She had a couple of hours until she was due at the taverna for Spyros's cooking lesson—and a gander at the goings on at Metaxas's shop across the street. By now the police were sure to have found the body, and she could pump Spyros or Takis for information.

The Acropolis in the distance seemed to draw her to it, and she itched to climb the hill to the crumbled ruins. Takis and Niki had tried to get her to visit the site with them the day before, but for some reason, Welcome wanted to go there alone.

Besides, she told herself, a nice brisk walk would clear the cobwebs from her brain.

A man in a black sweater watched the redhead pass, then stepped from the shadows of a column and crushed out his cigarette in the receptacle that held a great number of his butts.

Someone had been upstairs; he was sure of it. After he'd taken care of that traitorous devil, he'd heard the scraping of boxes, the creak of the window and the sound of feet on the outside stairs. But by the time he made his way to the storeroom and past the barricade, the person had fled.

After a quick search of the premises, he'd found a woman's coat and a hat near the rugs. In the pocket of the coat were directions to Metaxas's shop. The directions had been torn from a pad with the hotel's name and logo at the top: the Grande Bretagne.

The hat gave up a single long hair. Red.

Perhaps this was the woman, he thought. The coat

seemed to be the proper size for her, and she was the only one he had seen around the hotel with hair that exact shade.

Perhaps the coat and the hat belonged to the observer of his handiwork, perhaps not. No matter. He dared not leave a witness. There was only one way to be sure.

He fell into step behind her.

Six

Dreams surely are difficult, confusing, and not every-
thing in them is brought to pass for mankind. For fleet-
ing dreams have two gates: one is fashioned of horn
and one of ivory.

Homer
c. 700 B.C.

Welcome truly meant to stride straight for the
Parthenon, which was situated on the highest part of
the Acropolis and clearly visible from anywhere in the
city, but she became sidetracked by the scores of sights
and sounds and smells that surrounded her as she
walked along.

Whole streets were devoted to shops that sold only
one thing: pots and pans or bridal wear or children's
clothing. Others sold rugs of exquisite design that
begged her to stop and run her fingers over the weave.
An entire block housed furriers, while other streets offered fabrics or souvenirs. She brushed past a Gypsy
woman insistently hawking lace shawls, and soon found
herself in front of a tiny treasure of a church. Agia
Dynamis, the replacement for her lost guide book informed her.

When she stopped to read about the colorful history

of the little Turkish church, Welcome felt an odd sensation and glanced over her shoulder.

Was someone following her?

She turned casually and looked carefully. Nothing
seemed out of the ordinary. Greek shoppers and awed
tourists filled the sidewalks, chattering over the horns
and engines of traffic noise. Her imagination, she was
sure.

Walking on, she passed the Mitropoleos, Athens's cathedral, which was impressive only because of its size,
and turned left toward Odos Pandrossou. She had only
to follow the bouzouki music playing full blast to find
the city's famous bazaar street.

As she skirted the bargain hunters, Welcome again
had the feeling that she was being followed. Strange,
she knew, given the throngs of people shopping in the
bazaar. Still she paused several times at various open-
air stalls, fingered the merchandise, and scanned the
crowd for a familiar face. Once she thought that she
saw the same man twice, but he went inside a door
and she didn't see him again.

Ordinarily she wasn't so jumpy or suspicious. She
was used to people staring at her. They either recognized her, thought they recognized her but couldn't
figure out from where, or merely stared because she
was an especially tall woman with wild red hair and a
distinctive look. She knew that. Most of the time she
simply tuned out people's reactions to her and went
on with her business. But since yesterday—Lord, had
it been only yesterday?—she'd become super-sensitive.

The bazaar street spilled onto a square which was
the site of a lively flea market and a subway entrance.
Everything imaginable was for sale in the flea market.
She even saw a framed picture of John Wayne alongside live goldfish in jars, mountains of books, and
shelves of old car parts. Welcome had about decided

to stop for a cup of coffee when she saw the Tower of the Winds.

Making her way through the crowd around the square, she proceeded to the tower, a structure dating from the Roman period her guidebook said. Once a working water clock, it was named for the gods of the four winds carved on its sides, and the tall marble octagon fronted the ruins of the Roman agora. After the bustle of the bazaar and the flea market, the area was an oasis of peacefulness, deserted except for an artist in a straw hat sketching the tower, and there was a young couple, arms entwined and oblivious to the rest of the world, walking among the broken columns of the agora.

Little remained of the marketplace built by the Caesars centuries after the Greek agora. Grass and small white wildflowers grew in the patches between the worn and broken stones of the floor.

As she stood quietly beside one tall pillar, a peculiar feeling wafted over her. The tower and the agora rippled as if painted on a wind-blown gossamer curtain that cloaked the real landscape. Behind the curtain, the stones were gone and in their place appeared a rocky stream that wound its way through an olive grove.

She heard playful feminine laughter, then the deeper laughter of a young man. Suddenly she could see him running toward her, and her heart almost stopped as he neared. Clad in a short chiton and sandals, he was more beautiful and more dear than Apollo himself. His eyes were as sparkling blue as the Aegean; his hair as gold as Athena's helmet. He smiled and reached out his hand to her; she lifted hers to him.

A crack above her head sent marble splinters flying.

"Dammit! Get down!"

The hand jerked her to the ground. A heavy body fell over her.

Another crack.

Shouting.

Welcome struggled to rise.

"Dammit! Stay down," he growled against her ear. "Do you want to get your head shot off?"

She recognized that voice. The spook from Metaxas's shop. "Who's shooting?"

"How the hell should I know? I just got here. Stay down until I can check it out."

She lay there prone for the longest time, waiting.

For an eternity, she waited.

And waited.

"Miss, miss. Excuse me," a very British voice said. A hand shook her shoulder.

She looked up.

The artist. The one in the straw hat who had been sketching the tower.

"Miss, I say, are you ill? Shall I call a doctor?"

Welcome pushed up with both hands and looked around. No spook. No shooter. Nobody.

She stood and dusted her hands on the seat of her jeans. "No, I'm fine, thank you. At least I think I am. Unless that big galoot broke one of my ribs when he fell on me."

"A big galoot?" The artist looked puzzled.

"I suppose you might call him a bloke. A man."

He looked even more puzzled. "What man was that?"

"The one that jerked me to the ground and fell on me when somebody shot—" She stopped when she saw his expression change from puzzlement to incredulousness. "You didn't see the man?"

He shook his head. "I'm afraid not. Heard a car backfire, but I didn't see a man. And I was watching

you quite carefully. You have marvelous bone structure, you know. Wouldn't by any chance be a model
for the magazines, would you?"

She nodded.

"Thought so. Thought I recognized you. I was gathering up my nerve to ask you to let me sketch you
there by that bench. And then I was hoping that you
would join me for tea, maybe a bite of lunch later."

"I'm sorry. I have an appointment in a few minutes."

"Well, there you have it. Are you sure that you're
all right?"

Hell, no, she wasn't all right. She was about to have
a screaming fit, but she didn't want this Brit to know
it. She gifted him with a dazzling smile. "I'm right as
rain, sir. Thank you very much. Good-bye."

He finally took the hint and toddled back to his can-
vas stool. She reached to pick up the sweater that had
slipped from her shoulders and noticed that a few
small slivers of marble clung to the dark yarn. She
searched the face of the column beside her.

Two fresh nicks marred the surface. One about an
inch above her head, the other about nose high.

She hugged herself and shivered.

Car backfire, my aunt Het! Somebody had taken two
shots at her. And if the spook hadn't yanked her out
of the way, the second one would have opened a new
hole in her head.

Her first thought was to call the police. Her second
was that they would think she was nuts when the only
witness wouldn't corroborate her story. Her third was
to get the hell out of there.

She got the hell out of there. Fast.

As soon as she reached the square, she flagged a
taxi and finally made the driver understand that she
wanted to go to the Grande Bretagne. Strange that in

Greece, everybody spoke perfect English except the taxi drivers.

While he drove, she sat huddled in the back shivering.

She had a thing or two to say to Philip Van Horn.

"I don't care if the Queen of England is listening!" Welcome shrieked. "Dammit, somebody tried to shoot me! And my white knight keeps running off before I can talk to him. Who the devil *is* he anyway? You got me into this mess. Now get me out of it!"

"Calm down, love. You're babbling. Don't fret yourself for one minute. I'll have someone pick you up and take you to the airport immediately."

"The *airport*? I don't want to go to the airport. I have to do the brochure for the hotels. If I leave without doing the photos, Meri won't understand. And I can't tell her the truth. She'll worry, and I don't want to upset her in her condition."

"Then what do you want me to do?" Philip asked. "I'd come, but I wouldn't be much use in a wheelchair."

"Send somebody. What about the blond guy?"

"What blond guy?" Philip asked.

"The one that keeps getting me out of scrapes. Big guy. Blondish hair going a little gray, square chin, nose a little out of kilter. Looks like an ex-jock."

"Doesn't sound like anybody I know."

A sinking feeling rippled over Welcome. "He's not one of yours?"

"No."

"Swear?"

"Swear."

That feeling rippled over her again. Who was her guardian angel?

Then it struck her.

Ram. He was one of Ramson Gabrey's security men. Ram always had a gaggle of security personnel guarding Meri and Welcome every time they went on a shoot. The guys were always undercover, but they were always there. It made Meri furious, but Ram wouldn't budge on the practice. Meri had canceled, but she supposed that Ram had kept the guards in place since it was his business they were concerned with.

"Welcome? Are you there?"

"Oh. Sorry, Philip. It just occurred to me that Ram Gabrey probably has part of his security force on me. I feel much safer, but I'm still pretty nervous. That guy meant to kill me."

"Look, stay in today. By tomorrow I'll have someone there, and you can explain to her what's going on. If the person I have in mind is available, she can be your temporary photographer."

"Can she really take decent pictures?"

"Of course. Will you be okay until tomorrow?"

"Yes, I think so."

Just as she hung up, there was a knock at the door. Welcome must have jumped two feet.

She hurried to the door and looked through the peephole. A bellman stood there with flowers. She let him in. He presented her with another two dozen yellow roses.

Again there was no card.

Why was Philip sending her more roses?

Or had he sent them?

After a room service lunch, which she only picked at, Welcome discovered that she was so sleepy that she could barely keep her eyes open. Not surprising given the night she'd had.

As soon as her dishes were cleared away, she locked and bolted the door, shoved the chair in front of it, and curled up on her bed.

Something tickled her nose, and she roused slowly, aware of the scent of wildflowers filling the room. Stirring to look, she discovered that hundreds of tiny yellow and white blossoms lay scattered over her like a diaphanous blanket.

Then she felt his presence, a charismatic energy that vibrated the air and set her heart singing. He came into view; her breath caught, and a smile sprang to her lips. His familiar masculinity worn like a chlamys about his broad shoulders, he moved toward her, an answering smile on his lips, one so bright that it leapt and warmed like a spark from the sun.

He held out his hands, she grasped them, and he pulled her from the bed into his embrace. With practiced ease she snuggled close, the curves of her form fitting perfectly against the hollows of his.

"How I have longed to hold you thus," he murmured.

"And I have longed to be held. It's been so long. Years and years and years since we parted, since we've touched."

"I was such a fool to—"

She halted his words with two fingers against his lips. "We will not speak of foolish things. The past has fallen into dust. I feel only joy that you are here now." As if in response to her words, tremendous waves of delight welled up from her heart and spilled into bubbling laughter. "Oh, you're here. You're here." She hugged him again. "I have a million questions, but first I must show you something. Come."

Giddy with excitement, she took his hand, and pulling him along after her, they flew from the hotel. Across Syntagma Square, past churches and the cathedral and shoppers in the bazaar they went. She didn't stop until she had drawn him into the middle of the ruined Roman agora.

"Look," she said, her arms outstretched as she laughed and

whirled around the cracked and crumbling marble floor. "Just look. Do you remember this place?"

"Should I? It looks like a mess to me now." He sat down on a hunk of stone that had once been a wall, rested his chin on his fist, and drew his brows together. "As I recall, Julius Caesar give yon tower to Athens as a planetarium. And this—" his hand gestured over the agora "—Julius and Augustus Caesar built to house the shops and markets. And there," he added, pointing, "was the public toilet." He broke into a broad grin. "How was that for remembering?"

"Oh, you!" She gave him a playful swat. "You know very well that I was thinking of the time long before the Romans came." She sat on the stone beside him, slipped under his arm, and rested her head on his chest. "Do you remember when first you saw this place?"

"Yes, I remember." He rubbed his cheek against the top of her head. "None of these houses were here then. Nor was the Tower of the Winds or the agora. There was a stream, coming from that direction, that ran along here." He pointed and traced a path with his finger. "And a grove of trees grew here. Olive trees, I think. I used to chase you, and you would run and hide in the groves."

A warm glow came with the memories. "I never ran very fast," she said.

He chuckled. "But I did. Because when we were older, when I caught you, I would kiss you. I'm sure that running after you was what made me so agile and fleet-footed."

She stiffened slightly in his arms.

"Is something amiss?"

"I—I must go. I hear a call."

"I don't hear anything. Are you angry with me after all?"

"We'll not speak of the past. It is over and done with. I truly hear a call. I must go."

"Don't go, love. Don't—"

* * *

Welcome was jolted awake by the ringing phone. She groped for the receiver, then mumbled a sleepy, "Hello."

Silence.

"Dammit! *Hello.*"

Again silence.

She slammed down the receiver, then snatched it up again and dialed the hotel operator. "I have been receiving some annoying telephone calls. From now on, I want all my calls screened. *Nobody* is to be put through without giving his name and your checking with me first. Is that possible?"

"Certainly, miss. We are distressed by your problem. May we be of other service?"

"No. No, that's all. Thank you."

Welcome hung up and dropped back against the pillow. Damn whoever was bugging her! Not only was it getting on her nerves big time, but the call had interrupted the loveliest dream. A significant dream, she felt. The raucous jangle of the phone had ripped the images from her head, and she couldn't remember a bit of it now.

Only a pleasant afterglow clung to the edges of her consciousness. A slight, hollow ache throbbed in her chest.

She tried to go back to sleep, to recapture the dream, but she was wide awake.

The phone rang again.

Takis was calling, the hotel operator informed her.

Oh dear, her meeting with Spyros had flown from her head until that moment. She apologized to Takis profusely and asked him to apologize to his grandfather. "I had a family emergency arise, and I haven't had a moment to call."

She felt lower than worm dirt for lying and even

lower when Takis expressed his sincere concern about her situation and offered his assistance.

"No, no," she said. "Everything is under control now. Ask Spyros if we may reschedule for tomorrow."

Spyros himself took the phone after Takis relayed the message. "You okay, Welcome? Takis says you sound bad. Forget tomorrow. You come today. We'll drink wine and cook fried chicken steak and cheer you up. Come, come, my family says. Be with us. I have never seen my Niki so happy since she meet you. We drink wine and sing and dance and maybe we break some plates, eh? You know about breaking the plates? I send Takis on his motor scooter to pick you up. Okay?"

Welcome hesitated. Philip had told her to stay in her room, and it seemed to be a fine idea at the time, but the idea of staying cooped up and staring at the same four walls for the next twenty-four hours or so sounded less and less appealing.

"A taxi would be better?" Spyros asked.

"No. Takis's scooter will be fine."

"He pick you up in half an hour, okay?"

Philip would probably kill her if she left the hotel—if somebody else didn't beat him to it.

But she couldn't imagine anything happening to her when she was going to be surrounded by a bunch of people the entire time. Surely she would be safe with the Katrakises.

"Half an hour will be fine."

Seven

*The wine urges me on, the bewitching wine, which sets
even a wise man to singing and to laughing gently and
rouses him up to dance and brings forth words which
were better unspoken.*

Homer
c. 700 B.C.

A full moon rose over the old city, and the evening
was pleasantly cool. Wade heard a variety of languages
blended into a happy chatter as tourists strolled along,
visiting the brightly lit shops, the tavernas, the night-
clubs. Well-dressed young men stood outside various
establishments waylaying passersby and touting the fine
menus or the exceptional entertainment.

There was an excitement in the air along with the
familiar, lively music so stereotypically Greek that Wade
Morgan half expected Anthony Quinn to spring from
a doorway and break into a Zorba dance.

As they made their ways down one of the winding
streets of Plaka, Shark sniffed the night air. "You smell
that?"

"What?"

"If I didn't know better, I'd swear I smell chicken-
fried steak and gravy cookin'."

Wade snorted. "Around here? Not likely. But I tell

you, I could handle a couple about now. Do you know how long it's been since we ate?"

"I guess I do. My belly's stuck to my backbone. That little dab of fancy stuff we had at the hotel," Shark said, checking his watch, "nine hours and fifteen minutes ago is long gone. Where's that place the fellow at the hotel told us had Greek soul food?"

"On the next block, I think. You know, this area sort of reminds me of the French Quarter in New Orleans."

"Yeah, except for the strip joints, restaurants with decent food I know the name of, and people who speak English, it's a lot like the French Quarter."

Wade laughed. "Come on, Shark. Where's your spirit of adventure?"

"Left it in a locker at LAX. Could you tell me yet what we're doin' here?"

"Damned if I know."

"Ah, sirs, you look for good dinner?" one of the street hustlers asked. "Taverna Katrakis is the best place to eat in all Athens. You like chicken? We got the plumpest. Our lamb is the finest. We got *moussaka;* we got *kokoretsi;* we got *dolmade.* Look at our menu. Take a look. We got anything you want. Anything. Best in Athens."

They looked at the menu, then at each other. "Can you read that stuff?" Shark asked.

"Not a word."

"Me neither. You got any barbecued ribs?"

"Ribs? No," the young man drawled as if considering. He suddenly brightened and flashed a big grin. "But we have chicken-fried steak. We are the only taverna in Athens to serve chicken-fried steak."

"You're shittin' me," Shark said.

"No shittin'. We have chicken-fried steak and also

the cream gravy so thick that a spoon stands upright in the bowl. That is the very best kind, you know."

"*Greek* chicken-fried steak?" Wade hooted with laughter. "This I gotta see." He turned to Shark. "You game?"

"Man, right now I'd even eat some of that stuff wrapped in grape leaves. I'm 'bout starved to death."

They followed the hustler to the door, then a waiter seated them at a table near a small stage. The taverna was only about half full, but there was an atmosphere of camaraderie like in a neighborhood tavern back home. Smoky, savory smells and the hum of light-hearted conversation filled the room. A Sony tape deck above the bar played more of the *Zorba the Greek* music.

They each ordered beer and a chicken-fried steak special dinner.

As the waiter left, a raucous burst of laughter came from a large table by the bar. Wade glanced over and saw a tall redhead wearing an apron jump to her feet, raise her glass high, and say something that he didn't catch. The people at the table clapped and cheered. Two of the young men sitting at the table rose and walked to the stage.

The redhead applauded wildly.

Shark nudged Wade. "You see that tall woman with the red hair?"

"Yeah, I see her." *See her?* Hell, he couldn't take his eyes off her. She was dynamite.

"She look familiar to you?"

"She ought to. I've been pattin' her butt every day for ten years."

As Takis and his friend danced on the small stage, Welcome climbed on her chair, clapped and whistled and cheered. "Opa!" she shouted, tossing a flower at the pair. "Opa!" If breaking real plates hadn't been outlawed, she would have loved to smash a stack on the stage.

Welcome was having a blast. For the past several hours, she and Spyros and his family had been drinking wine and learning to cook chicken-fried steak. It had taken some doing to convince Spyros that the meat couldn't be fried in olive oil and remain authentic. Amid much laughter, they had turned out some fine round steaks, tender and crispy-coated and so large that they hung over the platters. The home fries and the gravy were downright scrumptious as well. She'd filled up on a big helping—and a lot of wine.

A lot of wine.

"Opa!" she shouted, laughing and raising her glass high.

Takis gestured for her to come and join their dance. Although she hadn't a clue as to the proper steps, she didn't have to be asked twice. She downed her wine and grabbed Niki to join them as well. The four of them stood in a line, arms out and clasping their neighbors'. Her Greek friends showed her the steps, and she soon got the hang of it.

To the bittersweet rhythm of the bouzouki strings, they moved and dipped and stamped and yipped until Welcome felt she would weep with the joy of the dance. Losing herself in the emotion of the music and the movement, she became one with the music, the moment, and the friends and danced on and on until she thought her heart would burst.

When the last strain died, the Katrakis family and friends rose and cheered. Spyros smothered her in a bear hug. "Wonderful! You have the soul of a Greek, my daughter. *Ella!* Come! Customers have ordered the chicken-fried steak, and we must prepare it for them."

He thrust her wineglass into her hand and propelled her toward the kitchen.

"Ahhh-haaaa!" she yipped, holding her glass high. "Ahhh-haaaa! San Antone!"

"Good gawdamighty!" Wade whispered on the breath he'd been holding.

"Man. Did you see that woman?"

"See her? Hell, I feel like I've been run over by a Peterbilt truck loaded with bananas."

That was an understatement. The minute he'd spotted her, something had come over him, a feeling of such intensity that for a minute he was sure he was having a heart attack. He'd never felt anything like it. And the more he watched the redhead, the more powerful the feeling became.

By the time she left the room, his guts were turned inside out, and he was horny as hell. But his reaction hadn't been just a case of raging testosterone; his testosterone had been raging since he was fourteen. This was something different. Something—hell, he didn't know—something . . . profound.

"Man, what's the matter with you? You look like you been hit up beside the head with an axe handle."

Wade blew out a breath and nodded toward the door she'd exited. "She's the matter with me. The redhead."

Shark grinned. "Fine-looking woman. You planning on gettin' you a piece of that?"

"Watch your mouth, my friend. That's the woman I'm gonna marry."

"Marry? Man, you flipped out? You ain't even met her yet. You don't know nothing about her. You don't know her name. All you know about is her ass."

Wade's gut tightened. "I told you to watch your mouth," he said sharply.

Shark put out his hands, palms up in surrender. "Hey, hey, I didn't mean nothing by it, but I don't understand what's got into you. In the twenty-five years we been friends, I ain't never heard you mention *marrying* nobody. Now here you are—talking about marrying some lady you ain't even *met?*"

"I've been waiting for her."

Shark raised one eyebrow and took a big swig of his beer. "If you say so, man."

Wade took a pull from his bottle. "It does sound crazy, doesn't it?"

"Crazier'n old Pap Menefee back home."

"Shark, what can I tell you? I don't know how I know, but I know. She's the one I've been waiting for all my life, and I'm gonna marry her."

"What if she's already married? Did you ever think of that? What if she's got a husband?"

"Then I'll kill him."

Both of Shark's eyebrows shot up. "I almost believe you mean that."

"Believe it. That lady is mine."

Shark let out a low whistle. "I just hope the lady is willing."

"She will be."

When the redhead approached their table smiling, Wade rose and grinned from ear to ear. In an automatic response, his hand came up and stroked her butt.

She slapped the fire out of him. "Keep your hand off my derriere, you neanderthal. I appreciate your saving my bacon twice, but after all, that's what you're paid to do. If I called Ram and reported you, you would be out on your keister in a New York minute."

"Ram? Who's Ram?" Wade asked, totally mystified.

"You know very well who. Ramson Gabrey. Your boss. You're made, so there's no need for you to deny it. For once, I appreciate Ram's paranoia about security. When that guy shot at me today, I damned near wet my pants. Where did you disappear to anyway?"

"Shot at you? What the hell are you talking about? Who's Ram?"

She rolled her eyes at Shark who sat there grinning like a possum. "I don't know who Ram is, either," Shark said, throwing up his hands.

Glancing heavenward, she made an exasperated face. "What a pair of hams. But if that's the way you want to handle it, okay. I've played this game before. We'll pretend that we just met by accident. God knows, for once I'm glad to have a couple of bruisers hanging around. But you," she said, sticking her finger in Wade's face, "keep your hands off my butt. If I want to be touched, I'll let you know. Enjoy your steaks," she said, nodding to the two platters the waiter had placed on the table. "I cooked them myself."

She wheeled and strode away.

"Close your mouth and sit down," Shark said.

Wade sat.

Shark snickered. " 'Spect we don't need to reserve the church just yet."

"Did you make any sense out of what she said?"

"Best I can tell, she didn't like you pattin' her butt, she thinks we work for somebody named Ram, somebody shot at her, *and,*" Shark said, leaning close to inhale the aroma of his food, "I got a feeling that she's a damned fine cook." He picked up his knife and fork, cut a wedge of steak, and ate it. "She is. A damned fine cook. Reckon they got any catsup?" He craned his neck and looked around.

"Somebody *shot* at her?"

" 'S what the lady said."

"Well, gawd damn, I gotta find out about that." Wade got up to start toward the table where she sat.

"Whoa, hoss." Shark grabbed him by the elbow. "Sit down. She ain't going nowhere just yet. Let's eat and talk about this some. We may have stumbled into something we don't want to get involved in."

"Too late, my friend. I'm already involved." But he sat down and started eating. Shark was right; she was a damned good cook. Best chicken-fried steak he'd ever eaten, and he'd sampled many a one.

Welcome sneaked another glance at the guy with the dishwater-blond hair. During their first two encounters, she'd been too scared to pay much attention to the man, but she couldn't seem to keep her eyes off him now.

She couldn't believe that she'd slapped him for touching her. Over the years, especially when she went to Italy, her bottom had been patted and pinched thousands of times, and she'd never slapped anyone for doing it. Usually she had either shot the perpetrator a scathing look or ignored the incident, side-stepped, and gone on about her business. Occasionally she had torn a strip off the offender, verbally or by international gesture. She'd never *slapped* anybody.

Why this one?

Was it because when he'd touched her so intimately that she'd almost gone ballistic?

And why had she been so defensive with him? Actually, she could have thrown her arms around the big lug and kissed him to hell and back. The other one, too. Seeing their bulk and knowing that they were around to protect her should have made her feel ecstatic.

She didn't feel ecstatic.

She felt edgy. Anxious. A little scared.

Of him.

Not physically. She didn't fear any physical threat from him. Ram Gabrey's security force was too professional and too well screened. The threat seemed to be emotional, and scarier still since she didn't know where the feeling was coming from.

A sense of impending—not doom exactly, but impending *something*—hovered around her, flapping its wings like a big owl preparing to settle. Something about this man ignited an inner spark that suggested danger.

But then she'd been as tense as a whore in church since she'd passed by Metaxas's shop this afternoon and noticed that it was open for business as usual. She'd dragged Takis inside with her before they went to the taverna.

A middle-aged woman, dressed in black and with her hair done up like somebody's grandmother, had been at the counter.

Bold as brass, Welcome had marched up and said, "I would like to speak with Miklos about some glassware."

The woman had eyed her strangely and said, "I don't know any Miklos. What kind of glassware interests you?"

Wrong response.

Welcome had mumbled something, hooked her arm through Takis's, and hauled it in a hurry. But not before she'd scrutinized the counter for bloodstains.

There weren't any. The counter was clean as a whistle. Something very weird was going on. Or else, she had imagined the whole thing.

She didn't like to even consider the possibility.

Unable to help herself, she glanced at the blond man again.

He was staring a hole through her.

She quickly looked away, her face burning.

Lawdy, lawdy. Was she, Welcome Venable, a sophisticated nineties woman, actually *blushing*?

What was it with her? He wasn't her type. The man was obviously an ex-jock of some kind, like so many of Ram's men, and she didn't care for the jock mentality. Never had. Even in high school she'd quickly discovered that football players had egos the size of Greyhound buses and that their priorities were all screwed up.

If she had any sense, she would telephone Ram in Cairo and tell him to call off his dogs; then she would get on an airplane, go to Texas, and stay as far away from this man as possible. He was trouble, and she knew it.

Instead, she tossed back the rest of her wine and got up to dance with her friends, knowing full well that the man was watching her every move.

Welcome clung to Takis's waist, singing nonsense syllables to the top of her lungs as they rode to the hotel on his motor scooter. *"Opa!"* she shouted, thrusting one hand in the air.

Takis laughed. "I think you had a little too much *chima.*"

"Who, *moi?*" She spewed out a giggle.

"Yes, my friend, you. Tomorrow you will regret it."

She yawned. "Maybe so, but I had a *wonderful* time tonight."

They had continued the party until the wee hours, and she'd never had so much fun. Getting out had done her a world of good. She hadn't had time to think about—no, she wasn't going to think about it now either.

Where were her watchdogs? Close behind she assumed. The pair had stayed until the taverna closed. Mostly they just sat and sipped beer and watched. She had tried not to look at them—good security practice she told herself—but her eyes kept wandering to her rescuer. Several times she caught herself gazing at him and discovered that each time their eyes met, extremely provocative images began flitting through her head.

It had been the wine. Or maybe she felt this titillation because of the recent danger they had shared. Or maybe it was because she felt that she wanted to freefall into the depths of his beautiful, magnetic eyes and—

"Puh-lease!"

"Pardon?" Takis asked.

"Never mind. Oh, there's the old GB."

When Takis stopped the scooter by the front steps, Welcome climbed off, careful of the package of baklava that Aunt Irini had sent along with her. "Good night, sweet Takis. I had a dee-lightful evening." She kissed his cheek.

"I'll see you safely to your room."

He started to get off the scooter, but Welcome stopped him. She leaned forward and whispered, "No need, sugarplum. I have watchdogs." She giggled again, wiggled her fingers, and ran up the steps.

When she reached her room, she had to put the baklava on the floor to search for the key. She tried her waist pack, then patted all her pockets until she found the elusive little devil.

Verrry carefully she fitted the key in the lock, opened the door, and went in. The room was pitch dark. She pulled off one boot, switched on a dim lamp, then pulled off the other boot. She yawned again, tossed her jacket and key on the settee as she passed, and started peeling off her sweater as she headed straight for the bed.

The place reeked of roses.

Absolutely reeked.

Just as she reached for the button on her jeans, she saw why.

Her bed was covered with crushed yellow rose petals. They had been ripped from the two arrangements which now stood decapitated on the dresser.

She began to shake.

She couldn't stop.

Wanting to flee, she tried to move, but her feet seemed cemented to the spot, and her eyes glued to the ravaged blossoms on her bed. This was not the romantic gesture of a lover scattering petals across the coverlet; this was a deliberate demolishing, a taunting mockery. She could feel vestiges of malevolence in the air.

Dear God! Was he still in the room?

Her feet moved. Clenching back a scream, she ran to the door, flung it open, and collided with a broad chest.

The scream she'd been holding escaped. She struggled frantically against the arms that enveloped her.

"Whoa, whoa, sugar. It's just me."

Welcome composed herself enough to see that she had run into the pair of security men, and she slumped against the blond one who held her. "Oh, Lord. I've never been so glad to see anyone in my life. I've just had the bejesus scared out of me again. My heart can't take much more of this."

"Want to tell me what's going on?"

She gestured to the room behind her and tried to explain, but all she could seem to do was blather, "The roses. The roses."

"Shark, you go check. I'll take her to our suite."

Welcome allowed herself to be led along, grateful for the presence of the warm, muscled body next to hers. She couldn't seem to stop shaking.

She didn't know where she was going to sleep that night, but one thing for sure, it damned well wasn't going to be in that bed.

Eight

Hades is relentless and unyielding.

Homer
c. 700 B.C.

Cold fury engulfed him, and he swore silently as he stood among the brooms and mops and watched through a small crack in the door.

Three times he thought that he'd had her, and three times he'd been thwarted by some twist of fate. Now it was these big American men. The black one looked especially dangerous, not one to attack without a gun and some distance between them.

He'd never cared much for guns. They were bulky and noisy. Even with a careful sighting and the perfect shot, things could go wrong. Hadn't he seen evidence of that? He preferred a blade. Quick. Silent. One of his rested sleekly along his upper spine; the other was strapped above his ankle.

Ah, well, his opportunity had passed. But there would be another. While the black one was in her room, he slipped from the closet, left the hotel, and melted into the shadows.

Nine

These impossible women! How they do get around us!
The poet was right: can't live with them, or without
them!

Aristophanes
c. 450-385 B.C.

Welcome sat on the couch wearing a borrowed, oversized sweater, and huddled in her rescuer's arms. A
big girl all her life, she'd never been the delicate type
who needed a man's protection or was prone to attacks
of the vapors. But being held by this strong man, having him stroke her back and murmur soothing sounds
made her feel positively delicate and completely safe.

The fright began to wane, and she began to relax.
Her shaking stopped, the chill chased away by the soft
warmth of the man's cashmere sweater and the cloak
of his arms.

After a few moments, she felt better. Much better.
But being held felt so good that she lingered in his
arms a little longer, snuggled a bit closer, and rooted
her cheek against his chest.

She could feel his heartbeat. Strong and steady.

The black guy came in, and she sat up.

"Nobody in your room now, but looks like somebody
trashed your flowers for sure. Ripped all the petals off

your roses and threw them on the bed. Any idea who did it?"

"Not unless it was the guy who shot at me." She turned to the man who still held a comforting arm around her. "Did you ever get a look at him?"

He frowned. "I don't know what you're talking about. What guy? Did somebody really shoot at you?"

He seemed so genuinely mystified, that Welcome grew unsettled again. "Look, I know that Ram likes for his men to be unobtrusive, but this is ridiculous."

"I don't know anybody named Ram. Shark here doesn't know anybody named Ram. Just who is this guy anyhow?"

Her heart dropped to the pit of her stomach. She looked from one of the hulking men to the other. "You don't work for Ramson Gabrey of Horus Security?"

Both of them shook their heads no.

"Swear to God?"

"Swear to God," the blond one said.

The other raised his hand. "On a stack of Bibles a foot high."

She swallowed. "Then who *are* you?"

"He's D'Angelo Thomas," the blond one said. "But everybody calls him Shark. I'm Wade Morgan. I play for the Vulcans."

"The Vulcans?"

"The Los Angeles Vulcans. I'm their quarterback," he said with thinly veiled pride.

She pushed away from his brawn. "You're *football* players?"

"Well, don't say it like you stepped in something nasty," Wade said. "Yeah, I'm a pro football player, and Shark is my trainer."

"You don't work for Ram?"

"Sugar, we don't have any idea who this Ram guy is. The only Rams I know play for St. Louis."

"I'll bet that I can't hope that you know Philip Van Horn either, can I?"

"Nope. Never heard of him."

"Ohhhh, dear." Welcome leaned her head back against the couch cushion. "Then it was simply a coincidence that you were in Metaxas's shop when he was murdered?"

"*Murdered?*" Wade said. "Who was murdered? What the hell are you talking about, Red?"

"Don't call me *Red*. My name is Welcome, and you know very well what I'm talking about. I'm talking about the man whose throat was cut in his shop across from the taverna where you ate dinner tonight."

"What kind of a name is Welcome?"

"A perfectly good name. The one I've been called all my life. My driver's license says Mary Alice Venable, but I don't answer to anything but Welcome, and don't change the subject. Something fishy is going on here. I hope that you're not going to deny being in Metaxas's shop yesterday."

There was a painful silence.

Then Wade said quietly, "Sugar, Shark and I didn't arrive in Greece until this morning. Yesterday we were in California."

She glanced quickly from one man to the other. "What's going on here? I *saw* you with my own eyes. You were in a shop in Plaka, and you helped me get away from the killer. I didn't imagine you lowering me from that window. And I didn't imagine you knocking me to the ground when someone shot at me either."

Wade cut his gaze briefly to his buddy, then shrugged. "I don't know what to say. It wasn't me."

Her eyes narrowed. "But you can't deny that you were in Greece this morning when I was shot at in the agora."

"What time was this alleged incident?"

"There's nothing *alleged* about it. The bullets nicked the marble column I was standing by. It happened at about eleven o'clock."

"Ma'am, at eleven o'clock this morning, he was sound asleep in that room in yonder," Shark said. "I know 'cause I heard him snoring."

"Impossible." Still trying to make some sense out of things, she said, "You don't happen to have a twin brother, do you?"

Wade smiled. "Not that I know of."

She dug her fingers into her scalp and rested her forehead in her palms. "Oh my God, am I losing my mind?" she cried.

Wade pulled her close again and patted her back. "Shhhh, honey. You've had a lot of wine and got pretty scared about your flowers—"

She jumped to her feet. "Don't you condescend to me, you pea-brained jock!"

"Now, now, darlin'—"

"I'm not your *darlin'*. I'm not your anything. I don't know what in the hell is going on here, but I'm not drunk, and I'm not crazy! Get your hands off me. I didn't say that you could touch me."

Shark was grinning and his shoulders shook. "Heh, heh, heh."

Welcome whirled on Shark. "What's so damned funny?"

Shark sobered immediately. "Not a thing, ma'am. Not a thing. Sounds like there's some serious stuff going on here. Seems to me that we ought to call the police."

She rolled her eyes and made an exasperated noise. "And tell them what? That I saw a murder being committed and somebody shot at me, but the other witnesses didn't see a thing? Or shall I call the police and tell them that I've been getting crank calls, but I don't have any witnesses to that either. Or that somebody scattered rose petals on my bed? Now that's a good idea. They can see the rose petals. I can hear them snickering now."

"Well," Shark said, "if it was me, I'd at least talk to the hotel manager. Somebody's been in your room that shouldn't have been there, and they made a mess. I think I'd ask to be moved to another room."

"Good idea," Wade said. "I'll call." He glanced at Welcome. "Any objections?"

She started to object on general principles, but she was too weary for principles at the moment. "Go ahead." She plopped back down on the couch and pulled her knees to her chin.

After a few minutes on the phone, he hung up. "The night manager will be here immediately."

The manager arrived in less than five minutes, effusive in his apologies. Leaving Welcome in their suite, Wade and Shark went with the manager to survey the damage.

The manager was appalled that an unauthorized person had gained entry to Miss Venable's room and ruined her lovely roses.

"Come in here," Shark said, indicating the bathroom. "I guess she didn't see this, and I didn't mention it."

Wade stuck his head in the door. On the mirror, printed in lipstick was: BITCH.

"Uh-oh," Wade said.

"Yeah."

"Something serious is definitely going on. But what?"

"Are you thinking what I'm thinking?" Shark asked.

"That she's a mental case, and she might have done this herself?"

"Could be. Wouldn't be the first time a woman has pulled some kind of stunt to meet you. Remember that time in Vegas?"

Wade took a wad of tissue and smeared the lipstick off the mirror before the manager, who was calling hotel security, saw it. He couldn't have said why he wiped the word off, except that he felt very protective of Welcome. He didn't want this incident to get blown out of proportion until he could figure things out.

They spent a few minutes with the hotel security man and listened to more apologies from the manager. Apparently Welcome was considered a VIP; the poor guy was doing some major hand-wringing about something so dreadful happening to such a gracious and celebrated person. From what Wade could surmise from the shaken manager, Welcome was a big deal in the fashion world and traveled in tall company. He hadn't realized that she was famous, but then he didn't pay much attention to women's fashions, especially the European stuff.

Unfortunately, all the rooms were filled for the night, but the manager promised to move Miss Venable to a complimentary suite on the following day. "Perhaps I can find her another hotel until then," he added.

"Never mind," Wade said. "She can stay with us for tonight."

As he and Wade returned to their suite down the hall, Shark said, "How you think she's gonna take to spending the night with us?"

Wade shrugged. "Beats me, but I want her around so that I can keep an eye on her. She can have my room, and I'll sleep on the couch."

"Better yet, why don't I let her have *my* room, and

I'll sleep on the couch," Shark said, grinning slyly. "That way I can make sure nobody sneaks into her room while she's asleep."

"Hell, man, I'm not that big a louse! Besides, she'd probably cut my dick off if I tried anything."

Shark hooted with laughter. "You got that right."

The argument was settled when they opened the door. Welcome was curled up on the couch, fast asleep.

For several minutes Wade stood looking down at her, envying his own sweater as the over-large garment encased her body and nuzzled her skin. Emotion so potent that it was painful rose up out of nowhere and threatened to choke him. He'd been in heaven holding her, touching her—until she'd turned into a spitting bobcat.

He didn't begin to understand what was going on with her, what fantasies plagued her mind. Maybe she was nuts, but even if she was crazier than Pap Menefee, he would follow her to the ends of the earth and protect her with his life.

Whether she liked it or not.

Nothing had ever seemed so important. It was as if his whole life had led solely to this moment.

He resisted the urge to kiss her. He only allowed himself to touch one fiery curl of her hair. The strand wound itself around his finger and clung to it like a lover.

"I won't fail you, Red," he whispered to her sleeping form.

Slowly he withdrew his hand and spread a blanket over her. He made sure that the hallway door was bolted, then stole quietly from the room.

Ten

> *By convention there is color, by convention sweetness,*
> *by convention bitterness, but in reality there are atoms*
> *and space.*
>
> Democritus
> c. 460-400 B.C.

The moment he appeared, she knew. Her eyes opened, and he stood beside her smiling. He held out his hand, and without a word between them, she took it.

He pulled her up and into his arms. "Oh, my only love, how sweet to hold you again, to touch your softness, to smell your soul." He nuzzled his face against her sun-flamed hair.

She pressed closer, molding her shape to his, savoring the delight of his nearness.

"Is that music I hear?" he said.

"Music? I hear no music."

He laughed. "Listen closely."

Cocking her head, she listened with her sensitive ear, then smiled. "I believe that it is distant music."

"Ah, I thought so. Shall we go and find it and dance?"

From Syntagma Square they followed the haunting strains of the bouzouki that beckoned them back to Plaka. Now that the tourists were abed, the Greeks were out, and the tenor of the music changed. In an elevated area of the old city, a bittersweet melody wafted from a doorway, curled itself about them, and drew them toward the small, smoky boîte.

Inside, a man sat in a corner strumming a bouzouki as he sang impassioned words of lost love and desertion. Beside him, an accordion played a soft accompaniment.

"Beautiful," he whispered in her ear. His arms went around her waist, and he pulled her back against him as they watched the musicians and listened to the tearful song. She laid her head back on his shoulder and let herself drift with the bittersweet melody.

Bittersweet.

Ah, yes. Bittersweet.

Sensing that she was edging toward memories best left alone for now, he nipped her earlobe, ran his tongue along the inner shell of her ear, then whispered, "Come, let us go into the garden and dance."

As they moved outside to the deserted garden that was too chilly for most of the revelers, the music changed to a lively tune and he laughed.

"Did you—"

He kissed her question away and laughed again. "Come, love, let's dance and be merry."

Mirthful moonlight sparkled in his eyes as he held both arms straight out from his sides. Standing beside him, she clasped one of his arms, and they began to dance.

They danced on and on, laughing and dipping and clapping and stamping. "Opa! Opa!" they shouted and danced some more. "Opa!"

They broke plates as she had longed to do before. Stacks of plates. Then they laughed and clapped and shouted and danced in the deserted garden until the first gray glow of morning. Giddy with the joy of the moment, they fell into an embrace.

"Wonderful! That was wonderful," she said breathlessly. "Your dancing puts Terpsichore to shame."

"It is you who shames the goddesses. You are wonderful,"

he said, lifting her in his powerful arms and swinging her around. She threw back her head, and her gaiety rippled around the cypresses and myrtles. His movement slowed as he beheld her shining face, and his lips descended to hers.

"Wonderful," he whispered before he kissed her.

An aeon of emotion spilled from him; an aeon answered from her.

Her skin was like honey from the comb and as silky as her gossamer shift that vanished with a whisper. His garment faded as well, leaving only skin and sinew between them.

His lips were as enticing as a pomegranate and as passionate as a youth newly drunk from Eros's cup. His manhood pressed against her heated belly, then filled her hand like the lusty spear of a carved marble stallion.

Her breath caught; he groaned. Desire pulsated in the air and rustled the leaves as Eos sparked the first colors of a radiant dawn.

With thighs and calves akin to Helios astride the harbor of Rhodes, he planted himself and lifted her high. Her legs went round his girth, her arms around his thick neck; her lips never left his. His broad hands made a chair beneath her.

"Ah, my love," he murmured as he slowly lowered her onto his tumescence.

She breathed in a long sigh as she sheathed him as perfectly as an olive sheathes its pit, rejoicing to imbibe once again in her love's sweet ambrosia and to be filled with his essence.

They blended and moved, touching souls, kindling ecstasy, sharing heartbeats until their union burst into a dazzling array, as resplendent as the brilliant-hued aurora that rose over the horizon and painted the hills of Athens gold.

"Ah, my love, my only love," came a sigh on the wind.

Eleven

I call a fig a fig, a spade a spade.

Menander
c. 342-292 B.C.

The smell of coffee twitched Welcome's nose. A crash and a blistering hiss of curses jerked her awake. She sat up, brushed her mop of hair from her face to get her bearings, then groaned as a little man inside her skull bashed her temples with a tire iron.

She groaned again, eased back to a supine position, and vowed not to move so much as an eyelash, lest she die. Even though she hadn't glimpsed anything very familiar, at the moment she didn't give a damn where she was. She could be in a cathouse in Borneo for all she cared.

"Hangover?" a man yelled softly.

She vaguely recognized the voice. "Either that or I've just had a lobotomy." She winced and grabbed her head to hold it still after her words reverberated in her brain like a struck gong.

"Sorry I woke you. I dropped a coffee cup. I figured that you might have a doozie, so I had the concierge gather up the ingredients for my famous hangover potion. Here," Wade said, raising her head, "drink this."

She wrinkled her nose at the smell rising from the steaming cup. "What's in that mess?"

"Can't tell. It's a secret family remedy passed down from my old grandpappy. Drink up."

She took a tentative sip, then shuddered. "It tastes like a cross between burned peppermint and roofing tar."

He grinned. "You're not too far off. I had to make a couple of substitutions in the formula, but I think they'll do. Drink the rest of it."

After another swallow, which almost didn't go down, she shuddered again, harder this time.

"The concierge couldn't locate any sassafras, so I used peppermint instead. And in place of kerosene, I had to use a mixture of olive oil and lighter fluid—"

The sip she'd just taken spewed from her mouth. *"Lighter fluid?* Are you mad? If anybody strikes a match, I'll go up like bananas Foster."

Chuckling, Wade dabbed at the spattered brew. "Don't worry. It was burned off before I poured it. I think you've had enough. Now lay back and wait five minutes to let the potion do its work."

"I think I'd rather have a cup of coffee and an aspirin." She started to rise.

He gently pushed her back down. "Five minutes. Trust me. My grandpappy made potions as well as he made white lightning."

Her stomach churned; her head clanged.

An eternity passed.

"Can I get up now?"

"It's only been two minutes. I'll tell you when."

A second eternity passed.

"Time's up," Wade finally said. "Try sitting up. Slowly."

She sat up—very gingerly. Her head stayed on. Her

stomach was settled. The little guy with the tire iron had vanished.

"How do you feel?"

"Fine. I'm surprised, but fine. My compliments to your grandpappy."

He handed her a cup of coffee. "Try this. I added a little sugar and cream."

"Ahhh," she said after tasting it. "Pure ambrosia. Remind me never to drink *chima* again. Greek wine packs a wallop. At first it's like drinking punch, then while you're not looking, it hits you like a hand grenade."

When she'd finished the first, she held out her coffee cup for Wade to pour another, black this time. As he poured, she realized that she had fallen asleep on his couch wearing her jeans and his baggy cashmere sweater. Other memories from the night before crept in, some foggy, some clear. "My room—"

"You were asleep when Shark and I came back. The manager was very apologetic about the mess in your room. He's moving you to a complimentary suite today. I just talked to him a few minutes ago; your suite will be ready in a couple of hours. You'll be right next door to us as soon as count somebody or the other checks out and things get cleaned up."

"Thanks for coming to my rescue. Again." She held her breath waiting for him to deny coming to her rescue before. He let it pass.

"No problem. And hotel security thought it might be a good idea if you were registered under an assumed name instead of your own. They're going to keep a tight watch on the comings and goings in and out of your room. Security camera, I think."

"I appreciate everything you've done," Welcome said, rising. "Now if you'll excuse me, I think I'll go to my room to shower and dress. I'll have your sweater cleaned and returned as soon as possible."

"You don't have a room."

"Pardon?"

"You don't have a room."

"Of course I do. It may be a mess, but I have one."

"Nope. You're checked out. A maid packed your things and stashed them in my room."

Fury rose up in her like heat from the bad place. "Who the hell appointed you my guardian? How dare you make decisions for me!"

"Hey, Red, get down off your high horse. The security man suggested it, and you were dead to the world and snoring like a freight train."

"Don't call me Red, and I do not *snore."*

He grinned. "Yeah, you do, but don't worry about it. I do, too. My nose has been busted so many times that my septum is like a pretzel. Come on over to the table. We got breakfast waiting."

She tried to protest, but she seemed suddenly famished. "Just let me freshen up a bit and make a quick phone call, then I'll be ready. By the way, what name am I going to be registered under?"

"Who are you going to call?" he asked sharply.

"My photographer, if it's any of your business," she retorted just as sharply. "I'm expecting her today. We're here to work."

"Sorry. It's just that it doesn't make any sense to be incognito, then tell every Tom, Dick, and Harry where you are. I told the manager to use my last name. You'll be listed as Elizabeth Morgan from L.A."

She wrinkled her nose in distaste. "Of all the places in the world I'd rather not be from, Los Angeles heads the list. Which is your room?" When he pointed, she said, "I'll be right back."

Even before Welcome brushed her teeth or tackled the rat's nest that passed for her hair, she called Philip Van Horn and explained in cryptic terms her move and new identity. "And Philip, would you let Meri know about the changes? Tell her that a fan was harassing me or something, and I'll call later."

"Will do. And by the way, I was able to engage that photographer we spoke about. She should be arriving this afternoon. Her name is Soloma Jones. You can have complete confidence in her. Don't let her looks fool you, she's skilled in *every* aspect of her job."

Welcome buttered the last bite of her roll and popped it into her mouth.

"For somebody who wasn't very hungry," Wade said, "you did pretty well."

"To tell you the truth, I stay hungry. But with being a model all my adult life, I could never allow myself to admit it."

"Well, if you ask me, I think that you could stand a few more pounds," Wade said, then when he realized that he'd stuck his foot in it, he quickly added, "not that there's anything wrong with your figure now."

He was relieved when she laughed. "Thanks, I think. But you're right. A few more pounds wouldn't hurt. As soon as I'm finished with this job, my modeling days are over, and I plan to pig out on two pounds of sour cream pecan fudge."

"You're quitting?"

"Yep. I'm getting too old to keep playing dress up. I'm leaving it to the younger kids coming along in the business, and I'm going back to Texas to live on the family ranch."

"You don't seem very old to me, but I know the feeling. God, do I know the feeling. Pro ball is a young man's game, and I'm getting within spittin' distance of forty."

"Ever think of retiring?"

"Sometimes." He shifted uneasily in his chair. "Where in Texas is your ranch?"

"Near Athens."

"Athens, *Texas*? How about that? That's some coincidence. I'm originally from Athens, Georgia, and here we are in Athens, Greece. You ever been here before?"

"No, never have. I've lived in Europe for the past ten years and always meant to come, but somehow it just never worked out."

Wade emptied the coffeepot, apportioning the last of it between Welcome's cup and his. "Your folks still living in Texas?"

She shook her head. "My mom died when I was in high school, and my dad about five years ago. I didn't have any brothers or sisters. Just a bunch of cousins, but I had a gang of those."

"That's rough, isn't it? I lost my mother young, too, but I have an older sister who practically raised me. Mom wasn't even thirty when she died."

"My mother wasn't young," she said. "At least not nearly that young. My parents were in their late fifties when somebody left me on their doorstep."

A sudden fury came out of nowhere and spread all over him. "Left you on their doorstep? You mean that you were abandoned?"

"Yep. I was only a few hours old. I was wrapped in an old quilt, and a note was pinned to it asking the Venables to take care of little Mary Alice. My mom had desperately wanted a child but had never been able to have one. She was convinced that the angels had left me with her. The story goes that she kept repeating, 'You're very Welcome here, precious. Very Welcome.' "

Wade smiled at the tale. "So that's where you got the name."

She nodded, then grinned. "Until I was about four, I told people that my name was Very Welcome. It got shortened to Welcome and stuck."

He chuckled. "That's a great story. How did a ranch gal from Texas end up as a model in Europe?"

"It all started on a dare from my roommate in college, but I'll save that story for another time. Do you think my new accommodations might be ready? I need to shower and dress in something that I didn't sleep in."

"I'll check." While Wade was phoning the manager, Shark came in wearing a sweat suit and with a towel hanging around his neck.

"Mornin'," Shark said, nodding to Welcome and cutting his eyes to Wade.

As soon as Wade hung up, he told Welcome that it would be another half hour until she could move. "Why don't you use my shower? All your things are in my room, and there's a lock on the door." He winked playfully. He didn't feel playful. The notion of this gorgeous woman being naked only a few yards away made his old ticker go pitty-pat.

"I think I'll take you up on that." She rose. "Which way?"

"The door on the left." After she'd gone, he turned to Shark and blew out a silent whistle. "Man alive, she is some woman."

"Gets your old blood to pumping, does she?"

"She does that, but it's more. I've never met a woman so easy to talk to. And do you know that she sat here without any makeup on and it didn't seem to

bother her a bit? Most of the women I know would
rather die than do that."

"I been telling you that you've been messing with
the wrong kind of women. She say anymore about
shootin's and throat cuttin's?"

"Not a word."

"Maybe she just had a little too much to drink last
night."

"I hope that's all it is," Wade said. "She seems to
have forgotten about it this morning."

Welcome towel-dried her hair and pulled on the first
thing she could find in her luggage—leggings and a
mustard-colored tunic. The entire time while she show-
ered, she tried to figure out what was going on with
Wade. He seemed normal enough, but she honestly
didn't know what his game was. He said he was a professional player with the Los Angeles whoozits, but
what did she know about pro football? She never read
the sports pages even when she was in the States.

She did, by damn, know that he'd been in Metaxas's
shop on the day that the man had been killed. She'd
seen him with her own eyes, touched him, smelled him.
He hadn't been some kind of hallucination. He'd been
real. There was no way he could have been in California.

Deciding to do a little snooping, and not feeling one
bit guilty about it, she made a quick round of his room.
In the inner pocket of a sport coat hanging in the
closet, she found an airline ticket and some other
stuff—claim checks, receipts, and the like.

When she checked them carefully, a queasy feeling
washed over her. His ticket clearly showed his departure from LAX. Even allowing for the time differences,
there was no way he could have been in Athens the

day before yesterday. Her mind whirled, trying to come up with some scenario that would explain things. Maybe the airline had made a mistake on the ticket and—

Then she saw the dates on a claim check for a hotel garage in Palm Springs and her explanation evaporated. Her fist closed around the stub, and she held it to her chest as waves of chill bumps rippled over her.

What was going on here? Had she eaten some funny mushrooms? Was somebody playing mind games with her?

Her knees buckled, and she sank to the carpet outside the closet. Her brain raced from one explanation to another. She thought of everything from twins to an alien invasion, but nothing she came up with made any sense. Her first idea of course was that the tickets and the receipts were phoney. But what was the point? Why would anyone try to perpetrate such an elaborate hoax on her?

She needed to talk to Meri. Since the moment that Meri had walked into their room in college, the two of them had been best friends and confidantes. They had been through a lot of stuff together. Maybe Meri—

She stopped when she remembered that Meri had been through a similar situation when they had gone to Cairo on an assignment and Meri had first met Ram. But Meri had been *dreaming* about Ram for years, and when she saw him in the flesh, she'd thought she was losing it. And no wonder. But Meri had never seen Ram *in the flesh* when he wasn't there.

Meri and Ram's meeting was destiny, a reuniting of star-crossed lovers. But they were soul mates for gosh sakes. Anybody who was around them for five minutes could tell that. Wade Morgan damned well wasn't *her* soul mate. Oh, he was easy to talk to and fairly nice looking. Sexy and sort of appealing if you cared for the gridiron grunt type—which she didn't. The last person on earth she would be interested in was a professional quarterback. She knew enough about sports to know that guys like Wade were glory hogs who reveled in publicity and loved being in the limelight. Not her. Not any longer. She was through with that kind of life.

No, this was nothing like Meri and Ram. She was getting out of here fast and staying as far away from Wade and his buddy as she could.

All Welcome could think of was hurrying to take the photos for the brochure and hightailing it out of this crazy place before she went totally bonkers. She didn't know what was going on, and while there was probably some reasonable explanation, she was beginning not to care. She wanted to go home to Texas.

As soon as Welcome was situated in the new suite, she called Meri in Cairo. Naturally, the first thing Meri wanted to know was why Welcome was registered under a different name. Welcome was uncomfortable about lying to her best friend, but she made up some story about a man bugging her by calling and sending flowers with proposals.

After they chatted for a few minutes, Welcome said, "I have a question that sounds pretty weird, but I know you've had a few unusual experiences, especially when you and Ram first met."

"Yes?" Meri said hesitantly.

"Well, hell, I guess there's no way to ask this except straight out. Did you ever see, or thought you'd seen, Ram when he really wasn't there? When he couldn't possibly be there? And I don't mean in your dreams."

"No. I don't think so. Why? Welcome Venable have you met a man? A special man, I mean."

"No. Lord, no. Well, I mean I've met a man, but not *the* man. I could have sworn that I saw him and talked to him a couple of days ago, but it's impossible. He didn't arrive in Greece until yesterday, so I *couldn't* have seen him at the shop in Plaka, but I swear that if it wasn't him, it was his double."

"Maybe it was his double."

"I don't think so.

"Is it possible that you dreamed it?"

"I suppose that it's possible, but not probable. It's scary, Mer. Damned scary."

"I don't like the way you sound, Welcome. What's going on?"

"I'm not sure. Oh, by the way, is it possible that Ram has some of his security men watching me?"

"Let me ask." Meri's voice was muffled as if she'd put her hand over the mouthpiece. A few moments later, she came back on the line. "Ram says no. Welcome Venable, something fishy is going on. I can tell by your voice. Are you in any trouble? I've a good mind to get on the next plane for Athens. Hush, Ramson Gabrey, I'll do what I please. Listen, Welcome, don't you hang around there if you're in any danger. Forget that brochure. Get yourself to the airport and come here. We haven't been able to get together in a coon's age, and I miss you something fierce."

"I miss you too, sweetie. Say, have you ever heard of a football player named Wade Morgan? I think he plays for a Los Angeles team called the Volcanos."

Meri laughed. "That's the Los Angeles Vulcans. And of course I've heard of him. The Vulcans won the Super Bowl again this year with Morgan as their quarterback. Why? Is *he* the man you've met?"

"Well, I met him. Uh oh, there's someone at my door. Gotta go. I'll call later."

"See that you do. I want to hear *everything.*"

"There's nothing to hear. Promise. Talk to you later, sweetie. Be sure to drink your milk."

Welcome hung up the phone and hurried to the door. After checking the peephole, she opened the door. "Yes?"

"I'm Soloma Jones," the young woman said, sticking out her hand.

Welcome tried to hide her shock. *"You're* Soloma Jones?"

"In the flesh. But call me Solo."

Twelve

Appearances often are deceiving.

Aesop
c. 550 B.C.

Surely *this* little slip of a girl couldn't be the agent that Philip had sent to protect Welcome. About five feet one, Solo Jones had a mop of short blond curls, big blue eyes, and a beaming smile that produced a face full of dimples.

"My God," Welcome blurted out, "you look like a high school cheerleader."

"If I hadn't heard that about a million times, I'd be offended." She picked up a garment bag and another bag that appeared to hold photographic equipment and strode inside, kicking the door shut as she passed. "I'm sure Philip told you not to let my looks fool you. I'm thirty-four years old. I have two college degrees. And when the occasion calls for it, I'm a mean fucker. Which room is mine?"

Welcome let out a whoop of laughter. "Right this way, sweetie. I can see that we're going to get along fine. Where are you from?" she asked, thinking that she detected the traces of a familiar speech pattern.

"Here, there, and yonder, but I grew up in a small

town in Texas. I don't imagine that you've ever heard of it."

"Try me."

"Port Neches."

"Port Neches. Hmmm. As I recall that's close to Nederland and not too far from Beaumont. This is your room. Mine is over there."

Solo dropped her bags. "I'll check out the arrangement before I decide where to bunk. How did you know about Port Neches? Philip told me that you were a famous Paris model."

"Make that past tense. I *was* a famous Paris model. As soon as my project is finished in Greece, I'm going home to another Athens, the one that's about halfway between Corsicana and Tyler."

"You're from Texas, too? Well, I'll be damned. Philip didn't mention that."

"Probably his idea of a joke."

"How many rooms do you have here?" Solo asked as she opened the door to the bath and peeked inside. She seemed to be giving the area only a cursory glance, but Welcome saw the quick darting of Solo's eyes, and she doubted if the agent missed so much as a fly speck.

"The living room/dining room, a small kitchen, two bedrooms, two baths."

Solo strode through the suite checking out various nooks, crannies, and places of entrance/exit. Welcome followed along behind her. "This a connecting door?" Solo rattled the knob of a door off the living room.

"I assume so, but I haven't been here very long myself."

"Then you don't have any idea who's next door."

"As a matter of fact, I do. A couple of guys from the States: Wade Morgan and D'Angelo Thomas, also known as Shark. They're the ones who took me in last night."

"Wade Morgan? The Vulcan quarterback?"

Welcome rolled her eyes. "How come everybody's heard of him but me?"

"I take it that you're not a football fan." Solo opened a balcony door and peered out.

"Not particularly. About the only spectator sports I enjoy are tennis and rodeo riding."

Solo grinned. "I'm not much of a tennis player, but I used to be a heck of a bull rider."

"You?"

"Me."

"But you couldn't weigh more than a hundred pounds."

"A hundred and two, but my riding weight was about ninety-seven pounds. Most bull riders are small. I paid my way through college by rodeoing on the weekend."

Solo strode to her room. She seemed to stride everywhere, Welcome thought as she trailed behind.

"I did some barrel racing in high school," Welcome told her, "but I was only so-so. My mother was always terrified that I would break my neck, so I was too cautious to be very good. The closest I ever came to riding bulls was dating a bull rider. And come to think of it, he wasn't much bigger than I was. I switched my affections to a steer wrestler after a short time."

Solo went through her equipment bag and pulled out five gizmos. Suddenly she was all business as she said, "I'm going to attach these to the front door, the connecting door, the balcony doors off the living room and the other bedroom, and this window. Don't try to open any of them unless you want to raise a ruckus. They're delicate alarms and make one hell of a racket. And we'll switch bedrooms. You take this one."

"But the one I'm in has a better view—and a balcony."

"Exactly. This one, with only a window, is more se-

cure. And by the way, stay away from this window, th
plate glass windows in the living room, and the Frencl
doors. No need to give a sniper a prime target."

Welcome's eyes widened. "A *sniper?*"

"Just a precaution. As is this." She took a small bu
lethal-looking pistol from the bag, checked it, the
slipped it and its holster on the waistband of her jean:
"Let's fix some coffee, and I want you to tell me ever
detail of what has happened since you deplaned i
Athens."

"Every detail? I thought Philip filled you in."

"He did, but I want to hear it again. *Every* detail
Especially about Wade Morgan." Solo grinned and ru
ined her serious image. "The guy's a hunk."

"This is going to take a while. Shall I call room serv
ice for the coffee?"

"No need. There's an electric pot in the kitchen
and I carry my own coffee." She pulled out a foil ba
and held it up. "You like chicory? It'll grow hair o
your chest."

"I think I'll have tea. I carry my own brand, too."

While Welcome switched rooms with her clothes
Solo set the alarms. They brewed their drinks, and We
come related the whole story, every detail. Solo didn'
so much as raise an eyebrow during the telling, no
even when Welcome told her that Wade denied being
in Athens during the time of the murder. When she
reported the finding of tickets and receipts tha
seemed to corroborate his story, Solo only said, "Tha
can be checked out. Which hotel garage in Palm
Springs?" When Welcome informed her, Solo merely
nodded as if committing it to memory. "Go on."

"That's about it. A few minutes later, the manager
called and said my suite was ready. Wade and Shark
helped me move my stuff, I told them thanks, and

twenty minutes later you showed up. Solo, do you think I'm nuts?"

"Not that I can tell. I think you're stressed out, but under the circumstances most people would be. In fact, I think you're handling things remarkably well. Lots of women would take to their beds in hysterics. Men too, if the truth were told." She rose. "Let me make some telephone calls."

When Solo returned twenty minutes later, Welcome was pacing. "I set up a portable FAX machine in my bedroom. I should have reports back in an hour or so," Solo said. "Want to order lunch sent up?"

"No, I'd rather have lunch out. Listen, Solo, I don't take well to being cooped up. Never have. Say, are you really a photographer?"

"I've won a few awards. Want to see my portfolio and judge for yourself?" Solo didn't wait for an answer. She left the room and came back unzipping a black leather portfolio about the size of a notebook. Handing it to Welcome, she sat down on the far end of the couch.

Welcome leafed slowly through the book of eight-by-ten copies, whistling silently a couple of times, raising her eyebrows a couple more. When she was done, she glanced up and was surprised to see Solo's uncertain, expectant expression instead of her usual confident one.

"Wow. I'm impressed. Your work is dynamite. You have a real flair for composition. Ever done anything professionally?"

Solo's grin returned. "Yes, but not in the photography profession. I haven't done any sort of fashion work or anything like the brochure you're planning."

"I don't think you'll have a problem. We'll call my friend Meri and have her give you a few tips. The sooner we can get the shots and get away from here, the better I'll like it."

"Surely you don't mean to continue with photo shoots for the brochure?"

"I damned well do."

"Philip doesn't think that's a good idea, and neither do I."

"Tough tittie, sweetie. That's the way it's going to be. Grab your coat. I know a great place for lunch."

After the phone rang eight times, Wade let out a string of curses and slammed it down.

"What you got such a hard-on about?" Shark asked.

"I was trying to call Welcome."

"She's not there. I saw her and a little bitty blond gal get off the elevator in the lobby just before I came up."

Wade let out another string of curses. "She doesn't need to be running around by herself. When was this?"

Shark shrugged. "Five, ten minutes ago."

"Let's go." Wade started for the door.

"Where you going?"

"To find Welcome. If some nut case has it in for her, she shouldn't be out there unprotected."

"Hell, man, you crazy? This city is 'bout as big as L.A. She could be anywhere."

Wade raked his fingers through his hair. "What am I going to do?"

"I don't know about you, but I'm going to get me something to eat and take a nap. This jet lag is killing me. Come on. Let's see if we can rustle up some barbecued ribs or some greens and corn bread."

Wade laughed. "Fat chance."

Thirteen

Adopt the character of the twisting octopus, which takes on the appearance of the nearby rock. Now follow in this direction, now turn a different hue.

Theognis
c. 545 B.C.

Ah, there you are, *ma chère,* he thought as he watched from a sheltered spot. Her red hair moved and glistened like a beacon, drawing his attention to her as she spoke animatedly with the small blond one across the table.

So she hadn't checked out after all. After he had telephoned her room earlier, he was sure that all was lost, that she had fled Athens.

He smiled. All was *not* lost. Not yet.

He'd had to look no further than the hotel dining room to find her again. Luck was with him. He had always been lucky—until the redheaded bitch had crossed his path. Simply thinking about the complications she'd wrought in his life made him angry. And anger was not an appropriate emotion to indulge in. It clouded one's thinking, dulled the reflexes.

He wondered about the two large American men. Where were they today? When they had become involved, he had feared that the situation would be made more difficult. Perhaps they were merely guests of the hotel, not her intimate devotees—though he found it perplexing to imagine that they were not well acquainted.

Deciding to watch and wait until he made another move, he kept secluded, biding his time until the two had finished their meal.

Ah, at last they were done.

He hung back, secreting himself beside a group of tourists speaking German, and observed the women enter the elevator. Only three others were going up at the same time.

Watching the floor indicator, he noted the stops.

Three. Six. Seven.

Which?

She had been on the sixth floor before, and if she had moved, he imagined that it would be to another floor. Three or seven?

He could bribe another maid for the information, but he didn't want to attract any more attention to himself. The last woman he'd paid had been very nervous.

He would wait.

She would come down again.

Fourteen

*Thrice I tried to clasp her image, and thrice it slipped
through my hands, like a shadow, like a dream.*

Homer
c. 700 B.C.

"Look, Solo, I conceded the point about a photo
shoot on the Acropolis; I understand that it's too open
and too crowded, but the National Museum seems perfectly safe. Getting permission for pictures wasn't easy,
and the director is expecting us."

"I swear to God," Solo grumbled, then sighed and
picked up her equipment bag. "Guarding a head of
state isn't as complicated as riding herd on you is going
to be."

Solo frowned and groused softly for the entire cab
ride—which was thankfully short.

After Welcome gave her pass to the museum attendant and they were inside, she turned and said, "Look,
Solo, I know that you're just trying to do your job, but
I'm trying to do mine, too. I'd appreciate it if you
would cooperate with me. After all, I'm the one in
danger."

"Yeah, but it will be my ass in a sling if your brains
end up spattered all over one of those uncircumcised

dongs." Her head gestured to the myriad nude males on marble pedestals.

Welcome walked around and scrutinized a number of the marvelous statues that she'd only seen in books. "By damn, they are all uncircumcised, aren't they? I'd never noticed."

"The hell you say. Well let's get our shots and get gone."

Welcome felt the same way, but it wasn't uneasiness about the threat that made her anxious, it was something about the museum itself. Almost everything was marble, and the place was sterile and spartan. Oppressive. Cold. She shivered. It gave her the willies.

A guard, who was assigned to accompany them, politely led the way to the first designated area. He stood aside unobtrusively, but he eyed Solo the whole time and looked as if he wanted to get in her britches in the worst way.

The plans were to photograph Welcome perusing three of the most famous displays including two large bronzes. They shot the first against a galloping horse with a small boy on his back and moved on to the second, an excellent bronze piece depicting Poseidon posed as if he were about to hurl his trident. The trident was missing.

"Nice pecs," Solo said of Poseidon. "And look at those calves. The guy who posed for this must have spent a lot of time in the gym pumping iron."

"Most of the male models were also athletes," Welcome said as she picked up her bag to move to the third shot.

She stopped. How had she known that?

She shrugged. Must have read it somewhere.

Their next setup featured a marble group representing Aphrodite, Pan, and Eros. By that time, they had attracted the attention of several people in the museum, and despite the guard's admonitions, a group gathered to whisper among themselves and watch model and photographer work. Used to such audiences, Welcome simply ignored them and checked her hair and makeup as if she were alone in her dressing room.

Solo seemed extremely nervous. Her eyes darted over the crowd and around the large room. She took three photos with the lens cap on, then discovered her boo-boo, cursed, removed the cap, and promptly dropped it. The cap hit the marble floor like a reverberating shot and went rolling with a clatter.

While Solo and the guard chased the runaway lens cap, Welcome scanned the statues in the rest of the room. Her gaze froze on one. Her heart stumbled.

Nude, life-sized lovers leaned against a pillar, smiling at each other with rapt expressions while the young woman, seen in a three-quarters view from the back, fed grapes to the man from the cluster in her hand.

Welcome's spine came alive with serpentine sensations. Chill bumps raced over her skin. Her feet moved until she found herself at the base of the marble sculpture which elevated the figures about three feet off the floor.

An eerie feeling rippled over her as she stared at the female figure. A force tugged at her consciousness, urging her to merge into the scene and lend the magic of her presence to transform cold marble into living flesh.

A bizarre sensation.

For a moment she was afraid and wanted to flee, but she seemed rooted to the spot and the fear soon passed.

There was a brief humming, then, as if captured with the marble people in a timeless, pulsating warp, all the surroundings in the museum ceased to exist.

The scent of grapes permeated her awareness—the grapes she fed her lover. The sweet smell grew stronger, then stronger still. She could sense the cluster's weight in her palm and feel the stickiness of juice on her fingers.

The man's marble eyes began pulsing with warmth and love. She felt a thrill go through her. He held out his hands to her, and, automatically she offered hers.

Suddenly she was wrenched upward.

A shout.

A *thunk*.

Screams. More shouts.

"Damn it, Welcome," Solo yelled, "are you okay?"

Wade jerked awake, crying out, his heart racing and his face covered with sweat.

"Hey, hey, man," Shark said. "What's going on with you?"

Wade shook his head, then looked around wildly. He sprang to his feet, and the magazine he'd been reading fell from his lap. "Welcome's in trouble. I've got to get to her." He strode toward the door.

Shark grabbed him by the arm. "You crazy? She's in trouble? You don't even know where she is. You just dozed off and had a bad dream is all."

"Uh-uh. I'm going." He shook off Shark's grip.

"And just where you going?"

"Somewhere with lots of statues."

"Around here that don't mean jack-shit. There's statues in the bathrooms."

"A museum. Some kind of museum."

"Bet there's a dozen."

"Then I'll go to all of them, starting with the biggest." Wade yanked open the door. "I'm gone."

"Well if you're hell-bent determined, I'll go with

you," Shark shouted after him, "but would you at least put on your shoes first?"

"Welcome! Are you okay? Dammit, answer me!"

Welcome blinked several times before looking down at Solo, who seemed to be having a fit about something. Then Welcome realized that she was standing on the base of the statue, behind the male figure. How in the world had she gotten up there? God, no wonder Solo was having a fit. The museum guard was hanging on to Solo, who had her hand under her jacket and looked about ready to shoot the poor man.

If the museum director found Welcome climbing around on their precious antiquities, he would probably toss them out on their ears. If Solo shot the guard, there would be no question of it.

Welcome climbed down. "What's going on?"

"A crazy man! A crazy man!" the guard said, then babbled something in Greek. "Bang. Everybody scream, but no one is hurt. Is politics, crazy politics."

Puzzled, Welcome turned to Solo "Can you translate that?"

Solo wrestled her arm from the guard's grasp. "Some dude pulled a gun and a woman saw him and screamed. He took a wild shot, then ran out. I think he shouted something as he ran—some sort of political statement, I gather. I didn't see the man or hear him because Casanova here threw himself on top of me."

The guard grinned, obviously pleased with his quick actions. "Not Casanova. Yannis. I am Yannis Pesmazoglou."

Solo made an attempt to smile, but her teeth were ground together. "Let's get out of here," she said to Welcome.

"Why?"

"*Why?* You have to ask?" Solo cut her eyes to the statue of the lovers.

There was a nasty little crater blown in the marble woman's back. About heart high.

Welcome swallowed back the lunch that threatened to reappear. "For me?" she mouthed silently.

Solo nodded slightly. "I think we should call it a day."

Welcome shook her head and fought to remain calm. "No. In fact, this is probably the safest time to get that last photo. The man is long gone."

Solo argued, but Welcome held firm. It wasn't that she was all that brave—just sensible. She couldn't imagine that the man hung around. And truthfully, whatever happened with the statues unnerved her more than being shot at. Dear Lord, what had she seen?

Marble statues didn't suddenly come to life.

She was losing it for sure.

No, she didn't want to think about it, or she would go screaming from this place. There was no logical explanation for what she'd seen.

Hallucinations. It was hallucinations.

Brought on by stress probably.

She didn't actually buy that idea, but it was the only one she could come up with at the moment. *Forget it,* she told herself. "Let's get back to work," she told Solo.

"God, you're stubborn." Solo rolled her eyes. "Okay, if you're determined to do this, let's move it. Take your place."

Welcome was posed in front of Aphrodite and Pan when Wade and Shark strode into the room. Wade grabbed her arm, and his eyes looked wild when he asked frantically, "Are you all right?"

"I'm fine. But you just ruined that shot."

The museum director came running up, chest heaving. "Miss Venable, are you all right? You weren't injured, were you?"

"Injured?" Wade said. "What's he talking about?"

"I can't tell you how very sorry we are that something so terrible should happen while you are here."

"Terrible? What happened?" Wade asked more loudly.

"Oh, Miss Venable, a thousand apologies to you and Miss Jones as the representatives of Horus Hotels. Mr. Gabrey and his family have been most generous in facilitating a number of transactions for the museum, and we owe them our tremendous gratitude."

The director was wringing his hands. "Politics in Greece are insane. Even Greeks don't understand them much of the time. Always one group of fanatics or the other tries to draw attention to itself. The police have been called, and they will arrive shortly, but this was only for publicity, you can be sure. Only for publicity."

"This? This what? What happened, dammit?" Wade shouted.

Yannis leaned forward. "A man drew a gun and shot it. I covered Miss Jones's body—"

"That's it," Wade said, grabbing Welcome's arm. "We're out of here."

"Amen to that," Solo said.

"I'm not going anywhere," Welcome said. "We have work to do, and my business and my whereabouts are not your concern, Mr. Morgan."

"You're going back to the hotel."

"Oh God," she groaned, looking heavenward for strength, "how I hate Tarzan types. One night on your couch and one breakfast don't entitle you to tell me what to do. Watch my lips, Wade. I . . . am . . . not . . . leaving."

"Watch my lips," Wade shot back. He gave her a

quick, hard kiss. "Yes . . . you . . . are." With a single fluid move he scooped her up, and she was folded over his shoulder. When she tried to kick and yell, he gave her a swat. "Hush that caterwauling, honey." He held out his hand to the director. "Thanks for your concern, Mr.—"

"Mitropoulos."

"Mitropoulos. Sometimes my fiancée doesn't understand the gravity of situations. We'll be in touch." Wade turned to Solo and stuck out his hand again. "I don't believe that we've met. Wade Morgan."

"Solo Jones."

"This is my friend D'Angelo Thomas."

"Dammit, put me down you freakin' jock!"

"Just call me Shark."

"Ready to go, guys?" Wade asked.

Welcome shrieked.

Shark grunted.

Solo said, "Lead the way."

"I'm going to kill you," Welcome shouted as he strode from the museum. "I'm going to castrate you with a chain saw!"

He didn't break stride as he toted her down the steps and out to the curb. She switched to French and called him every loathsome name she could think of.

"I don't understand a word you're saying, darlin', but I'm impressed by your command of the language. Shark, flag us a taxi."

Shark did just that. Wade set Welcome on her feet, then gently but firmly pushed her into the back seat, climbed in behind her, and pulled her into his lap. She would have socked him except that her arms were pinned to her sides.

Solo slid into the seat next to them. "Thanks," she said to Wade.

"No problem."

Shark got into the front beside the driver and gave him directions.

"Exactly what do you think you're doing, Wade Morgan?" Welcome asked indignantly.

"I'm taking care of my woman."

"*Your* woman? Are you out of your ever lovin' mind? I am by no stretch of the imagination *your* woman."

"Oh, yes you are. You just don't know it yet." His mouth covered hers in a kiss meant to brand.

She struggled for a moment, then as his lips softened and his tongue gently teased its way inside her mouth, her struggles ceased. A feeling of rightness and wonderment melted her objections right along with her spine; she relaxed and sighed against his mouth.

His arms tightened around her, and the kiss began to swell from poignantly sweet to achingly sensual. Desire, bone deep and older than the colonnades of Athens, sprang to life with such sudden intensity that it stole her breath.

Her struggles began anew, but this time she wanted her arms free so that she could touch him, hold him as tightly as he held her.

His tongue plunged deeper. His mouth grew hungrier.

She moaned.

Someone cleared his throat. "I hate to break this up, folks, but we're at the hotel," Shark said.

Welcome immediately pulled away and looked around.

The taxi driver was grinning.

Shark was grinning.

Solo, to her credit, was studying the ceiling light and trying not to grin.

When it dawned on Welcome that she'd been mak-

ing out in the back seat of a Greek taxi, in broad daylight, with an audience, and with a professional jock
who collected women like some people collect match-
books, she was furious with herself. Dear God, what
had possessed her?

As soon as Solo got out, Welcome scrambled from
the taxi, stomping indelicately on Wade's feet as she
went. When he climbed out looking as smug as a teenaged boy after his first score, fury set her on fire and
steam spewed from her mouth.

She shook her finger in his face. "Don't you go getting any ideas from that, Wade Morgan. It was a temporary aberration. It didn't mean a thing, do you hear
me? Not a thing."

"What didn't, sugar?"

"That kiss, of course. Don't be dense. It was nothing.
Nothing."

His brows went up. "Really? Didn't seem like nothing to me. Want to try it over?"

Before she could protest, he grabbed her and kissed
her again. Her brain went completely haywire; her
body turned into cookie dough. She clung to him like
a blathering idiot and kissed him back.

A flash went off. Then another.

She thought it was the magic of the moment until
someone yelled her name. She pushed away from
Wade, and someone shouted, "Smile for me!"

"Damnation! Paparazzi. Just what I need." She tried
to get away, but Wade held on to her and smiled and
mugged for the photographer, who snapped another
shot and fled before Solo could stop him. Welcome
stomped on Wade's foot. Twice. "You imbecile!"

His smile died. "What did I do?" He looked truly
bewildered. Welcome only glared. "What did I do?"
he asked Solo.

Solo appeared ready to deck him. "Unbelievable
arm."

In their hotel suite, Solo went to check for FAX mes-
ges in her room, and Welcome paced in the living
oom. Her life was coming apart, unraveling like a
heap sweater, and she couldn't seem to do anything
bout it. It was bad enough that she'd been shot at
nd photographed by some damned paparazzo, but
hat on earth had made her kiss Wade Morgan the
ay she had? It wasn't as if she were deprived.

And as foolish as she felt about her reaction to
Wade, that paled beside her other concerns. Sexual
ttraction, even unwise sexual attraction, she could un-
erstand. Hormones, libido, pheremones, these were
atural phenomena easily explainable. Too, she'd
een preoccupied and had her guard down, she rea-
oned.

But it was the other stuff that had her shook. She
ouldn't get the incident with the statues out of her
nind. Should she tell Solo?

No. The whole thing was too outlandish to be be-
eved. Anybody, with the possible exception of Meri
nd Madam Zenobia with her Indian guide, would
hink she was out of her cotton-pickin' mind. Statues
lidn't come to life. Men didn't appear out of thin air.

But, by damn, those statues did seem real. The sen-
ation of being there was as real as—

She stopped, jolted by an idea.

Of course. Why hadn't she caught on earlier? Maybe
he *had* been there when the statues were created. Per-
aps in another time she had posed for the sculpting
f the female figure.

And that day in the agora when she saw a different
cene, an olive grove instead of buildings and pillars,

it might have been a memory. A memory of another life.

She'd once told Meri that reincarnation seemed like a reasonable concept, but actually, she'd never given the notion any serious consideration.

She considered it carefully now. It was the only thing that made any sense. She'd been so caught up in memories that they had seemed real.

But how had she gotten up from the floor to behind the male statue and out of harm's way?

God, this was too weird and too complicated. So many complexities chased in her head that she was getting a headache trying to puzzle things out. Aspirin. She needed aspirin. About to go in search of some she stopped when she heard a knock at the door.

Solo, just entering the room, said, "I'll get that," but Welcome's hand was already on the latch, and she opened it before she thought.

The man standing there charged inside and grabbed Welcome.

Fifteen

Thus have the gods spun the thread for wretched mortals . . . for two jars stand on the floor of Zeus of the gifts which he gives, one of evils and another of blessings.

Homer
c. 700 B.C.

Before Welcome could open her mouth, Solo had clutched the man's platinum blond ponytail, yanked his head back, and stuck her Glock in his ear.

"If you move except to release her, you're history, shrimp." She repeated the phrase in French and had started it in German when the man released Welcome.

He broke into a broad grin. "Ah, *chérie,* who is this delightful elf who has captured me?" he asked Welcome in a thick French accent. "I believe that she is a woman after my own heart. I may be in love." He dramatically splayed his hand across the front of his lime green fisherman's sweater.

"You may be dead if you don't cool it, you little peacock," Solo said, referring no doubt to his small size and his colorful outfit. He wore pants in a wild print that coordinated with his sweater, black combat boots, and several earrings in each ear. "On the floor. Face down. *Now.*"

Welcome was laughing so hard that she couldn't get a breath to explain who Jean Jacques was.

Jean Jacques widened his eyes and formed a playful O with his lips. "Ah, my little bird, if I were going to do that for anyone, I would do it for you, but I think not." He smiled, made a lightning quick move and the pistol was in his hand.

He had no time to gloat, for Solo made a move just as quick, and he was on the floor with her knee in his back and the muzzle against his nape. "Call security," she told Welcome.

"Wait. No, no. Wait," Welcome managed to choke out before she burst into a new fit of laughter.

"Just who the hell are you?" Solo asked him. "What is your—"

Before she could finish, she was on her back, wrists pinned to the floor, with Jean Jacques astride her. "I am your karma, the answer to your prayers," he said, then planted a good one on her gaping mouth.

Solo was silenced for only ten seconds before she bit his lip and let out a yell, then she was on top. "Dammit, you pint-sized dandy, you do that again and your ass is grass! Who the hell are you? What is your business here?"

Welcome couldn't stop laughing. Maybe it was hysteria, but waves of giggles erupted from her, one swell after another until she bent over and held her aching stomach.

He did a rapid maneuver and was once again uppermost. "I am Jean Jacques. I have come to protect Mademoiselle Welcome. And you." He wiggled his eyebrows.

"And who is going to protect us from you?"

"Now that, my sweet, is the question." A slow, lascivious grin spread across his face, then froze as somehing beaned him. His eyes rolled back, and he itched forward.

Wade stood in the open doorway, breathing fire. He'd just hurled a crystal rose bowl with his umpty-million-dollar passing arm, and Jean Jacques was out cold. While Solo scrambled out from under Jean Jacques's dead weight, Wade strode into the room and grabbed Welcome.

"Are you okay?" Wade asked, looking her over.

"I'm fine, but Jean Jacques is not."

"Who the hell is Jean Jacques?"

"That's what I'd like to know," Solo said.

Shark wandered in and perused the prostrate form with a suspicious eye. "Who's he?"

"He's Jean Jacques," Welcome informed them, "an old friend who was sent here no doubt by Ram Gabrey."

"Are we back to that guy again?" Wade asked. "Forget him. Want to go out to dinner with us?"

Jean Jacques groaned.

Welcome knelt beside him and gingerly examined the knot on his head. "No, we do not want to go out to dinner with you. He may have a concussion. I think we should call a doctor." She glared at Wade. "You caused this. Help me here. Let's get him onto the couch."

"I'll do it," Shark said. He lifted the small man as if he were a baby and laid him on the couch.

Solo called for a doctor, and Shark made an ice pack. Welcome scowled at Wade and made occasional disparaging remarks about his interfering nature until the doctor came.

By the time the doctor arrived, Jean Jacques had roused. "But I am fine, *mon amie*. Just a little bump on my—how you say?—noggin? A short rest, a cool hand upon my brow," he said, glancing up at Solo beseechingly, "and I'll be fine."

The doctor examined Jean Jacques and agreed with the diagnosis and care—except for the cool hand. He suggested the continuation of the ice pack, then left.

Jean Jacques groaned. Solo rolled her eyes, but Welcome sat on the couch by the injured man and patted his hand. "I'm so sorry this happened."

He gave a fluttering gesture with his fingers as if to shoo away her words.

Wade stood nearby, his hands in his pockets and a scowl on his face. "You want to tell me now who this character is?"

"I've already told you," Welcome said, totally exasperated. "He's *Jean Jacques.*"

"Am I supposed to recognize the name? It doesn't mean diddley to me."

"I'm not surprised. He probably doesn't recognize *your* name either. But I expect that he'll find out before he sues you for heaving a bowl at his head."

Jean Jacques raised one beautifully arched brow. "And exactly who is this big brute who bashed my head?"

"Meet Wade Morgan. He's the quarterback for the—"

"Los Angeles Vulcans," Jean Jacques finished, jumping to his feet. He grabbed Wade's hand and began pumping it. "Delighted to meet you. I'm a big fan of yours, and so is my friend, George Mszanski. Perhaps you know of him? He played with the Cowboys."

"George Mszanski? Sure I knew him. What's he up to these days? Say, this is my friend Shark Thomas. I'll never forget the last time I played against Mszanski. Remember that game, Shark? Must have been about five years ago."

Welcome looked at Solo, and they both made a wry mouth. "Look," Welcome said, "if you guys want to

alk about football, fine, but would you go somewhere
:lse to do it? I have a splitting headache."

"Ah, *chérie,* forgive our gaucheness," Jean Jacques
aid. "You go lie down, and I will escort the gentlemen
o the door."

"While *you* stay here?" Wade asked. He didn't seem
varm to the idea.

"Certainly."

"No," Solo said to Jean Jacques, "since you seem to
)e nicely recovered, I'll escort all of you gentlemen to
he door, and you can return to your own rooms."

Jean Jacques smiled slyly. "But I have no room in
he hotel."

"Then to wherever you're staying."

"I'm staying here. On the couch."

"Like hell you are," said Wade and Solo at the same
ime.

Jean Jacques glanced toward Welcome and lifted his
)rows in a question.

She sighed. "He can stay here and sleep on the
:ouch tonight. We'll talk later, Jean Jacques. I'm going
o lie down now." She left them all yammering at each
>ther and headed for the aspirin bottle. Jean Jacques's
sleeping accommodations were the least of her con-
:erns.

Reaching for a bag on the dresser, Welcome noticed
he roses for the first time. Yellow roses again. She
eaned close to touch a bud and inhale the scent. Who
had sent them? Philip?

She looked for a card and was surprised when she
found one attached among the stems. Philip never sent
a card.

This one said only YOU'RE *MINE.* An array of emotions swept over her: puzzlement, apprehension, then
anger when she realized who must have sent them.

Wade Morgan. This was some more of his "my

woman" baloney. She made a face. Brother, what a
line that one was. "In your dreams, Tarzan," she muttered. She was tempted to toss flowers, vase, and all
out the window.

But she couldn't. She adored yellow roses.

And if she would allow herself to admit it, Wade
titillated her senses just a wee bit, too.

Later that evening Welcome, Solo, and Jean Jacques
sat around the dining table in the suite polishing off
the last of their dinner. As Welcome had suspected,
Meri was worried about her, and Ram had sent his
security chief to look into things.

Solo eyed his wildly conspicuous garb. *"You* are the
director of an international security firm?"

Jean Jacques grinned. "Nobody else ever suspects it
either, my dove. That's why I'm so effective. Exactly
what has been going on here?"

Welcome glanced at Solo who shrugged as if to say,
"It's your call as to how much to tell him."

Welcome gave Jean Jacques an edited version of the
events including witnessing the murder, the phone
calls, the incidents with the roses, and her being shot
at. She didn't mention either the bracelet, her business
at Metaxas's gift shop, or statues that came to life. Nor
did she mention seeing Wade—or his twin brother—
when he couldn't have been there.

Jean Jacques listened without interruption to the
whole tale. When she had finished he gave a low whistle. "I think Meri's instincts were right. She had reason
to worry. What do the local police think about the
situation?"

"Wellll . . . I haven't exactly talked to the police."

He inclined his head slightly. "I see. Any particular

reason? When one witnesses a murder, the logical thing to do is call the police."

"Wellll . . . there are complications."

"Hmmmm. Why were you in the shop, *chérie?*"

Her eyes darted away. "I—I was browsing."

"Ah. I suspect that you were either meeting a married lover or doing a bit of an errand for Philip Van Horn or one of his cronies."

"How did you—" Welcome quickly clamped her mouth shut.

Jean Jacques chuckled. "How did I know about your running errands for Philip? You forget that my men and I tailed you and Meri all over Egypt last year. I saw you with him several times, and I know that you are friends. Philip's connection with the CIA is a poorly kept secret. Even the *Mabaheth,* Egypt's secret police, suspected that you were acting as his courier. But about your doing favors for him this time? I guessed."

"Damn!"

"Exactly." Jean Jacques's jaw tightened. "This time wasn't a harmless couriering of papers or money. This time he's landed you in a serious situation. He ought to have his *couilles* cut off and pickled. At least he ought to come get you out of this mess he's landed you in."

"He can't," Welcome said. "He was in an accident in Paris. He's in the hospital."

"Then he could send someone."

Welcome glanced at Solo

"You?" Jean Jacques asked.

"Me," Solo said. "And I can assure you that I'm qualified to handle the situation."

He laughed. "*Ma chère,* you are an adorable little kitten to be sure, but—"

"Watch it," Welcome said, leaning closer, "your

chauvinism is showing. Solo was with the Secret Service for several years before she went private. She's a partner in a highly respected security firm, the same as someone else present that we can name."

"Sorry. I, of all people, shouldn't judge by appearances. Welcome, I don't understand why you're still in Athens. The solution seems very simple to me. Pack your bags and take the next flight out. Or better yet, Ram can send his jet to pick you up and fly you to Cairo."

"There you go," Solo said. "That's what I've been trying to tell her."

"It's not that simple. First, I want to finish the layout for the new Horus Hotel brochure that Meri and I are doing—"

"To hell with the brochure! Ram would be furious if he knew you were endangering yourself over a silly brochure. And I know that you don't need the money. Go pack. Now."

Welcome drew in a deep breath. "There's another reason that I'm not ready to leave yet."

"Morgan?"

"Wade? Lord, no. Where did you get such an idea?"

Jean Jacques only smiled. "Then tell me the reason worth risking your life for."

"It's—it's something that I can't explain."

"Try."

Welcome took a deep breath, then glanced back and forth between the two pair of eyes focused intently on her.

The breath escaped. She couldn't tell them.

How could she when she couldn't explain it to herself? But instinctively she *knew* that she was on the threshold of something of great consequence in her life.

Great consequence.

Major significance.

She didn't know exactly what it was, but she somehow perceived that she would find it in Athens. A tremendous force inside her urged her to stay, to find her—Her what?

Destiny sounded so corny, but destiny was the closest she could come. Kismet? Providence? Whatever. Somehow it was connected to the mystery of the statues in the museum and the scene in the Roman Agora—though she didn't understand exactly how. No, she wasn't leaving yet. She couldn't. Every whit of her being shouted, *stay!*

Welcome dragged out her best lighthearted smile and tapped Jean Jacques playfully on the nose. "I'm not through sightseeing, sweetie, and I have tons of shopping to do. Did you know that they have the most wonderful flokati rugs here? They would look great at the ranch house."

Jean Jacques looked dumbfounded. *"Shopping?* You're going to endanger your life to go *shopping?"*

She gave a trill of laughter and brushed off his curt question. "Ah, *mon beau gosse,"* she said, chucking Jean Jacques's cheek, "you obviously don't understand a woman's passion for shopping. And I've seen some urns that the girls at the agency would love. I must buy a case of them. They're decorated with marvelously virile men, handsome, broad shouldered, and so—so *ready.* Hung like rutting stallions. You would adore them."

He made a disgusted sound. "Forget about urns and *les bijoux de famille.* Dammit, Welcome, a man is trying to *kill* you."

"Then we can't let that happen, can we? Perhaps if we can find out who he is, we can prevent it. You and Solo discuss it. I'm sure you can come up with a solution. I'm off to get my beauty sleep now. Don't forget that tomorrow we go to Delphi."

"Thank God for that," Jean Jacques mumbled.

Welcome made a speedy exit, then stopped, hung onto the doorjamb, and leaned out for a parting shot. "Oh, J.J., you might tell Solo your background. I think she would find it *very* interesting. Why you grew up practically neighbors."

In her bedroom, Welcome had just laid her earrings on the nightstand when the phone rang. She grabbed it in midring. "Hello."

Silence.

"Hello."

More silence. Then, a whispered, "Bitch!"

She slammed the phone down, and seconds later Solo charged into the room. "I heard. I was on the extension. Did you recognize the voice?"

Welcome shook her head. "This is the first time he's said anything. Before he only breathed." A sudden thought struck her. "Solo, how did he know to call me here?"

Sixteen

He knew the things that were and the things that would be and the things that had been before.

Homer
c. 700 B.C.

This time it was she who sought him out, relishing the clandestine game of slipping by the sleeping guards and stealing into the room that held his dense, muscular body. Careful not to stir an atom or ripple a wave of air, she approached his form on the bed.

But he was not there!

A low chuckle came from across the room, and she quickly glanced in that direction. He sat on a table in the corner, swinging one leg and hugging the other under his chin. His eyes glistened with the laughter that lit his face and flashed around him like fireflies on a summer's night.

"I've been waiting for you," he said.

"And how did you know that I would come?"

"I knew." He smiled and approached her. Lifting her chin, he touched his lips to hers. "I knew because you're my woman. For now and for always." He cocked his head, awaiting her reply.

She let him wait, fighting her own laughter. Finally she shrugged. "Perhaps. We shall see. Come. Tonight I would see the Acropolis, stroll its rocky crest, and bathe in the moonlight."

"I like the bathing part. Especially if we do it together. It has been a very long time since we shared a bath . . . of water or of moonlight." He took her hand, kissed her fingers, and they flew from the hotel, from the Square to the ruins of the grand temples atop the city's high fortress hill.

The place was deserted, quiet except for their voices which sounded like whispers of wind through the pale stones. They stood before the soaring columns and crumbled remains of the Parthenon, plundered of its great artistic treasures by Roman and Byzantine emperors, by barbarian invaders, by British archaeologists.

Much of the great edifice might be standing yet except for war, for the occupying Turks who twice stored their gunpowder in the marble recesses. They were blown to bits, first when lightning struck the powder room, and again later when a Venetian named Schwartz scored a direct hit on the Parthenon magazine.

"No wonder the Greeks hate the Turks," he said. "Remembering the beauty that was here, I could almost hate them myself. How Pericles must cringe to see his grand conception reduced to this state. How Phidias must weep to see his statues ruined or lost. See that likeness of me on the frieze? The whole face is gone."

"I know not if Pericles cringes, but I doubt if Phidias weeps. He put his talents to painting chapel ceilings and sculpting again in Rome. His work from that era endures yet. Of late he designs aircraft and spacecraft and is busy dreaming of flying these machines to distant planets."

"How do you know these things about Phidias?" he asked.

"Our paths crossed in Rome and again briefly some years ago when I visited NASA on a field trip with my classmates. He has not changed much; he was always obsessive and given to excesses. He is . . . not among my favorites."

"Nor mine, but I have to grant him that he gave me my
freedom."

She pulled away. "He gave me mine as well—after a fashion." Bitterness tinged her words.

"But where did you go? I came looking for you. Those in
the household said you had been gone a year or more."

"You were too caught up in the games. You waited too
long, came too late."

"But it was the games that provided my freedom. You know
that."

"I know no such thing. You loved the running and the
wrestling and the throwing. You reveled in the masculine company and the attention while I—" She stopped and drew a
breath. "Those days are done and gone. Let us not speak of
that time again." She moved into the inner part of the Parthenon. "Look. Do you remember the ivory and gold statue of
Athena that stood here?"

Behind her, he wrapped his arms about her waist and nuzzled the side of her neck. "How could I forget the endless,
unmoving hours you spent standing on that block while
Phidias worked? It is your face, your form I see in the past's
looking glass."

His breath against her skin stirred the embers of encounters
long ago, and as always, his nearness thrilled her anew. She
skipped away, laughing. "We came to bathe in moonbeams,
not to relive former times. Come."

Hand in hand they darted from the shadows of bygone
glory and played in the dozens of pools of light, splashing
and laughing and teasing, relishing being on the same plane
again after spending so long apart.

For almost twenty-five hundred years they had shared no
lifetime on earth. While wounds healed and other lessons were
learned, they had existed one here and one there, then reversed,
serving as always as spirit guardians to the other part of
their soul so dear.

How he reveled in her close company! How he ached to

make her his once again. Given a chance, he would banish her lingering doubts, dissolve the barriers between them, and they would be one for eternity.

Covered with glistening moonbeams that beaded on his skin like drops of mercury, he pulled her to him, delighting in her copper and silver glow. His warm lips covered hers, and they blended with a soft sigh.

A heartbeat later, a bright star streaked across the sky.

Seventeen

Know thyself.

Inscription at the Delphic Oracle
The Seven Sages
c. 650-600 B.C.

"See anything back there, Solo?" Jean Jacques asked as he drove the van up the winding road.

Solo put down her binoculars and shook her head. "Looks clear to me. Since we went through Thebes, the only thing I've seen that's still following is that tour bus you passed. And it was packed with people."

"Good. That's good."

Welcome relaxed. They were free for a while. Jean Jacques's plan had worked. Solo had awakened her an hour before dawn with the scheme he'd devised. She had dressed and packed a single bag quickly, then she and Solo had met Wade and Shark at the elevator. She hadn't been too thrilled with that part, but Jean Jacques had convinced her that they needed the extra muscle along since his force was thinly spread for a few hours yet.

The four of them, all wearing hats and sunglasses, had ridden the elevator down to the second floor. They got off and their places were taken by four other people wearing hats and sunglasses: a busboy in a red wig, a petite cashier in a short blond one, and two men that hotel security had rustled up to play Wade and Shark. The security chief went along as well—an extra passenger to explain the stop.

According to the plan, the decoys continued downstairs, and with heads ducked and collars turned up, hurried through the lobby into a waiting limo that drove to the harbor and a private yacht anchored there. Welcome, Solo, Wade, and Shark went down the service elevator, hurried through the cleared kitchen, and went out the back door to where Jean Jacques waited with a tinted-window van.

Now it seemed that their ruse had worked. Four hotel employees were spending the day on a yacht, and the five of them were on their way to Delphi for an overnight trip.

Welcome had barely recognized Jean Jacques with his earrings gone and his hair tucked under a maroon baseball cap. Wearing jeans, running shoes, and a black fisherman's sweater, he looked like an ordinary person. Only the compact automatic weapon in the seat beside him belied his conventionality.

"Want me to drive for a while?" Shark asked. He sat in the front seat with Jean Jacques

They had arranged themselves in the van according to security needs as well as leg and bulk room. Wade and Welcome shared the center seat, and Solo was in the back with the bags and equipment, partly because of her size but mostly because of her being an experienced lookout.

"No, thanks. I'm used to the highway. I've driven through these mountains before."

Shark nodded at the sense of his statement. "Never been here myself."

"I have. Many times. When I danced in the Athens Festival or in other Greek theater performances." Jean

Jacques's French accent was gone, replaced by a slow American Southern drawl.

"You a *dancer?*" Shark asked.

"Used to be a pretty fair one." Jean Jacques didn't elaborate and nobody pressed him. Maybe the Uzi by his leg discouraged the questions or comments Welcome might have expected from men like Wade and Shark.

Welcome yawned. "Any coffee left?"

Wade shook the thermos by his feet. "Not in here."

Shark tested a second one beside him. "Here either."

"I could use some more caffeine." She yawned again and stretched. "Or some more sleep."

"There's a place about a half hour from here where we can stop. Aráchova, a quaint hillside village. One of my men is ahead of us checking it out. We can have breakfast and all the coffee we can drink. And," Jean Jacques added, winking at Welcome over his shoulder, "they have excellent flokati rugs."

"Great. The rest of you can have breakfast, and I'll shop."

"We'll all have breakfast," Solo said firmly. "Then we'll all shop."

Wade patted his shoulder. "Use this for a pillow and snooze until we get there. Or you can curl up and use my lap."

"Uhhh, I don't think so. But thanks." Instead, she rolled her down jacket into a sausage, wedged it between the headrest and the window, and snuggled into a nest facing away from Wade.

Earlier she'd tried to convince Wade to sit in front and let Shark share the middle seat with her, but they had both merely smiled slightly and taken their present seats. Sitting in such proximity to him had made her antsy. Each time he shifted positions, and he seemed to shift exceedingly often, his leg brushed hers.

And he was a toucher. Every time he spoke to her, he punctuated his words with a pat to some portion of her anatomy, usually her thigh or knee, and he let his hand linger, stroking until she thought she would go mad. Twice he'd stretched his long arms across the back of the seat, and his thumb had made lazy circles on her shoulder cap. Both times she'd glared at him until he moved his arm.

"Oops, sorry," he'd said, acting as innocent as a baby about his actions, insinuating that his contact had been purely accidental and guileless.

Fat chance.

Wade Morgan knew exactly what he was doing every time he touched her. How could he not know when the tension between them generated enough electricity to light Athens for a month? Every graze of his leg, every circle of his thumb sent rashes of chill bumps over her skin in unending waves. Sitting close to him was pure torture. Even breathing the same air was titillating. All her senses were acutely attuned to his presence. She'd never had anybody affect her quite so viscerally or so profoundly. Her libido had gone berserk, turned recalcitrant, and strained against her control.

Welcome didn't like the feeling. She didn't like it a damned bit. She punched at her coat-pillow and wiggled around, trying to get more comfortable. Her brain controlled her life, not sexual urges.

She was not about to get involved with a professional athlete who lived for awards and adulation of the crowds. Nope, not on your life. The man she was looking for would care more for her than playing fields and prefer a quiet evening sitting on the porch to a press party.

You could count on that.

Take it to the bank.

Drowsy, she began to relax. A brief scene flicked into her awareness, loud, bright, like a frame or two of film and sound, seen, heard, then withdrawn. A short time later it came again, as if a door to a movie theater had briefly opened, then closed.

The vibration of the van and the sound of the motor were as soothing as a train ride, and she continued to relax.

"Please," she begged, *speaking loudly to be heard over the roar of the crowd, "please let me in. I must see Marco."*

The gatekeeper barred her way. "Begone! No women except the priestesses of the temple are allowed in the stadium while the games are underway. You should know that."

"But I am only a slave, and my master has sent me with a message for Marco," she said, flinching not at the lie. "And with this watered wine for his refreshment." She held up the ewer she carried.

"Slave or no, no women are allowed." He moved to close the gate.

"Wait! Wait!" Frantic to speak to Marco before the household discovered her missing, she pushed against the closing portal. "Would you kindly deliver the libation to him? And inform him that Astrid waits outside the gate with an important message."

A cheer went up from the crowd inside, and the gatekeeper glanced over his shoulder, his impatience to return to watching the contests obvious.

She caught his hand. "Please, I beg of you. Do this and I will pester you no more."

Another cheer went up, louder, more exuberant.

"Here, give it to me and begone!" He snatched the ewer

from her hand, spilling some of its contents in his haste to slam the gate.

The summer sun was high overhead when she sat down on a stone to wait. She beseeched the gods to hear her prayers and send Marco to her. He was her only hope. The bronze bust of the foreigner was almost done. Another day, maybe two and the work would be finished. He would sail back to the northern land from whence he came.

And, if the snatches of conversations she heard were true, Astrid would go with him.

She did not want to go with the foreign man to a distant country, no matter what riches he promised her. She wanted to remain in Attica. With Marco.

For years, since they were both brought into the sculptor Phidias's household as children—he one year, she the next— they had been inseparable. At first they had clung to each other because of fear and bewilderment at finding themselves slaves in an alien land; later, because of a genuine fondness. They were like two halves of a whole, confidants, friends . . . then lovers as they grew older. As youths they had sworn a solemn oath to watch over and protect one another forever and always. They had renewed that vow often, promising that one day they would be free and live happily together always.

Marco had been free for two years now. As a result of his athletic prowess and the great esteem Marco had brought to his sponsor, Phidias had granted his freedom. When Astrid had last seen Marco some months past, he had promised that soon he would petition Phidias for her freedom as well. If he won the events in the Athens games, her master was sure to look favorably on his request. If he won again in Delphi the following year, Phidias, as Marco's sponsor, would grant any petition.

But she could not wait for the games in Delphi. She could not even wait for the completion of these games in Athens. There was no more time. By week's end she would be forced to leave with the man who had offered Phidias an enormous sum for her.

When she had overheard the first price proposed, she was staggered. And terrified that Phidias would agree. Her master had refused the offer. The following day, the foreigner had offered more, the day after, even more.

She trembled at the notion of belonging to the foreigner. She did not like the predatory way he looked at her, or the way he tried to touch her when no one else was around. Only Marco had ever been allowed to touch her so intimately. Fearing for her situation, she had hidden behind the myrtle bush outside the studio, clutched the ewer she carried, and eavesdropped shamelessly.

"I fear my flame-haired model has obsessed you," Phidias said quietly as he worked.

"I fear so, too. I must have her, sculptor. Name your price."

"Hmmm," Phidias had said. "I will think on it. Come, it is time to depart for the games."

From her years in the household, she knew that when Phidias said that he would think on it, his answer was sure to be yes. Frantic, she had secreted herself in an alcove until the men departed and tried to devise a plan.

Now she waited.

The sun moved to the west and cast long shadows. Still the crowd roared and cheered beyond the gate.

Her throat grew parched.

Still she waited.

At last the gates burst open and men spilled from the stadium, laughing and shouting. She stood on the rock to search the throng.

There! There!

Marco, laughing and naked except for a crown of laurel leaves, rode the shoulders of a band of joyous men.

"Marco!" She waved and screamed his name over and over, willing him to look at her. At last he turned his head and

their eyes met. She gestured frantically for him to come to her.
He laughed and blew her a kiss.

"Welcome." Someone shook her. "Honey, we're stopping."

She roused, her heart beating wildly, the remnants of a dream clinging to her consciousness. An important dream. She fought to grasp it, but the harder she tried to catch it, the more elusive the dream became, withdrawing and hiding behind shadowy recesses until it was lost. She was left with only an aching sadness and a feeling of deep despair.

"You awake?"

She glanced up and was shocked to find herself snuggled in Wade's arms and with a death grip on his shirt front. "Yes, I'm awake."

She immediately unclenched her fist and tried to sit up, but Wade held on to her, his brow furrowed. "Honey, what's wrong?" he asked softly.

"Wrong? Why nothing's wrong."

His thumb traced an arc beneath each eye. "Then why the tears?"

She sniffed. "I don't know. Maybe I'm allergic to something." She pushed away and smoothed her hair.

"I don't know about you guys," Solo said, "but right now I could eat a rhinoceros, horn and all."

"Me, too," Shark said. "I like a big breakfast. I don't understand all these European types who don't eat nothing but a little roll and a thimble full of coffee sludge."

Jean Jacques laughed as he pulled off the main highway and into a parking area beside a modest-looking building, one of several red-roofed buildings perched down the mountainside. "This place is used to tourists in all their diversity. Their food is bountiful and excel-

lent—just don't expect bacon and scrambled eggs—
and the view is unbelievable."

The whole troop piled out of the van and went inside. Only a few people were scattered among the tables in the dining room. A lone man sat at a table for
six near the windows which commanded the best view
in the place. He and Jean Jacques exchanged brief
nods, and the man moved to another table near the
door.

Welcome and Solo exchanged their own nods, and
Welcome said, "I'll have coffee, juice, and a roll."

Solo said, "Order the same for me, and one of everything else on the menu. If you'll excuse us, gentlemen?"

They followed the signs to the ladies' room to
freshen up.

In trying to find her makeup to repair the damage
from her earlier tears, Welcome fumbled through her
big shoulder bag and kept dropping things. When her
blusher landed on the floor and the case cracked, she
leaned against the sink and hung her head. "Damn!"
Why were her fingers shaking so?

"Are you okay?" Solo asked.

"Sure. Fine. Just a little jumpy still."

"Nobody followed us. I'm sure of that. I think you
can relax, at least for a while."

When they returned to the table a few minutes later,
it was filled with food: sausages, breads, yogurt, cheese
pies, stewed fruit, juices, jams, honey, and blessed coffee.

Everybody ate their fill while they looked out over
the valley below and the other mountains beyond. The
view was breathtaking, and sitting there, Welcome grew
keenly aware of the people throughout centuries of
civilization who had passed this way going to visit the
Oracle at Delphi.

A scene blipped into her thoughts, then out again. But for a moment she had felt herself in an ox cart as it rumbled over a road, and she had been looking at the same view that she was observing now.

Odd, she thought. She shrugged and dished herself another helping of yogurt and honey, trying to act normal when she felt as if a bucket of bees was loose inside her.

"You're awfully quiet," said Wade, who had taken a chair next to hers.

"I have a lot on my mind."

"I can understand that. But it looks as if we eluded the guy who's bothering you. By using the decoys today and in your suite tonight, J.J.'s men plus the hotel's security should be able to catch him if he tries anything else."

Although Wade and Shark hadn't been told everything, Jean Jacques—rather, J.J. as he had suggested that everyone call him—had filled them in with a highly edited version of a crazed stalker pursuing Welcome.

"I know." She cradled her coffee cup in her hands and stared out the window, her anxiety unabated. Strangely, thoughts of the killer weren't the source of her apprehension. Something deeper, more nebulous was the cause. A part of her wanted to flee from this navel of the earth as the ancients called it. Another part, the stronger part, bade her stay and meet the challenge.

"Ready to go?" J.J. asked the group.

Welcome drew a deep breath. "Ready."

Eighteen

Of all the oracles in the world [Delphi] had the reputation of being the most truthful.

Strabo
1st century B.C.

"That's the last shot on the roll," Solo said to Welcome. "Ready to take a break?"

"I'm ready to take a nap," Welcome said, pushing herself up from the steps of the Sanctuary of Athena, "but not here. This cold marble is murder on the derriere." She rubbed her bottom. "I think I'll take a stroll to walk out some of the kinks."

"I'll go with you," J.J. said, swigging the last of his soft drink from the bottle.

"Me, too," Solo chimed in.

"Look, you two, I appreciate your concern, but I'm perfectly safe here without a bevy of bodyguards. Actually, I'll like some time to myself. I'm just going to walk up to the top of the hill over there."

"How about we follow twenty paces behind?" J.J. said. "We'll be very quiet, and you can pretend that we're not there."

"Make that fifty paces, and you're on." Welcome took her jacket from Shark and handed him her makeup bag. "Mind stowing that in the van?"

"Will do. Say, isn't it time for lunch?"

She laughed. "Is food all you think about?"

"Not all," he said, grinning, "but it's way ahead o. whatever's in second place. You seen Wade?"

"Not since we were at the Temple of Apollo." Welcome cringed when she recalled what had happened there.

"Wonder where he could've got off to?"

"Maybe he went into the museum," Solo said.

"I'll check," Shark said.

"Find him and let's meet back here in twenty minutes," J.J. said.

Welcome wondered about Wade's absence as well. During the shoot at the temple, she'd been keenly aware of him. His eyes had seemed to devour her as he watched her every move. She had become so nervous from his scrutiny that she'd cursed and stalked off in a huff—a professional first for her. Welcome had never been a temperamental model and had never allowed such egocentric shenanigans by any of the models from her agency.

When she'd returned, she had apologized to everyone except Wade. He was gone. He probably thought that she was a real prima donna snot.

What was happening to her? She was behaving completely out of character, she mused as she brushed back a scrubby branch and started climbing the rocky path to the summit where the theater and stadium were supposed to be.

In order to select photo sites, they had taken a brief guided tour when they first arrived at this mystical center of the ancient world. The entire time of the tour and every moment since, an eerie feeling of déjà vu drifted around in her brain, making her feel lightheaded and chilled.

She pulled on her jacket, stuck her hands in her

ockets, and trudged on up the hill. As she ap-
roached the top where the remains of the theater
tood, the eerie feeling grew stronger.

A very faint hum seemed to vibrate the air.

Those brief blips of curious scenes came again. Like
he sweep of the radar arm on a weather map, other
mages momentarily found substance, then faded.
ounds came too, like the jumbled voices of people
n fair day.

As she neared the ruins of the amphitheater, she
topped abruptly. A flash, and for an instant, the struc-
ure stood in its former glory, the corners and edges
f the marble blocks distinct and pristine instead of
lulled and crumbling. The lone black goat pulling at
veeds growing from the crevices vanished, and in his
lace were throngs of people in arced rows of seats
nd a cast of players in the bowl. Excitement filled the
ir and leapt in her breast.

As quickly as the scene had come, it went, leaving
nly memories like the dissipating wisps of an old jet
rail.

She had walked this path before.

She *knew* it.

The roar of a huge crowd rang out, and she startled,
er eyes going immediately to the stadium at the crest.

But there was no crowd. No sound except the crop-
ing of the goat and the faint chirp of a bird or two.
rom her high vantage point, she scanned the area
or tourists, but none were nearby. Below, the Key
ours guide herded her charges aboard the bus—for
unch no doubt. J.J. and Solo were about thirty yards
ack, leaning against a rock and talking. They waved;
he waved back. Shark was by the museum, leaning
gainst a rail of the porch.

The roar came again, and her head jerked around.

Her gaze went to the stadium. She cocked an ear and listened with every fiber of her being.

Nothing.

A trick of the wind.

She started to climb upward to the arena. Her heartbeat accelerated, and her eyes went out of focus for a moment.

She stumbled.

When she looked down, her feet had changed. They were smaller and shod in crude leather sandals. She wore a short tunic caught with cord around the waist, and her legs were slender and coltish. Excitement bubbled from her, and she felt her hair. It was clipped short and fell in ringlets about her face. She laughed and moved along with the crowd of men to the stadium.

Welcome stopped and shook herself. Her heart was running away.

She looked at her feet, and her size nine Bally boots looked back at her.

Was she going nutty? Or were these memories?

A simple walk to the top of the hill suddenly became very scary. Did she dare go on?

Hell, yes.

Her backbone stiffened, and she strode to the summit of the deserted ruin. For a moment she hesitated at the gate, reluctant to pass through, but only for a moment. She climbed a low wall and sat in a small niche on one side of the stadium.

A blip.

Naked men, muscular bodies glistening in the sunlight, raced around the track.

Another blip and they disappeared.

A blip.

A javelin thrower. One arm extended, the other drawn back. Back muscles bunched. Bare flanks taut.

he sun catching the sheen of sweat and oil and turn-
ng his finely carved body to shimmering gold perfec-
ion.

Her breath caught, and she was filled with emotion
o powerful that she cried out from the intensity of it.

The sound caught his attention, and he looked at
er.

A blip.

The magnificently nude javelin thrower was gone.
Wearing jeans, a blue polo shirt, and a khaki jacket,
Wade Morgan stood in his place. His arms were posi-
ioned as if throwing a javelin. Or a football.

Obviously embarrassed to be caught in his charade,
is arms dropped, and he walked slowly to the stands
where she was. He climbed the crumbling tiers and
at down beside her. Leaning forward, he rested his
elbows on his spread knees and clasped his hands. He
didn't look at her. His eyes stayed on the playing field;
his gaze bemused as if he watched some spectacle un-
olding there.

Finally he broke the silence, saying softly, "You know,
feel a strong kinship with the men who competed
here so long ago. It's as if their energy and their cour-
ge permeated the stones around us. How many years
has it been since games were held here? A thousand?
Two thousand? Yet even after all these centuries, I can
almost feel the athletes' exhilaration, sense their
grunts of exertion, and hear the crowd's roar."

Fury ripped through her, unreasonable, blinding
fury. It came from out of left field and set her on fire.
"You love that don't you?" she lashed out, her voice
shaking with rage. "Above all else, you cherish the adu-
ation of the crowd!" She jumped to her feet, about
o bolt.

He grabbed her arm. "Astrid, wait!"

Her fury doubled, and she twisted from his grip.

"Drop dead, you muscle-brained bastard!" Seething, she clattered down the stone bleachers and hurried away.

Wade rushed after her. "Dammit, woman! Would you wait? What did I do?"

Welcome didn't wait. She didn't acknowledge his questions. She made a very crude remark under her breath and kept going.

Unfortunately she wasn't the athlete that Wade was. He caught her before she reached the wall. "Dammit, would you wait!" He grabbed her and turned her to him. "Would you tell me exactly what set you off? I must have done something, but I swear to God I haven't got a clue as to what."

"You—you—you called me the wrong name," she stormed, grasping at a reasonable excuse for her irrational anger.

He looked totally bewildered. "No, I didn't."

"You damned well did. You called me Astrid. One of your other women no doubt."

"Astrid? Who the hell is Astrid? I don't even know anybody by that name. What's going on with you?"

"Nothing's going on with me. Would you please let go of me?" She gave him a look that would wither weeds. It didn't faze him.

"I'm not letting go until you tell me what's going on. I feel like I'm in the middle of an Italian movie, and I don't know the language or the plot. Now what set you off? Was it something I said? Something I didn't say? Something I did? Something I didn't do? Help me here. All I remember doing is sitting there spilling my guts about a very profound feeling I was having, and the next thing I know you're spewing fire in my face."

"I—I—" She kept working her mouth, but the words wouldn't come out. Her insides were wrapped in knots,

HERE'S A SPECIAL INVITATION TO ENJOY TODAY'S FINEST HISTORICAL ROMANCES— ABSOLUTELY FREE! *(a $19.96 value)*

Now you can enjoy the latest Zebra Lovegram Historical Romances without even leaving your home with our convenient Zebra Home Subscription Service. Zebra Home Subscription Service offers you the following benefits that you don't want to miss:

- 4 BRAND NEW bestselling Zebra Lovegram Historical Romances delivered to your doorstep each month (usually before they're available in the bookstores!)

  - 20% off each title or a savings of almost $4.00 each month

  - FREE home delivery

  - A FREE monthly newsletter, *Zebra/Pinnacle Romance News* that features author profiles, contests, special member benefits, book previews and more

- No risks or obligations...in other words you can cancel whenever you wish with no questions asked

So join hundreds of thousands of readers who already belong to Zebra Home Subscription Service and enjoy the very best Historical Romances That Burn With The Fire of History!

And remember....there is no minimum purchase required. After you've enjoyed your initial FREE package of 4 books, you'll begin to receive monthly shipments of new Zebra titles. Each shipment will be yours to examine for 10 days and then if you decide to keep the books, you'll pay the preferred subscriber's price of just $4.00 per title. That's $16 for all 4 books with FREE home delivery! And if you want us to stop sending books, just say the word....it's that simple.

It's a no-lose proposition, so send for your 4 FREE books today!

and she felt as if the top of her head was about to blow off. "I don't know what's the matter," she said. Her face screwed up, and she threw herself sobbing into his arms. "I think I'm going crazy."

"Shhhh, darlin'. Shhhh." He sat down on the wall and pulled her onto his lap. "Don't cry. We'll get this all worked out."

"I'm not crying," she wailed against his chest. "I never cry. I'm tough as nails. Ask anybody."

"Right, sugar." He patted her back, and she kept blubbering like a fool.

"I keep seeing things that aren't there. I've been doing it for days."

"Has anything like this ever happened to you before?"

She shook her head. "Never. Not to me. I'm steady as a rock and—"

"—tough as nails," he finished for her. "I know." He held her close, stroked her back, and moved his lips across her temple until she quieted.

Being in his arms felt so wonderful and so secure that she didn't want to move. She could have stayed there for an eternity, cloaked by his spicy male scent and the warmth of his body. Even the strong beat of his heart under her palm was reassuring.

As tall as Welcome was, few men made her feel delicate and petite. Wade did. And she discovered that she liked the feeling, loath as she was to admit it.

She liked feeling cherished and protected by his size and his strength.

She took a deep, shuddering breath and snuggled closer.

How perfectly she fitted against him. How content she felt.

She sniffed.

Wade patted over his body with one hand. "Sorry,

sugar, I don't have a handkerchief." He pulled a paper cocktail napkin from his jacket pocket and offered it to her. "Will this do?"

She nodded then dabbed at her eyes and nose. "Thanks." She should have moved then. She should have gotten up and gone down the hill.

But she didn't. She sighed and settled back into the comfortable cranny that she'd found, satisfied to stay there forever.

"Feeling better?"

She nodded. "Much."

"Welcome?"

"Yes?"

"Look at me."

She drew back slightly and looked up. His gray-green eyes were filled with such deep and indescribable emotion that she was stunned. His head bent slowly, and his mouth descended to hers. When their lips met, when their tongues touched, she was swept away. Lost in a torrent of sensation.

Magic happened.

His every touch thrilled her, sent tremors rippling over her. His mouth moving against hers was sweeter than nectar from the gods. Aching to pull him closer, her arms went around his strong body, gripping, straining to blend with him into a single pulsing entity. Desire of overwhelming intensity throbbed in her womb. Longing swelled her breasts.

The kiss could have lasted seconds or hours or centuries. Time ceased to exist.

Only a repeated clearing of a throat brought her back to reality. When Wade's head came up, scowling at the intruder, Welcome felt dazed, disoriented.

"I hate to break this up," J.J. said, fighting a smile, "but a new busload of tourists is headed this way, and I don't expect that you want an audience. Too, Shark is about to start eating tree bark if we don't find him something better."

Wade nodded curtly. "We'll be along in a minute." When J.J. left, he lifted Welcome's chin and kissed her briefly. "You okay now?"

"I think so." That was a lie. She wasn't okay at all. If she was confused before, her mind was in chaos now. She didn't want to get involved with someone like Wade, but it was too late. She was involved.

"Sweetheart?"

"Yes?"

"Will you—"

Her heart raced in anticipation. "Will I what?"

"Never mind. You would think *I* was crazy. We'd better get going. I hear the thundering herd coming this way." He dropped a quick kiss on her mouth and lifted her off his lap.

"I *hate* it when people do that."

"Do what?" he asked, dusting off the seat of his jeans. "Start something and then not finish it."

A gleam came in his eyes, and a slow grin spread over his face. "Oh I intend to finish it."

Nineteen

When toilsome contests have been decided, good cheer is the best physician, and songs, the sage daughters of the Muses, soothe with their touch.

Pindar
518-438 B.C.

Welcome held her glass high. "To new friends and old."

"Hear, hear!"

The five of them clinked their glasses together and downed another measure of local wine. Despite a continuing overlay of creepiness about the area, Welcome felt very relaxed and content when compared to her anxiety of the past few days. They had finished the photographs, including what promised to be some great ones of the sunset over the ruins. Nobody had shot at her except with a camera; nobody had trashed her room or made obscene phone calls.

Earlier the group had gone back to the local hotel to rest and change for dinner. The hotel in Delphi was a far cry from the GB in Athens, but their rooms were clean and comfortable. And the view from the side of the mountain was spectacular. Asserting that she was in no danger here, Welcome had tried to hold out for a private room, but J.J. and Solo nixed the idea. The women had to share a room with two double beds, and J.J. insisted on taking the adjoining room with a connecting door. Shark and Wade were in rooms across the hall.

They had gone to dinner at a wonderful, unpretentious restaurant and had eaten mounds of thinly sliced grilled lamb chops with herbed rice and vegetables. The bread was fresh from the oven and the olives scooped from a barrel. Bouzouki music played from an endless tape. The wine flowed freely, as did the laughter.

There were less than a dozen diners left at the tables when there was a lull in the conversation, and Welcome grew aware of the tempo of the music. She turned to J.J. and caught his hand. "Dance for us, Jean Jacques." When he shook his head modestly, she squeezed his hand. "Please. For me."

He smiled and kissed her hand. "Ah, *chérie.* how can I refuse? Join me?"

"Later."

J.J. rose, tossed his cap aside, and walked to the small dance floor near their table.

Shark leaned forward. "Is he really gonna dance out there all by himself?"

"Yep. Watch. He'll blow your socks off."

And he did.

Jean Jacques stood unmoving in the center of the floor for a moment, and the room grew quiet. He closed his eyes, breathed in the music, the mournful strums, then he raised his arms like a rousing Phoenix, and the music flowed through him as he danced.

Welcome had almost forgotten how very good he was until she watched, spellbound. The mood of the music dictated the movements he improvised, a perfect blending of traditional Greek steps and modern ballet that captured her core and sent her soaring.

"Man, oh, man," Shark whispered, "would you look at that? That dude is something else."

"Lord, look at him jump," Wade said. "He'd make a hell of a pass receiver."

Solo didn't say anything. She only sat, mouth agape, with her eyes glued on the magnificent Jean Jacques.

The song ended with J.J.'s head thrown back and his fists thrust into the air.

There was a moment's silence, then everybody applauded wildly. The cheering sounded like a room full instead of the twelve or fourteen who had watched.

"Opa!" a waiter shouted.

"Opa!" Welcome shouted, jumping to her feet. "Opa!"

The tempo of the taped music changed, and J.J. grinned and started clapping to the beat. He motioned the others up.

Welcome started to the floor, urging the others to join them. They all chickened out, but she was caught up in the enchantment. She and J.J. danced. After a few minutes they were able to coax Solo onto the floor, and later, Shark, who was surprisingly light on his feet.

But Wade steadfastly refused. "I'm not much of a dancer," was his excuse.

"I don't believe you," Welcome called from the floor. "Come on up," she urged.

But he held out. "I'd rather watch."

"He's shy," Shark said.

"Oh, yeah. Sure," Welcome responded, not believing a word of it.

Wade sat on the sidelines, feeling like twelve kinds of fool. But he would have felt like a bigger fool if he'd gotten up there. Not that he couldn't dance. While he wasn't in the same league with J.J., he could hold his own with the average guy.

Another reason kept him in his seat. He was horny.

as hell. Watching Welcome dance, watching that gorgeous body move so damned seductively had done its number on him. With every toss of that fiery mane, every shake of her shoulder, every swivel of her hips, his pants grew tighter. He couldn't believe his own re-action; he hadn't been so turned on just watching someone since he and Pete Rogers had sneaked into a porno movie when they were fourteen.

He'd wanted her before, but after kissing her today, he couldn't think of anything else. God, how he wanted her. He wanted her naked and hot, writhing under him while he—

He clenched his fists and jerked his eyes away from her. Dammit, thinking like that wasn't helping the situation. He tried to get his mind on something else, but it wouldn't stick. He was obsessed by her. He wanted to run his tongue over every inch of her and drive himself—

Abruptly, he stood, his chair scraping loudly, then strode from the restaurant.

He had to get some air, walk around, get hold of himself. He chuckled at his own double entendre. He wasn't quite to that point, but close. He had to do something before he embarrassed himself in front of everybody.

Wade drew in several deep breaths, hoping the crispness would clear his head.

Still her image swam in his mind. Her head thrown back, laughing, naked, her skin aglow with inner fire. Her breasts rosy, her nipples hard—

Dammit! What was happening to him? No woman had ever affected him like this.

He started jogging toward the ruins.

He found himself ascending the path to the stadium, his way lit by the silvery fullness of the moon. When he reached the field, he circled the track once, then stopped, straining to listen.

For a moment he thought he'd heard cheering.

He shrugged. A trick of the wind.

Another turn around the track, and he felt his tension ease a little. He kept running, stripping off his jacket as he ran. He tossed the jacket aside, then shed his shirt. Running with the wind against his bare skin felt great, but still not quite right. He felt encumbered somehow, slowed.

He stopped and stripped off his shoes and socks, his pants and shorts and ran in the buff.

God, how glorious.

Swift as a deer, he circled the track again and again.

The crowd roared, urging him on.

Faster he ran, his feet barely touching the ground, until a final burst of speed sent him across the finish line, his arms raised in victory.

He made a final tour of the track, trotting to cool down, basking in the cheers of the gathered throng.

The cheers subsided, then faded to a hollow echo. He looked up at the stands.

The crumbling bleachers were empty.

A trick of the wind.

Chest still heaving, he looked down at himself. Good Godamighty! What the hell had gotten into him? Here he was, a grown man, running around in the middle of the night as naked as a jaybird. And hearing things, to boot.

He looked around quickly, hoping to hell that nobody had witnessed his idiocy.

Not a soul was around. Thank God for that.

A chill breeze nipped his butt, he became aware that the ground was rough under his feet. Dammit to hell! Had he really been running barefoot on this rocky field? He probably wouldn't be able to walk for a week.

Gingerly, he picked his way over to where his clothes lay strewn and dressed quickly. When he was done, he tossed his jacket over one shoulder and started back down the path to the hotel. Surprisingly, his feet felt fine.

The rest of him felt weird.

Very weird.

"Good night!" Welcome called to Shark and J.J. as Solo unlocked their door. "Sleep tight. Don't let the bedbugs bite." She giggled and fluttered her fingers.

"Shhh," Solo hissed, tugging her into their room and closing the door. "Some people are trying to sleep."

"Old duddy-fuddies. 'N that's what Wade Morgan is—an old duddy-fuddy." A giggle exploded into a snort. "Fuddy-puddy. Duddy-puddy. Party-poopa." She giggled again.

"Do you want the bathroom first?" Solo asked.

"Go 'head. I'll wait. Opa!" She clapped. "Opa! Party poo-pa!"

"Shhh. Lady, you're snockered."

"Yep. Snockered again. This country does it to me. Last time I was snockered was . . ." Welcome screwed up her face trying to think. "A loooong time ago. A loooong, long time ago." She fell back on her bed. "Years and years and years ago. Before Greece. Before Wade. Ol' poopa."

The room began to spin. Her stomach began to roll. She jumped up. "Changed my mind," she mumbled as she brushed past Solo and bolted for the bathroom.

She stirred slowly, feeling sluggish until she rose and moved away from the bed. She looked around hoping to find him waiting, but there was only a faint trail indicating that he'd been there earlier. Perhaps he'd lingered across the hall until she roused.

Checking, she found that he wasn't there.

The stadium.

She sighed. Of course. Where else?

How tempting it would be to ignore him this night, to curl up in limbo and rest. But no, the urge to be with him was too great. Besides, he would only seek her out later.

She flashed to the crest of the hill and into a seat in the middle of the grandstand.

He was on the field, balancing a javelin in his hand. Elbows on her knees, chin resting on the heels of her palms, she watched the beautifully nude form as he poised on his toes. He drew back, ran a short distance, and hurled the spear with all his might. It flew from sight.

She applauded, and he looked up and saw her. He smiled.

"It must have gone halfway to Athens," she said.

He laughed. "At least. I didn't realize that you were here."

"You were engrossed in your games again. Too enthralled to notice me."

He joined her on the crumbling marble seats, nuzzled her cheek and nipped at her earlobe. "Impossible. No games are as enthralling as you."

She stiffened slightly. "Sweet words."

"True words." His lips moved across her soft shoulder.

"Why the hasty retreat earlier?" she asked.

He whispered in her ear, and she laughed. "The flesh can be difficult."

"You can't imagine."

"Oh, yes I can," she said smugly. "I tried manhood once or twice if you recall."

He chuckled. "I recall." Leaning back, he gazed out over the stadium. "Do you remember our first visit here?"

"I remember. You were only a boy, and it was your first time to compete in the games. We journeyed for several days

to reach here, and I was furious when Phidias said that I couldn't watch you run."

His countenance brightened. *"Because you were a girl."*

"But I got in anyway and saw you win."

"By wearing my chiton and cropping your hair."

"Phidias never knew of my caper, but he was livid when he saw my hair. I told him that when I was out looking for the cat, I had gotten into a batch of burrs and they tangled in my hair so badly that there was nothing to do but to cut them out. I'm not sure that he believed me."

"Me either. Phidias was a wily old duck. He was very fond of you." He gazed again over the stadium. *"I won my last contests here. And received many gifts. By then I had won the games at Olympia and in Athens and amassed a great purse with a small house and groves besides. I went to Phidias to beg or buy your freedom, but he said that you were gone. I demanded to know where, but he turned a deaf ear. Nothing I said would move him."*

"I had been gone over a year by then. I left the day after the citizens carried you on their shoulders when you won the decathlon in Athens."

"You knew then that I won?"

She nodded and dropped her eyes. *"I knew. I heard the shouts. I saw you outside the gate and waved."*

"And I blew you a kiss."

"Yes. You blew me a kiss." A bitter knot formed in her core; she willed it away and smiled. Rising, she caught his hand. *"Come, let us visit the theater and dance among the stones. Let us recite the words of Homer or play thespian upon the stage."*

"A wonderful idea. I shall play the satyr and you shall play the lovely maiden." He grinned lasciviously and rubbed his hands together.

"Why can't I play the satyr this time?"

"Because my precious one, you make such a lovely lovely maiden." He reached for her.

She laughed and flitted away to the bowl of the amphitheater.

They romped until the first fingers of dawn dripped golden honey over the marble blocks and pillars, then they joined in a jubilant burst of joy.

Renewed, replete, they reluctantly parted with a sigh. They yearned to spend every hour together, waking, sleeping, loving. But for now they must await another night.

Soon, the oracle's voice whispered.

Soon, the poet echoed.

Soon, their hearts promised.

"Rise and shine, lover boy." Shark's gruff voice penetrated the deep fog. He smacked Wade's rump. "Rise and shine. We're gonna do five miles this morning."

Wade groaned. "I don't need to run. I must've done twenty last night." He pulled the pillow over his head.

"Is that where you went? You should have stayed with us. Welcome and J.J. taught Solo and me all the steps, and we had a good time. A real good time. Why did you leave?"

"Because I didn't want to look like a fool. I don't have that natural rhythm like you do."

"That's true." Shark grinned. "I'm not half bad, but man, that J.J. That mother can *dance*. Where you suppose he learned to dance like that?"

"No idea." Wade yawned and stretched. "Some ballet school I imagine."

"*Ballet*? You think he's a fruit?"

"I don't know, but if the way he looks at Solo is any indication, I'd guess not. Has he hit on you?"

Shark grabbed Wade's pillow and whacked him with it. "Hell no. You're the pretty boy around here. Now get you white ass out of the bed."

Wade groaned and rolled out. He expected his aging bones to be sore after last night's punishment. But except for a minor twinge or two, he felt fine.

Hell, he wasn't so old. Not any older than Montana. And Blanda had played into his forties. He still had a few good years left in him. He'd call Barney later and see if he'd been able to goose the Vulcan's front office into a satisfactory contract.

After a pot of coffee from room service, Welcome felt considerably better. She thought briefly of asking Wade to fix his potion, but she wasn't that bad off.

Why had she drunk so much again? She rarely had more than a glass or two of wine. Was it nerves?

Or was it because Wade had left in the middle of the evening when she'd thought that they had something going? She didn't understand why he'd left.

Maybe he'd been sick.

Of course, That was it. She'd noticed his pained expression. He wouldn't be the first tourist to fall victim to Plato's revenge.

Relieved by the explanation, she dug through her bag for a suitable outfit.

Solo glanced up from the guidebook she was reading. "You about ready for breakfast?"

"Give me ten minutes."

"*You* can get ready in that length of time?"

"Sweetie, models are the fastest dressers on earth. I could be ready in five minutes, but I want to take a shower."

Ten minutes later, Welcome, in full makeup and wearing jeans and a sweater, pulled on her jacket. "Ready?"

"Yep. Let me give J.J. a ring. Wade stopped by while

you were in the shower. He and Shark are going to meet us in the restaurant in a few minutes.''

Welcome's pulse quickened at the mention of Wade's name. Surprised at her reaction, she knew that she was developing a very bad case for him. She, of all people, was falling for a professional *athlete*. She smiled. Would wonders never cease?

But Wade Morgan was different.

He was . . . well, different.

She stuck her hand in her pocket and felt something. She pulled out a crumpled cocktail napkin and smiled when she remembered where it came from. Wade had given it to her for a handkerchief.

What was written on it? She frowned and looked carefully at the airline napkin. Lisa McKay, Holiday Inn, Athens. Xenia Hotel, Delphi.

Well, hell. So that's where the rascal snuck off to.

So much for different.

Twenty

*The sun too penetrates into privies, but is not polluted
by them.*

Diogenes the Cynic
c. 400-325 B.C.

He opened the door of his hotel room a slit. Something was going on, some unusual activity, but he
couldn't see exactly what. Holding the door open further, he leaned out to peer around the alcove. A room-
service cart. With breakfast he supposed. Although he
had finally wrangled a room on the sixth floor of the
GB, its location wasn't the ideal vantage point for
watching her suite.

And he needed to watch. The flame-haired bitch
would be back. He was sure of that. Most of her luggage was still in her room. He had paid the larcenous
maid. He had laid out a thousand drachmas for that
bit of information.

Being on this floor was convenient too in that he
had an excuse for coming and going frequently, for
passing her suite or dawdling in the hallway. As a guest
he attracted no undue attention, although he'd had a
close call last night. Someone else had been trying to
discover her whereabouts as well.

He was still seething about the ruse she and her

fucking partners had executed the day before. Only by coincidence had he seen them sneak from their rooms before dawn. By the time he'd pulled on his pants, they were on the elevator. He'd run down the stairs and reached the lobby only in time to glimpse them enter a limousine.

A glimpse had been enough. He'd seen the red-head's profile.

Duped! Somewhere between the sixth floor and the lobby, they had escaped. *"Oh, merde alors!"* he cursed. She would pay for his vexation. She would pay.

The woman under the covers roused. "Come back to bed," she urged, her voice thick.

Fat cow! He wanted to strangle her and toss her out the window. But he forced himself to smile and turn on his considerable charm as he approached her. After all, this was the hotel's telephone operator. She could be of use to him.

Naked, he slipped into bed beside her and touched her intimately. He nipped her inner thigh and murmured, *"Ah. un chat parfumé."*

She giggled inanely, and he wanted to puke.

After this, *le con* had better be useful.

Twenty-one

The days that are still to come are the wisest witnesses.

Pindar
c. 518-438 B.C.

During breakfast Welcome was cool to Wade, answering his direct questions with terse replies but otherwise ignoring him. He might have chalked it up to one of those woman things except that she was the gay señorita with everybody else. Even Shark had noticed it, lifting a brow and giving Wade a pointed look when she supplied one of her icy responses. What the hell was wrong with her?

Was she pissed-off because he'd left the party the night before? Whatever it was, he meant to get to the bottom of it.

After breakfast they all walked over to the museum. They had decided to spend an hour or two there before heading back. Welcome wanted time to stop in a couple of the mountain villages for some kind of fuzzy rugs that J.J. told her were a bargain.

They got to the museum just after it opened and before any of the tour buses arrived, so they had the place almost to themselves. Wade finally was able to speak to Welcome alone as she studied the famous bronze charioteer.

"Want to tell me what's going on with you?" Wade said.

She looked at him as if she'd stepped in dog doo. "I don't know what you mean."

"Come off that. Something's wrong, and I don't know what. Talk about *men* not communicating. Honey, communicating with you is like playing twenty questions with a goal post."

"I suppose Lisa is easy to communicate with."

"Lisa? Who's Lisa?"

She took something from her pocket and slapped it in his hand. "This Lisa."

He scowled at the crumpled napkin. "What's this? And who the hell is Lisa?"

She rolled her eyes and made a wry mouth before she turned her back on him and began scrutinizing the charioteer.

Solo walked up, and Wade turned to her. "I don't know what she's talking about half the time. Do you know who Lisa is?"

Plucking the napkin from his fingers, Solo glanced at it. "Lisa McKay?"

"Who's Lisa McKay?"

"An airline stewardess maybe?"

"What the hell are you talking about? You're as bad as Welcome. I feel like I'm doing an old Abbott and Costello routine."

Grinning, Solo pointed out the writing on the napkin. "There is her name with her hotels. Since it's on an airline napkin, I figured that maybe it belonged to someone you met on the plane, probably a stewardess."

Wade was bewildered. "Beats me who Lisa is. I don't even know how the napkin got there. I only found it when I was looking for something for Welcome to blow her nose on."

Welcome turned around. "You didn't spend last night with her?"

"With someone I don't even know? How could I? Where did you get that idea?"

"Why did you leave the restaurant last night?"

"Yeah, Wade," Solo chimed in, "why did you leave? We were having a great time."

"I, uh, I was having a problem."

"What kind of a problem?" Solo cocked her head and grinned, obviously enjoying his discomfort.

Godamighty! Did he have to spell it out? "A, uh, delicate problem of a physical nature."

"You had Plato's revenge?" Welcome beamed. "Poor baby." She tucked her arm through his. "Are you feeling better this morning?"

"Oh, much better, thanks." If believing that he had a case of the runs made Welcome all smiles again, he wasn't about to tell her any different.

"Listen," Solo said, "I have some medication in my room if you need it."

"Thanks, if I have a problem again, I may take you up on that."

Solo wandered on to look at another exhibit. Wade said, "Did you really believe that I was with another woman last night?"

"The thought crossed my mind."

He grinned. "And you were jealous?"

"Certainly not." She unlocked her arm from his and strolled across the room.

He almost laughed out loud. By damn, she *had* been jealous. That was a good sign. He hurried to catch up with her. "What's that say?" He pointed to a sign written in French and Greek.

"It says: 'Football players must be kept on a leash.' " When he gave her a dubious look, she laughed. "It says: 'Please do not touch the displays.' "

"Why do they have it in French but not in English?"

"Because for many, many years, French was the common and diplomatic language for a big part of the world. Lots of Europeans prefer French to English. Does that sort of thing happen often?"

"What sort of thing?"

"Women leaving notes in your pockets."

He shrugged. "Sometimes. I guess when you're a little bit of a celebrity, people do nutty stuff. I imagine that you've had similar things happen."

"Unfortunately, yes. But in a few weeks I'll just be an ordinary person again. Notoriety is not one of the things I'll miss. Don't fans just run you crazy?"

"Not really. Most of them are pretty nice folks. Did I mention that I've been a fan of yours for ten years?"

"Of *mine*?"

"Yep. Although I didn't know your name. I have a picture of you hanging on my bathroom wall. It was from an old *Sports Illustrated,* the swimsuit edition."

"You're kidding."

"Nope."

She smiled. "That was from a lifetime ago. It was one of my first modeling jobs. I'd just been in the Miss America pageant—"

"You were Miss America?"

"No, no. I was only a runner up."

"The judges must have been blind."

Welcome laughed. "No, but an opera singer will beat a fiddle player every time."

"Not in my book. Do you really play the fiddle?"

"I used to, but I'm a little rusty. My dad taught me. He was great."

They walked on through the museum. Welcome read the signs to him while they looked at the various collections. They bought a few postcards then went back to the hotel to pack.

* * *

When all their luggage was loaded in the van, J.J. pulled Welcome aside and said, "I just talked to one of my men in Athens. Our ruse seems to have worked. Someone suspicious was prowling around on your floor last night."

"Did they catch him?"

"Unfortunately, no. He slipped by them. I think, and Solo agrees, that it would be wise to stay away from Athens for another day or two at least. I know you have some work to do there yet, but what if we rearrange your schedule and go on the cruise of the islands now instead of later?"

"It's fine with me, but I'll need some other clothes from my suite."

"Make a list, and I'll have a maid at the GB pack them for you. Do you have any objections to Shark and Wade going along with us?"

"If they don't mind playing Agatha Christie games. This can't be much of a vacation for them."

J.J. chuckled. "Oh, I have a feeling that they wouldn't miss it for the world."

"But their suite is just sitting there unoccupied, and, sweetie, the GB ain't cheap."

"Don't worry about it, love. Horus is picking up the tab. And before you protest, remember that Meri's peace of mind is a thousand times more valuable to Ram than the price of a hotel suite. The guy's rolling in dough. And your Mr. Morgan isn't exactly a pauper. Don't sweat it."

"Fine by me." Welcome climbed in the van. "Let's go buy some rugs, people."

* * *

As it turned out, Wade and Shark were anxious to stay with the group. "Never been on a Mediterranean cruise," Shark said as they drove along the mountain road. "Never thought I'd see the day. Sounds cool."

"If you're going, I'm going," Wade told Welcome. "It does sound like fun. Besides, I've got to protect your pretty little backside." He tapped her nose for emphasis.

"That's not my backside, sugar. And nothing about me is little."

"Actually," J.J. said, "this isn't a very good time of the year for cruising. It will be chilly on the water. In a month or two we could go swimming or sunbathing, but try it now and you'll freeze your *couilles* off."

"Then it's a good thing I don't have any," Welcome said, "because I have to do some swimsuit shots. As I recall, one of the near islands has a nice beach."

"That would be Aegina. When we stop for lunch, I'll call and make the final arrangements. One of Ram's Greek friends has offered us the use of his yacht and crew for as long as we want."

"A yacht?" Welcome frowned. "Meri and I had planned to take a typical tourist cruise ship. After all, most of the people we're aiming the brochure for can't afford to hire a private yacht."

"But a big cruise ship is the very devil for security purposes, especially without a dozen men or more. Let's opt for the safer vessel and see if we can't work around the problems."

"This isn't the same yacht that the decoys took, is it?" Wade asked.

"Nope. Different one. Different marina. But that's a good point. And the decoys are still in your rooms, toughing it out with television and room service," J.J. said, grinning. "Wade, do you and Shark need anything from the GB?"

"If we're going to be gone another night or two," Shark said, "I could use another change of clothes."

Wade agreed, and Solo said, "I'll need a couple of things too, plus some film."

"Make a list of everything you need, and I'll have one of my men slip it out of the hotel and stow it on board." He pulled to a stop on the bumpy road of a small mountain village. "Here we are, Welcome. The finest flokati rugs in Greece, and at the best prices, are for sale right here."

The van, considerably fuller with Welcome's purchases, took a slight jog toward Thebes. "Thebes is the setting for *Oedipus Rex*," J.J. told them. "There, on Mount Parnassos," he said, pointing to a spot, "is where Oedipus was supposed to have slain his father."

"Is that the dude who married his mama?" Shark asked.

"The very one. There's not much else special about Thebes except that there are a lot of gypsy encampments surrounding it, and they have an excellent restaurant. You guys about ready for lunch?"

Shark grinned. "I wouldn't mind some cornbread and a mess of collards."

"And a little red beans and dirty rice?"

"Yeah, man."

J.J. laughed. "You won't find it here, I'm afraid, but their seafood is excellent. The owner's son is an old friend of mine."

The food was indeed excellent. Wade was about to pop and Welcome groaned and said, "If I keep eating the way I have been in the past few days, I'll look like a porker in the bathing suit shot."

Wade eyed her appreciatively, "Sugar, you're a long way from being a porker."

She craned her neck, looking around. "Where's J.J.?"

"I think he's making another phone call. Which reminds me, I need to make one myself." Barney, his agent, was probably about ready to shit a brick by now. Wade was supposed to have heard from him yesterday. "Excuse me."

Wade gave Welcome's shoulder a squeeze, got up, and went looking for the telephone. He met J.J. on the way. "Listen, I need to call my agent in L. A. in the worst way. Think I could use the phone here? I'll use my credit card."

"No problem. Just use the owner's office. Down that hall, second door on the left."

Wade found the office and placed the call, but he had trouble getting through to Barney's office. He'd forgotten that, with the time difference, it was four o'clock in the morning in Los Angeles. And Barney would kill him if he called him at home at that hour.

Instead, he phoned the hotel to check for messages. Sure enough, Barney had called six times. "If he telephones again," Wade told the operator, "tell him that I'm going on a cruise for a couple of days, but I'll get back to him tonight—or it will be in the morning where he is."

"What is your destination, sir?" the operator asked.

Wade didn't dare tell anyone where they were going, not even the hotel operator. "I'm not sure yet. Just tell him that I'll be in touch."

When Wade rejoined the group, J.J. was outlining their departure plans. "We need to give them about two or three hours to collect our gear from the hotel and have it stowed. The captain and the crew are making the boat ready and taking on provisions. By the time we have baklava and another cup of coffee and drive to the marina, everything will be ready for us to get under way.

"By the way, Welcome, do you know a young Greek named Katrakis?"

"Takis? Yes, I know the whole Katrakis family. Why?"

"He's been pestering the front desk since yesterday trying to locate you. Seems that he didn't believe them when he was told you checked out. Hotel security nabbed him when they caught him sneaking around on the sixth floor."

"Good Lord! With everything that has happened, I forgot all about Takis and Niki. They were supposed to pick me up yesterday."

"Well, he's in jail," J.J. said.

"In jail?" Welcome exclaimed. "J.J., Takis doesn't belong in jail. We have to get him out. He's just a kid who befriended me. God, what his grandfather must think! He must be worried sick. I have to call Spyros at once."

Twenty-two

Gray-eyed Athena sent them a favorable breeze, a fresh west wind, singing over the wine-dark sea.

Homer
c. 700 B.C.

Welcome leaned over the rail and waved her hat. "Yoo-hoo! Takis! Niki! Over here."

Solo jerked the hat from Welcome's hand and yanked her back into the main salon. "My God, I don't believe you. Why don't you just take out an ad announcing where you are?"

"Oh, sweetie, don't be such a drag. After the zigs and zags we've taken, nobody could be following us. And I just felt so awful about Takis landing in the pokey that I had to do something to make it up to him. Niki, too. She's such an angel, and I don't want her to think that I don't care about her. She wants to be a model, and I think going along with us and doing a shoot or two will be great experience even if she does have to cut a few classes. Why are you so jumpy?"

"I don't know," Solo said, rubbing her arms. "I just have a bad feeling about this boat and this trip."

"Any particular reason?"

"Nothing concrete. Just a . . . sort of a hunch."

"J.J. seems to think everything is okay," Welcome said. "Have you discussed your hunch with him?"

"Sort of."

"And?"

"I don't think he takes me seriously as an operative. Because of my appearance, I'm sure. *Him*, of all people."

Welcome smiled knowingly. "You're not falling for him a little, are you?"

"Who? J.J.? That strutting pipsqueak in a platinum ponytail? You've got to be kidding. No way. But speaking of falling for people, where is Wade? I thought he had attached himself to your hip."

"I've been tossed over for a yacht. He and Shark are on the bridge with the captain."

"What is it with men and boats?" Solo asked. "My dad had a small inboard for bay fishing that he treated like a baby and spent a fortune on." She looked around the opulent salon with its white leather couches, intricately carved rosewood tables, and plush carpet. "But I can't imagine what the upkeep on this baby would be."

"Megabucks. But from what I understand, Theo Dalaras isn't hurting for cash."

"Is Dalaras the owner? He must be in the same league with people like Onassis was. Do you know him?"

"No, never met the fellow, but I've read about him and heard Eduard speak of business dealings with him. I didn't even know that Ram and Dalaras were acquainted."

"Who's Eduard?" Solo was examining a barstool, squinting and scrutinizing it closely.

"The guy I used to date in Paris. What's so interesting about that barstool?"

"I was just wondering what it was made from. I saw

a biography of Onassis on TV once, and they said that his yacht had barstools made from the foreskins of whales."

Welcome made a face. "Oh, gross."

"Exactly. I want to know what I'm sitting on."

Welcome peered closely at the padded seat. "Looks like silk jacquard to me."

"It did to me, too, but I've never seen a whale's foreskin, and I didn't know if the owner of this boat used the same decorator."

"I think you're safe." Welcome laughed as J.J. escorted a wide-eyed Takis and Niki into the salon. "Hello, my friends," she said, gathering the young people into a hug. "I'm so sorry, Takis, about the trouble you landed in because of me. Does your grandfather forgive me?"

Takis looked sheepish. "Grandfather doesn't know about the trouble."

"You didn't tell your family that you were in jail?"

"Only our cousin and me," Niki said. "He was too embarrassed. Grandfather would have—how do you say?—hit the house top."

"Hit the ceiling? Gone through the roof? I understand, and I'm so very sorry. Things have been complicated. Did J.J. explain?" She glanced at J.J. who gestured that he had explained after a fashion. "Did your grandfather object to your coming on the trip with us?" she asked the brother and sister.

"Not at all," Niki said shyly. "He is very fond of you."

"And I of him. This is my friend, Solo Jones." After the introductions were made, Welcome said, "You'll meet Wade and Shark later."

"Shark?" Takis said hesitantly.

"A nickname. From his football playing days I imagine. Come, I'll show you your rooms. Isn't this boat great?"

"It is . . . fantastic," Niki said, her wide brown eyes missing nothing. Her long dark hair was pulled back on the sides and caught with a clip at her crown, showing off her good bone structure. With an exotic beauty already molding her features, Niki was prettier than most of the Greek women Welcome had seen. The sultry facial characteristics that made Greek males so exceptionally handsome didn't ordinarily translate well into a feminine version, but Welcome suspected that the camera would love Niki.

"I've never seen anything like it," Takis said. "Well, that is, I've seen such boats, of course, but I've never been aboard one as a guest. I've brought my camera. Is that okay?"

Niki giggled. "He wants to take pictures and impress his friends."

After the *Ionna* was well underway, Wade and Shark wandered into the salon where Solo and J.J. were snipping at one another. They clammed up as soon as they noticed that they had an audience.

"Where's Welcome?" Wade asked.

"Showing the teeny-boppers to their rooms," Solo said. "I can't believe that J.J. actually brought them along. What if something happens to those kids?"

"Nothing is going to happen," J.J. said. "Every precaution possible has been taken. Unless this weirdo has a network more extensive than one of those James Bond villains, there's no way he could lock onto us. That's a sea out there, for Chrissakes."

"J.J.—"

"Oh, hell, I know they shouldn't be along, but have you ever tried to argue with that redhead when she has her mind made up?" He glanced around the room. "Are there any snacks anywhere? My stomach says that lunch was a long time ago."

"Mine's been talking to me too," Shark said, opening a cabinet behind the bar. "Here's some peanuts and some cashews. Fix you something to drink, folks? I was a pretty fair bartender for a while a few years ago."

"I'll have a scotch and water," J.J. said. "A double."

Wade and Shark opted for beer and Solo had mineral water. "*Somebody* needs to stay sober around here."

"I'll drink to that," Welcome said, entering the salon. "Is there a cola in the fridge?"

"There's every kind of drink known to man stocked back here," Shark said.

"How about a Diet Dr Pepper?"

" 'Cept that. But here's a Diet Pepsi." He popped the top and poured the drink over ice. "Where are your young friends?"

"One of the crewmen who's about their age is taking them on the grand tour. What time do we arrive in Aegina? I was hoping to get some shots of sunset over the harbor."

"We've had a slight change of plans," J.J. said. "Because of all our delays this afternoon, it will be almost dark when we get to Aegina, so instead of debarking, we're going to anchor in the bay of Aghia Marina, have dinner, and spend the night on board. There's a beach there, and it will be a perfect spot for your swimsuit pictures. At sunrise, if you like. We can spend the entire day tomorrow on the island, or longer if we want to. Now, if you will excuse me, ladies, gentlemen, I'm going to my cabin for a nap. I'll see you at dinner in a couple of hours. The dress is casual unless you would prefer otherwise."

"I didn't bring my tux," Shark said.

"Me either," said Solo.

"Then casual it is."

After dinner Welcome got another cup of coffee and left the others to watch a video movie in the salon. She walked onto the deck and leaned against the railing to look out at the moonlight on the bay water. Lights from the hotels and houses ashore made a glowing arc around the dark water. There was only a slight breeze, but it was chilly. She held her cup in both hands to warm them and sniffed as her nose grew cold.

She shivered slightly and wished that she'd brought along a jacket. As if a genie had heard her request, warmth cloaked her shoulders.

"Mind if I join you?" Wade asked as he settled the jacket on her.

"Not at all. Especially since you brought my jacket. You must have read my mind. It's nippy out here."

"I was watching you through the window. You looked cold. Want to go back inside?"

Welcome shook her head. "I'm not interested in the movie, and it's too soon to go to bed."

Wade turned her to him. The breeze played with the curly tendrils around her face, tossing the strands to and fro. With one forefinger, he raked aside a long spiral that fluttered across her lips.

"Is it?" he asked as he slowly lowered his mouth.

"Is it what?" she asked.

"Too soon to go to bed."

Before she could answer, his mouth covered hers, and she forgot the question.

He drew back, and she tried to follow his magnificent mouth, standing on tiptoe to maintain contact. "Is it too soon?" he whispered against her lips.

"Too soon?"

"Too soon to go to bed. Too soon to make love with me?"

I was born to make love with you, a reckless part of her thought. Making love with this man who set her sense aflame was tempting. Very tempting. She had a feeling that they would be dynamite in bed. Maybe that wa why she was a little bit afraid. "Yes. Too soon."

"I'll wait," he murmured. "But in the meantime I'm going to kiss you. A lot."

"Please do." She sighed against his mouth, and hi tongue stemmed the sound.

Gentle turned into hard, hot, and heavy.

His big hands stroked her buttocks intimately, then lifted her so that her face was even with his as his lip and tongue continued their sweet plunder.

The kiss went on forever, and she could feel the hardness of his arousal between them. She reveled in his blatant desire, and her own need grew steadily. The raggedness of their breathing and the soft groans o their craving drifted over the dark water.

"Dear God, how I want you," he said, nuzzling her chin atilt and kissing the hollow of her throat. He rolled her body across his, moving sinuously against her. He set her down and his broad hands stroked up her sides to cup her breasts. "I want my mouth here." His thumbs flicked over her hardened nipples. He stroked lower. "And here."

"I—I—" She kissed him again, lost in a maelstrom of sensation, engulfed in overwhelming emotion. Never had she felt such intense yearning. She wanted to strip naked right there and have him make love to her on the deck. Grabbing handfuls of his hair, she rubbed herself against him. "Do it," she ground out "Do it."

Twenty-three

Full of wiles, full of guile, at all times, in all ways,
Are the children of Men.

Aristophanes
c. 450-385 B.C.

As he stood in the shadows and watched them, his fingers itched for his blade. With them locked in an embrace and oblivious to everything else, how easy it would be to dispose of them both. A quick slash for him, then a single thrust for her, small splashes when they went overboard, and he would be done.

How simple.

How tempting.

He longed for this business to be done. His hand closed around the hilt and gripped it tightly.

But alas, he would have to slip into the water as well for the crew would be sure to search the vessel diligently and find him if he remained on board. Unfortunately, he was not a strong swimmer, which might be surprising to some since he had grown up near the sea. But even if he had been half fish, he did not want to risk shock from the cold water.

He would wait.

And watch.

And listen.

Frustrated at having the woman slip from his grasp and disappear before he could terminate her, he had been resolute in his conviction to find her.

He had used his brain. He waited. He watched. He listened. He spread around a few drachmas for others to do the same.

His vigilance had been rewarded. A small slip, and he had been there to seize the opportunity. These Americans were so naive. Locating the *Ionna* at Paleó Phálero, slipping on board, and stowing away had been simple for one such as he. By the time they arrived, he was already provisioned and comfortably hidden.

Tomorrow when they went ashore, he would follow. Even if she spotted him, with his disguise, he thought it unlikely that she would recognize him. After he disposed of the woman, he could easily lose himself on the island, at peace once again and able to continue his pursuits without the persist disquiet of unfinished business.

Seeing them move apart, he melted back into the shadows.

And waited.

Twenty-four

Equal to the gods seems to me that man who sits facing you and hears you nearby sweetly speaking and softly laughing . . . When I look on you a moment, then can I speak no more, but my tongue falls silent, and at once a delicate flame courses beneath my skin, and with my eyes I see nothing, and my ears hum, and a cold sweat bathes me, and a trembling seizes me all over, and I am paler than grass, and I feel that I am near to death.

Sappho
c. 612 B.C.

Welcome wanted to weep with frustration when Wade drew away. "What are you *doing?*"

"Trying my damnedest to stop before this gets out of hand. You said it was too soon. And you're right. I understand."

"Ignore what I said. Come here." She grabbed his collar with both hands and pulled his head down.

He struggled. "Honey, I'm trying to be a gentleman here."

"Forget manners." She gave his collar another yank.

"Sugar," he mumbled against her hungry mouth, "I don't have any condoms."

Her mouth lost its appetite, and she relaxed her grip on his collar. "You don't?"

He shook his head. "No, sorry."

"Well, that's a fine how-do-you-do. I can't believe it. In this day and age, I thought *everybody* was always prepared."

"Ordinarily, I . . . well, I thought Shark . . . and he thought I . . . and . . . well, hell, I don't have any." He waited a few seconds and said timorously, "Do you?"

She sucked in a deep breath, held it forever, then let it out. "Nope." She burst into a fit of giggles.

His deep laughter joined hers, and he hugged her close. "Aren't we a fine, sophisticated pair? Want me to check with J.J. or the ship's captain?"

"Good Lord, no. I'm not that blasé about my sex life. It may be the nineties, but I'm an old-fashioned girl at heart."

"You?"

"Yes, me." She pulled away and moved a few paces along the deck. "Does that surprise you?"

"I don't know. Some, I guess. Although I suppose that it shouldn't. With all the stuff going around now, people are nuts to be bed hopping. A lot of athletes I know still haven't gotten the message, but what happened to Magic Johnson and a couple of others sobered me up good. If it helps any to know, I don't mess with the groupies who throw it in my face or with someone I meet casually in a bar or at a party or on an airplane. I'm disease free and have the lab results to prove it."

"Me, too. It's not as if I don't trust you, and exchanging medical reports over dinner might not seem like romantic foreplay, but—"

"It's sensible."

"Yes."

"I agree." Wade looped his arm around her neck and pulled her close. "Want to go watch the rest of the movie or stay out here and neck some more and make ourselves miserable?" He rubbed her nose with his.

"What a choice." Welcome chuckled. "How about a minute or two more of misery, then we'll join the others for the movie."

"Sounds good to me." He gently kissed her eyelids, her nose, her cheeks, then his lips brushed their way to her mouth.

The fire between them had not been extinguished, only banked. When they kissed, the flame burst to life like the *whoosh* of a match to gasoline. Their mouths and tongues and hands went wild.

After a frenzied moment, Wade pulled away. His breathing ragged, he said, "You miserable enough yet?"

She leaned her forehead against his chest and laughed. "Lord, aren't we a pair? Is the deck where we're standing scorched?"

"I wouldn't be surprised. Are you sure that you don't want me to talk to the captain? After six years with this boat, I'll bet that the guy is prepared for every contingency."

"No, I don't want you to ask the captain. We're adults. We can wait. Let's go inside."

"You go ahead. I'd better stay out here for a while. I have a problem . . . of a physical nature."

She smiled and coyly twirled a bit of chest hair peeking from the V of his shirt. "Need some of Solo's medicine?"

"I don't think that it would help much. And I can't get off this boat and run five miles like I did last night."

"Last night?"

He nodded. "Honey, the truth is that I left the restaurant last night because you had my friend in the same state that he's in right now. Rock hard and ready."

"But you didn't even touch me last night."

"I didn't have to. I've always heard that the mind is the most powerful erogenous zone, and now I believe it. Darlin', just watching you and thinking gets me so hot and bothered that I nearly explode. Damn, I want you in the worst way. I've never had a woman affect me the way you do. I feel like a randy teenager."

The feminine side of her swelled with pride on hearing his words. It was a heady feeling knowing that she had that sort of impact on him. Of course he was no slouch in the arousal department either. Wade Morgan was one terrific hunk, a real studmuffin, she thought, allowing herself to admit her attraction to his fantastic physique.

And hot wasn't the word for his kisses. In no time at all he could melt the lace on her panties and fuse the hooks on her bra.

"I know the feeling," was all that she would allow herself to say. She tried to back up a step, but his arms were locked around her waist. "I'm not ordinarily so . . . so enthusiastic."

He grinned. "You are enthusiastic. And I like it. Babe, if we ever make it to a bed, we're gonna set the mattress on fire."

"Uhhhh . . ." Welcome cleared her throat. "I think I'd better leave. This conversation is causing more problems than it's solving."

"Right."

She waited. "Wade?"

"Yes, honey?"

"I need to go inside."

"Okay."

She waited another few seconds. "I can't until you let me go."

"I know. I keep telling my arms that, but they don't want to move."

"You're crazy."

"Yep. Crazier 'n a peach-orchard boar. About you. Will you marry me, Miss Venable?"

She laughed and kissed his cheek. "Not tonight. But it was very sweet of you to ask."

"I wasn't being sweet. I was being serious. Will you marry me?"

"Hmmmm." She pretended weighty thought. "I think I'll pass on marriage. But," she said lightly, giving him a huge wink, "I'll say yes to a flaming affair." She kissed her finger and touched his lips. "See you inside when your friend cools off." She laughed and wiggled her fingers.

He stood and watched the provocative swing of her hips as she walked away. His friend stirred anew.

Damn, he thought, she was some kind of woman. And he couldn't believe that she'd thought that he was kidding. The first and only time he'd ever proposed to anyone in his entire life, and she thought he was kidding.

He wasn't.

He was dead serious.

He meant to marry Welcome Venable. Somehow, some way. He knew in his gut that they were born to be together. All he had to do was convince her.

At least the sexual chemistry was there.

It was a start.

"You are a vixen," he said, pulling her to him.

She laughed gaily and danced away. "A little suffering is character building. Besides there are difficulties yet to be over-

come. We'll see how the flesh reacts this time. Come, let us rouse the dolphins and play.''

Leaping to the rail, she cupped her hands to her mouth and trilled a sweet sound, then dove into the dark waters. He followed, slicing deep until he reached the sandy bottom of the bay. He found her sitting on a rock, waiting, and appearing more lovely and enchanting than any mermaid of yore. Odysseus's sirens paled beside her.

He watched from afar as the dolphins came, answering her summons like loyal subjects of a queen. They circled, closer and closer, gently vying for her touch. She laughed softly, speaking to them and stroking each in turn.

"Come," she said, motioning as she slipped on the back of one of the graceful beasts.

He mounted the back of another, and they rode as if on an undersea wind. The animals raced out to sea and back again. They leapt and arced and danced on their tails. They cavorted like happy children, sang their birring songs, and delighted the pair on their backs.

Until first light they played, chasing the reflections of stars and scattering the ribbons of moonlight rippling over the water. Laughing, he abandoned his briny steed and joined her behind the great dorsal fin of hers.

"Poseidon trembles with envy to behold me thus," he whispered against her ear as he drew her close and caressed the sweetness of her form.

"No more than Athena envies me." She leaned her temple against his jaw and reveled in the sensations he wrought as his hands made their magic upon her. Turning astride the slowly swimming dolphin so that she faced him, she lay back against the smooth gray fin and savored the tingling intimacy of his touch.

Light emanating from her pleasure tinted the bay about them with a phosphorescent hue and trailed behind them like glowing silver threads. He lifted her up and onto his rod, and the water swelled with the echo of her sighs.

The dolphin birred and began to swim faster. His pace quickened until his shape was a shimmery projectile plowing through the deep, lovers joined astride on his back. He surged from sea, arched, then plunged into the depths. Again and again the beast sprang and twisted and dived, and they rode the rhythm in a mystical ménage à trois that roiled the water and uncovered golden treasures and alabaster urns resting in the murky silt.

Like Pegasus, the dolphin flew and they soared, reaching for the universe until the first fingers of the new dawn kissed them with fire. They fused into a wondrous pause of anticipation, then burst into ecstasy like a comet streaking across the ageless skies.

Slowly they glided back to their starting place.

"How glorious," she whispered into the sea.

"It was always thus between us," he said, holding her close as the dolphin slipped away.

She sighed, not wanting to think of that time, and disengaged from him. "Not always. Not after we were parted in Athens. All was black."

"Was the blame mine?"

She averted her gaze. "I cannot say."

"Then it must have been. Where did I err?"

"It is not my place to point out such things." She blew tiny bubbles that broke against his face and smiled when he wiggled his nose. "The choices will come again."

"I'll make the right ones this time."

"I hope so. We'll see." She broke away and rose to the deck of the boat.

He followed her, a dark band gripping his heart. "Help me here, my own. There are hazy spots in my memory. I know that there is a strong imperative concerning you in my core. It drives me, but it also haunts me, mocks me. What is this demand so deep in my spirit?"

"Perhaps it is the oath we took in the temple, the vows we made over and over again before the gods. Do you remember?"

He smiled. "Of course I remember. Our first vows were made when we were but frightened children, clinging each to the other. I promised that I would look after you always and keep you from harm. Forever and always."

She touched his cheek. "And I promised to be your guardian as well. Oaths thus taken bind us in spirit more powerfully than the roots of the olive trees grip the earth. Sacred vows cannot be lightly broken."

Puzzled, he said, "Did I break my vow?"

Gently she touched her lips to his. "Someone comes. I must go."

Welcome stirred when she heard the soft rapping. She grabbed her robe, hurried to the door, and peeked out.

J.J. stood on the deck, his platinum hair loose and blowing in the breeze. But it was not her door he knocked on, but Solo's, which was close by. Solo had stuck her head out as well and was speaking with J.J.

When J.J. saw Welcome, he smiled. "Sorry to disturb you, but I wanted to invite you ladies to see the dolphins if you were awake. I've been watching them for several minutes. I've never seen them so frisky, and they're only a few yards from the boat. I thought Solo might like to get some pictures of them."

Welcome hid her smile. She would bet that J.J.'s growing interest in Solo had more to do with his early visit than any burning desire for dolphin watching.

She raked her fingers through her hair, and hurried to the rail while J.J. went to rouse the others. Solo took several photographs of the dolphins as they frolicked like children, leaping, and arcing, and dancing if they were a trained troop.

Enchanted by their antics, Welcome leaned out over the railing. "Opa! Opa!" she shouted, laughing and clapping for their performance. One big fellow surged from the water and nudged her hands, then made a series of chattering sounds as if he were laughing, too.

"I think he likes you," Wade said from behind her.

"Isn't he grand? Aren't they all grand? Imagine what it would be like to get on his back and ride through the ocean. God, how magnificent that would be!"

Wade draped one arm casually over her shoulders and whispered in her ear. "I can almost picture you astride that big one's back."

A sudden, sensual thrill raced through her.

"Man," Shark said, "those babies are something else. I've never seen any in the ocean act like that. You'd think that they'd been trained at Sea World."

"I think they're naturally playful," Solo said, "and I suspect that boats around here toss them treats."

They continued to watch the dolphins for a few minutes before the group dived and sped away. As if savoring the vestiges of the exciting episode, the people on deck were quiet for a moment, then started chattering.

Everyone broke to dress for breakfast and for the day on the island. They had decided to save the swimsuit shots until later when the sun had warmed the beach sand, if not the water. While they dressed, the captain weighed anchor and sailed to the other side of the small island so that they could land at the harbor town of Aegina, the usual docking place for tourist ships.

The plans were for Solo to take various candid shots of Welcome, Niki, and Takis as they explored the island during the day, and the *Ionna* would pick them up back at Aegis Marina in the late afternoon.

The door that had opened slightly as they spoke, slowly closed. Soon they would be anchoring in the harbor, and he would steal ashore. He would pick the time and the place carefully, do the job, and melt away to blend with the tourists.

Twenty-five

Who shall bell the cat?

Aesop
c. 550 B.C.

What they saw when they arrived in the Aegina harbor was a scene from a picture postcard of a typical Greek isle. At the entrance, a tiny whitewashed chapel stood guardian, and the curving waterfront was lined with shops and tavernas and terrace cafés. Colorful skiffs moored at the quay were laden with piles of fruits, vegetables, and fish ready to market. Already tourists and locals alike were out stirring as the group from the *Ionna* stepped onto the pier.

The owner of a souvenir shop rolled out his green and gold awning while the proprietor of a similar small shop next door washed his sidewalk and shouted at the driver of a horse-drawn carriage leisurely parked in front to move on. Welcome didn't have to understand Greek to get the meaning of the heated exchange which included loud words and universally recognized hand gestures.

The red-wheeled carriage moved along a few feet and stopped near an open café with brightly colored cloths on the tables and boxes of yellow flowers by the porch. While the placid horse munched from his grain bag, the driver leaned back and munched on his apple. Welcome knew a great shot when she saw it, and motioned Takis and Niki forward. She pointed out the carriage to Solo, sent Wade back aboard the yacht for a breakfast roll, and whispered instructions to Niki and Takis.

The two young people acted like pros as they casually strolled in the direction of the carriage. They stopped in the street, turned to each other and laughed as Niki playfully fed the roll to Takis. With the produce skiffs, the restaurant, and the horse and carriage driver in the background, Welcome could already see a caption in the brochure about Greece and its obsession with good food.

They had taken several shots when the driver noticed them. He hurriedly tossed aside his apple, straightened his fisherman's cap, and jumped down from his perch.

"A fine carriage, no?" he said, grinning broadly and flashing a goodly amount of gold bridgework. "Come, Aristotle and I will take you on a tour of the waterfront and point out all the best shops. You want to know the history of our beautiful island? I, Manos Mercouri, can tell you every detail. You know of our ceramics? I can show you things you will see nowhere else in Greece."

J.J. turned to Welcome. "Interested?"

"Sure," she said. "Sounds like fun. But there are seven of us."

"No problem," Manos said. He put two fingers in his mouth, gave an ear-splitting whistle, and waved to another carriage down the street. "My cousin George. He is almost as good a guide as me."

The others in the group were game for a carriage ride, so J.J. made the deal to hire the two. Welcome, Solo, Wade, and J.J. squeezed into Manos's black and red carriage and Shark escorted Niki and Takis. With the driver's dialogue running all the while, they toured not only the waterfront but also the city's graceful boulevards lined with many fine old homes, built in the early 1800s shortly after Aegina became the first capital city of Free Greece.

They laughed at the unusual ceramic decorations atop walls and on the stuccoed sides of small buildings; some were humorous caricatures of hatted, mustachioed men or pompadoured women, all with mouths open wide as if in shock, in mirth, or in song. They stopped frequently to snap pictures of Welcome, Niki, and Takis at various points of interest.

"What are you going to do with all those pictures?" Wade asked. "You must have shot five or six rolls so far this morning."

"More," Solo said. "I know it must seem like a lot, but that way we're assured of having a great many good ones to choose from."

Welcome said, "If a photographer takes a hundred exposures, there may be fifteen or twenty that are very good, if the photographer is exceptional. Of those, perhaps four or five are outstanding. And if he or she is very skilled and very lucky, one will be magical. In the profession, we're always looking for that magic."

After a visit to a pottery factory where some of Aegina's famous pitchers were made, both carriages were overflowing with Welcome's purchases. Some were for Takis and Niki's family, others were wrapped for shipping to various friends or to herself in Texas, and some were to take to Meri. Solo had even bought one of the beautiful pieces for herself.

"Is it lunchtime yet?" Shark asked at the next stop.

Everybody laughed but agreed that food would be great. The carriages deposited them back at the waterfront, and they thanked their drivers effusively for the grand morning.

Wade looked down at the pile of packages at their feet and said, "Why don't we get rid of these before we eat?"

"Good idea," J.J. said.

After a minute of two of discussion, they decided that Niki and Takis would take the ones that needed to be mailed to the post office; Wade and Shark would take the others to the *Ionna*; and Welcome, Solo, and J.J. would go ahead and get a table at the restaurant that Manos assured them was the best in town.

Even though the situation seemed secure, Welcome knew that both J.J. and Solo's first concern was her safety. She noticed that neither of them volunteered to tote packages, and they'd both stuck to her side like twin cockleburrs. And neither of them missed much. Their eyes were always moving over the scene, and they got edgy around crowds.

A big cruise ship must have docked not long before because the restaurant was covered up with tourists. They were told that there would be a fifteen-minute wait for a table. J.J. left his name, and they went back outside to wait and browse the nearby shop fronts.

"I'm going to go in here for a minute," Welcome said, pointing to a small, narrow-aisled shop. "I see some great-looking belts. I'll be out in a sec." She heard Solo muttering behind her as she hurried inside the shop which was crammed with merchandise.

She squeezed past a cluster of Japanese tourists to get to the belts, which didn't look nearly so good up close. But the hats on the rack next to them weren't bad. She missed her brown fedora.

"Knife!" Solo screamed.

Welcome looked up to see a man bearing down on her.

Holy shit, it was *him!*

Her heart flew to her throat. When she caught the flash of a knife in his hand, Welcome screamed too and yanked the hatrack across the aisle as a barricade. Backing up, she hurled everything she could find at him while Solo battled to get by the tangle of panicking Japanese.

Jaw set, eyes hard, he came at her relentlessly.

She kept throwing things, but it was hard to do damage with hats, belts, and stacks of T-shirts advertising Greek olive oil.

As a last resort she grabbed a big tub of island-grown pistachios, flung the nuts at him, and used the tub as a shield against a slash of his knife.

She heard a noise like a hundred banshees and, from the corner of her eye, saw J.J. bounding across the top of display counters and merchandise tables. He made a flying leap and locked his legs around her attacker's neck just as Solo broke loose and got there. Welcome dived under the nearest table and dragged the tub with her.

"Drop it!"

A strangled gurgle.

"Move and I'll blow your fucking head off!"

The clatter of an object on the tile floor.

Welcome peered around the tub just as someone kicked the knife away. It skittered toward her, caromed off her galvanized shield, and slid to a stop six inches from her nose.

Her eyes grew wide.

She swallowed the bowling ball in her throat.

That knife was one wicked-looking mother.

"Somebody call the police!"

"On your knees, asshole! Now."

That was Solo. No question about it. And the other voice was J.J.'s. Three pairs of legs were all she could

see from her fort. The middle pair bent to pray—or
to keep from having a hole blasted in his head. Welcome didn't doubt for a minute that Solo would do
it.

"You okay, Welcome?"

She tried to speak, but nothing came out.

"Welcome?"

" 'Kay," she finally managed just as a god-awful bel-
low shook the rafters.

"Welcome! Out of my way, dammit!" There was
crashing and banging as if Godzilla approached.
"Wellll-come! Move you little pissant! Wellll-come!
Dammit, where are you?"

Wade.

"Here," she squeaked.

"Where?" he roared as he neared the rear of the
shop.

"Under the table."

She saw a table nearby upended, and its contents
crashed to the floor.

"Not that one," she yelled. "This one."

Was that J.J. who snickered?

Wade squatted and peered under. "Goddammit,
woman, I almost had a heart attack when I heard you
screaming. Are you all right?" He crawled in next to
her.

"No," she said, wrapping her arms around the tub.
"No, I'm not all right. Somebody just tried to skewer
my gizzard with this." She held up the vicious, razor-
sharp knife. "And I think that I'm going to throw up."

Keeping a death grip on the tub, she leaned over
and did just that.

Welcome couldn't stop shivering.

The police had carted the killer off to the pokey

over an hour ago, but still she shivered. Sitting beside Wade on one of the big couches in the *Ionna*'s salon, she wore fleece sweats, two pair of wool socks, and had a blanket around her, but her chin quivered like aspic in an earthquake, and her teeth clacked like wind-up joke dentures.

"Come here, darlin'," Wade said, pulling her into his lap. "Shark, toss me another blanket. We gotta get our girl warmed up."

Solo refilled a brandy snifter and handed it to her. "This will help."

As Welcome sipped from the glass, she glanced up to find five pair of eyes focused on her. She suddenly felt like an utter ninny, a prize wimp. She'd always prided herself on being tough as nails, and here she was falling apart over nothing.

Well, it wasn't exactly nothing. But thanks to J.J. and Solo, she hadn't been hurt. If you didn't count the skinned place on her elbow. Wade had kissed that little scrape and apologized a hundred times, as if it were his fault. A skinned elbow she could live with; a severed jugular, she could not.

She was one lucky lady.

She sucked in a deep breath and demanded that the shivering stop. Miraculously, it did.

Takis and Niki sat on an opposite couch, still as statues, their big brown eyes grown to enormous proportions. She held out a hand to each of them, and they jumped to her side.

"I'm so sorry, my friends," she said to the pair. "I had meant for this to be an adventure for you, not a disaster."

"But it has been an adventure," Takis said, then grinned broadly. "What an adventure! I'm only sorry that I missed the best part. We didn't get back from the post office until after the police had arrived."

"Speaking of police," Shark said, "isn't it about time for J.J. to be back from the station?"

As if on cue, J.J. walked in. For a moment he stood there solemnly, and everyone became quiet. Then he laughed, did a little jig and punched the air. "We nailed that sucker!"

"Who was he?" Solo asked.

Everybody hit him with a dozen questions until J.J. held up his hands. "Let me get a drink, and I'll tell you the whole story."

"I'll fix the drink," Shark said. "You start the tale."

"Maybe I'd better go back to the beginning," J.J. said, "for those of you who don't know the whole story. It all started when Welcome witnessed a murder the day after she arrived in Athens."

"A *murder?* You did?" Niki asked, amazed. "But why did you not tell us? Did you go to the police?"

"Well, uh—"

"There were complications," J.J. interrupted. "And no body. She thought that the police wouldn't believe her."

"Where was this murder?" Takis asked.

"In the shop across from Taverna Katrakis. I—I was shopping there."

"Across from my grandfather's place? But who was killed?" Takis asked.

"I don't know. The owner, I assume. It scared me to death. I was barely able to get out the back way before he caught me. He would have caught me if it hadn't been for—well, I had a close call." Welcome still hadn't figured out how Wade had been there when he was in California. She meant to get to the bottom of that.

But not now. She snuggled into the warmth of his arms.

"But he knew that there was a witness," J.J. continued, "and somehow he traced Welcome to the GB and followed her."

"He harassed me and shot at me and nearly scared me out of my wits."

"What I don't understand," Shark said, "is why didn't this dude just make tracks until Welcome left the country?"

"We don't know," J.J. said, "and he's not talking. Maybe he's just cautious. He's suspected in at least two other murder cases, but the witnesses have disappeared."

Despite her best efforts, Welcome shivered again.

"Is he some kind of hit man?" Wade asked.

"Possibly. The police have identified him as Andreas Chroni, which may or my not be his true identity. His father was Greek, his mother Turkish, and he lived much of the time in France. He is believed to have strong ties to a group that translates roughly as The Black Night."

Takis whistled. "A group of political terrorists who are always into some very bad things. Remember the bombing at the Athens airport two years ago? The Black Night."

Welcome felt Wade stiffen, and his arms tightened around her. "Is it possible that some of this guy's cronies may still come after her?"

After he dropped that bombshell, she went a little stiff herself. "Yeah. Am I still going to have to look over my shoulder every moment?"

J.J. shrugged. "Who knows? Chroni isn't talking. But the police have given us a break. Being able to toss our host Dalaras's name around made the difference. By the way, the gift shop owner's body washed ashore yesterday and was found by some fishermen. If Welcome will positively identify their suspect as the man who killed Metaxas and attacked her today, the police will 'overlook' her failure to report the murder and will hold our man for forty-eight hours until they allow him to contact anyone."

"Which means?" Wade said.

"Which means," Solo answered, "that she has forty-eight hours to finish her business here and get the hell out of Dodge."

"That about covers it," J.J. said.

"Forty-eight hours, hell," Wade said. "Let's head this boat back to Athens and pack. We can be out of this part of the world before sundown."

"Nope."

Wade looked at Welcome as if she had less sense than a pile of dried possum poop. "The hell you say."

"You heard me. I came here to get photographs for a brochure, and by damn, that's what I'm going to do."

"Even if you get your throat cut or your head blown off?"

"But I'm not going to. J.J. said that this guy usually works alone, and he's locked up. I've got more bodyguards than the queen of England. I'll be okay for a couple of days."

Wade tried to argue with her. J.J. tried. Solo only rolled her eyes and saved her breath.

They finally compromised. They would spend what was left of the afternoon on Hydra, another island nearby, stay the night on the *Ionna*, then return to Athens early the following morning for Welcome to make her statement to the police there. She would have the rest of the day to shoot scenes for the brochure, so long as she was ready to leave on a five-forty flight to Cairo. She wouldn't return to the GB; one of J.J.'s men would pack the rest of Solo's and her belongings and deliver them to the airport.

Welcome sighed. Even with all the chaos that she

had encountered in Greece, she wasn't ready to leave yet. She wanted to cook chicken-fried steaks again with Spyros and dance at the taverna. She wanted to see every museum and every ruin. She had . . . unfinished business, though she couldn't have for the life of her explained exactly what it was.

And then there was Wade.

had encountered in Greece, she wasn't prone to take
out, and raised to this rocking vessel of a sailboat, with
browsers and nodded at the spirited, sun-tanned faces
came arriving and expectantly she had . . . murmured
implied that she realized they totally about the
remained even after daylight was.
And even there she would be

Twenty-six

*Not fire nor stars have stronger bolts than those of
Aphrodite sent by the hand of Eros, Zeus's child.*

Euripides
c. 485-406 B.C.

Hydra's little harbor was even more picturesque than
Aegina's was. Fishing boats and nets and fishermen
abounded, and as the *Ionna* docked amid colorful
caïques, they could hear the bells in the clock tower
ringing four.

"Oh, look how lovely," Welcome said, "and it's so
late already. Let's hustle before we lose the light." She
was off the boat before it was made fast, and the others
were right behind her.

"She sure recovered in a hurry," Shark said.

"Didn't she?" Wade laughed. "She's quite a woman.
Most of the ones I know would have been in bed for
a week."

"Then you must know some wimps," Solo said, snap-
ping a series of shots with Welcome laughing at the
queue of burros lined up to transport goods and people.

"My God, look at the cats," Shark said. "I've never
seen so many."

"There are hundreds of stray cats here," Takis said.

'They hang around the harbor waiting for handouts
from the fishermen or hoping to catch a stray morsel
from the markets. For a dollar, tourists can even buy
food packets to feed them."

"Somebody was enterprising to think that one up,"
Wade said. He looked around. "Where are the cars?"

"There are no cars on Hydra," Niki said. "Everything is transported the old-fashioned way." She
pointed to the string of burros and to the carriages.

"Have you ever seen so many cats?" Welcome asked
as she joined them. "We need to get some pictures of
them. Niki, do you want to be in this shot?"

They photographed the cats and the burros and the
beautifully terraced homes with dogs lazing on the garden walls and cats hanging out in trees like squirrels.
They visited the upscale jewelry shops and art galleries,
hiked the cobbled street that led uphill from the harbor, and climbed a goat path behind a monastery for
a magnificent panoramic view and an unbelievable
sunset.

They hurried back to the street and began their decent as the lights began to go on in the town.

Her arms thrust in the air, Welcome whirled around
in the middle of the cobbled street. "Oh I love this
place. I think that it's my favorite of everywhere that
I've visited. J.J., can't we spend some more time here
tomorrow?"

"I suppose so, but then you won't have time to get
any more pictures in Athens."

"Oh, crap!" She heaved a big sigh. "And people will
expect pictures of the Acropolis and Hadrian's Arch
and a dozen other places. We'll have to have a wild
schedule to hit the major sites as it is. I need more
time."

Wade hugged her against him. "Sorry, sweetheart.

But if you'd like, we can come back here on our honeymoon and stay as long as you want."

She smiled and kissed his cheek. "Yeah, sure."

Back at the harbor, they stopped at a taverna for rest and refreshments. Shark ordered a snack that looked a lot like a full dinner to everybody else.

"You mess with me too much," he said when they all teased him, "and I won't let you have none."

They laughed and drank wine and ate fried Kalamarákia and zucchini from Shark's plate until all his food was gone, then they ordered another round of wine and another plate for Shark, which they again shared.

The evening grew later and the crowd in the taverna swelled. The group ordered more food and more wine, hesitant to leave the *joie de vivre* of the moment. Music began, and they danced together. Even Wade gave it a try and was able to get the hang of the movement with J.J. and Welcome's help.

"Opa!" Welcome shouted, clapping her hands.

"Opa!" Wade shouted, stamping his foot.

He'd paid the proprietor a hundred dollars for a big stack of plates, and when they'd coaxed J.J. to dance for the crowd, their gang had smashed every one of them. Wade couldn't remember having so much fun.

They closed the place down.

Arm in arm, the seven of them fanned across the street and walked to the *Ionna* singing "Deep in the Heart of Texas," led by Welcome and Solo, and stopping to stomp their feet at the clapping part.

On deck, the group said their good-nights and parted. Wade paused with Welcome at her cabin door.

"I don't want this night to end," she said, draping her arms over his shoulders.

"Me neither." He kissed her forehead. "And it doesn't have to. I made a purchase today."

She laughed. "So did I."

"Then we're doubly prepared. May I come in?"

"Would you give me time to take a shower and change?"

"Sure. I guess I'm pretty grimy myself. I'll be back in . . . ?"

"Twenty minutes."

Nineteen minutes later, there was a soft rap on the door as Welcome lit the candles on the bedside table. Feeling as nervous as a new bride, she slid her damp palms down the thighs of the turquoise caftan she wore and fluffed her hair. When she opened the door, Wade stood there smiling, his hair still damp, and looking good enough to eat in loose cotton slacks and a billowy white shirt that emphasized his broad shoulders and accentuated his masculinity. He carried champagne on ice and two glasses.

"Am I too early?" he asked. "I walked around the deck twice." He held up the ice bucket. "Look what I found. And it's the good kind."

She lifted the bottle and glanced at the French label. "The very good kind." She stood back and let him in.

He put the bucket and glasses on a small table by the window seat. "Shall I open it now?"

"I—I don't really want any more wine tonight. I wouldn't drink more than a sip."

"Me either. And it seems a shame to waste such a fine bottle of wine when all I want is you." He drew her into his arms and stood there for a moment doing no more than hold her. "This feels so good. So damned good."

"Mmmmm." She snuggled close, her head tucked

under his chin, her arms around him, and simply sa
vored his smell, his warmth, the rock solid strength o
him. "Why does it feel so right when you hold me?"

"I don't know, but it does, doesn't it?"

"Yes. We fit so perfectly that it seems incredible."

He brushed his chin over the top of her head. "
can't believe that we met only a few days ago. You are
as familiar to me as my own body. I feel that I've known
you forever. I think I must have dreamed of you al
my life." He kissed her forehead. "And now I've found
you."

"I wonder if that could explain it."

"What?"

"Dreams. Could I have dreamed I saw you that day
in Plaka when Metaxas was killed? But, no, tha
wouldn't make any sense. I *was* there. Metaxas *wa*
killed. Those are facts. But you were there too, Wade."
She drew back and looked into his eyes, the same gor
geous gray-green eyes she'd looked into the day when
he helped her out the back window. "I *saw* you, dam
mit. I *saw* you. I touched you, and you were as solid
as you are now."

He kissed her eyebrows and her lids. "Honey, I don'
know what you saw that day, but I was in California
What time of day was it?"

"Noon. Almost exactly."

"Well, if it was noon in Athens, it was, uh, ten hour
earlier in California, so that makes it two in the morn
ing. Darlin', I was in bed sound asleep. In Palm Spring
as a matter of fact. I'd played in a golf tournamen
the day before. Shark woke me up about four in th
morning, said I'd been making a terrible racket."

"And what about that day in the Roman Agora?"

"Asleep again," he said. "At the GB. We were wor
out from the trip."

"Hmmmm. Have you ever had anything like tha

happen to you? I mean, have you ever seen me or heard me before we met?"

He cleared his throat. "Uh, I may have. Once or twice."

"When? What happened?"

"Well, the first time was about five or six years ago, and I'm a little hazy on the details. The most recent was the fourth Sunday in January of this year, and I remember it clearly."

Her ears perked up. "Why do you remember it so clearly?"

"It was the final seconds of the Super Bowl game. We were right down to the nut cuttin'—on the eight-yard line and down by four points. You can't imagine how much was riding on that next play; I was sweating bullets.

"I prayed like hell before I called it, but damned if it wasn't a busted play. I could see myself going down like a dirty shirt, but all of a sudden I heard a sweet woman's voice telling me exactly what to do. I did it, and we won the game. Welcome, that was your voice. I heard it just as clearly as I can hear you now."

"You're kidding."

"Nope."

"What did you hear me say?"

"You said, 'Roll out to your right.' "

" 'Roll out to your right?' " She made a face. "That hardly seems earth-shattering. Certainly not in the same league with saving me from a killer."

"It may not seem important to you, but, babe, it saved my bacon that afternoon."

"Did you tell anybody about what happened?"

He shook his head. "You're the first. And you have to admit that it sounds pretty peculiar."

"Where were you, and what time was it?"

"I was in L.A., and I imagine that it was about six thirty or so in the evening."

"I was in Paris, and it would have been about . . . let's see . . . about . . . oh, blast, I never can get the time differences straight."

"It would have been about three-thirty on Monday morning," Wade said.

"And I would have been sound asleep. This is very strange. And the other time you mentioned. When did it happen?"

"I don't remember exactly. But it was during the winter. I was driving up around Lake Tahoe, and dozed off at the wheel."

"Dear God, Wade, you could have been killed."

"Tell me about it. But something, somebody woke me up. Somebody, a woman I think, yelled at me just before I went off the road and over a damned long drop. But I can't remember the details. I only remember that I had the devil scared out of me. I always figured that it was my guardian angel."

"What time of day was it?"

He shrugged. "I don't remember. After lunch, I think. I'd guess around two or three in the afternoon."

"That means—"

"It would have been around midnight in Paris."

"This is weird. I feel like I'm going mad," Welcome said, turning away and furrowing her fingers through her hair. "Have you noticed that when these things have happened, one of us is asleep and the other is awake? How can you explain that?"

"I don't know, love. I can't explain it, but I don't think you're mad. And I don't think that I am either. Maybe a psychologist could make some sense of it, or an astrophysicist, but I can't. Come here," he said, pulling her against him, "and let's forget all that stuff." He turned off the lamp so that only candlelight

luminated the room. "I'd rather be making love to
ou than trying to figure it out."

"But—"

His mouth covered hers and rational thought fled.
he didn't care about any of that stuff either. All she
ared about was the way his lips and his tongue felt
gainst hers.

Hot.

Wet.

Hungry.

Her fingers curled, and her nails raked down his back.
Her knee rubbed up and down his thigh restlessly as
he ached to climb into his skin, have his blood run
hrough her veins and her heart beat inside his.

"Oh, God," she groaned against his mouth, kissing
im frantically and trying to push closer, harder, to
neld their flesh.

He met her groans with his own. "You set me on
ire, woman. On fire." His hands were all over her; his
nouth trailed sparks to the V of her caftan. "How does
his come off?"

"Over my head."

It came up and off in one quick movement, and
Wade fell to his knees to press his mouth to her bare
kin. She cried out with pleasure at the sensation and
rabbed handfuls of his hair as the intimacy and de-
ight intensified.

"Wade," she gasped, "I don't think I can stand
his?"

"You don't like it?"

"Oh, noooooo. I love it, but," she panted, "I'm dy-
ng."

"Don't die on me yet, darlin'. I'm not finished by a
ong shot."

And he wasn't.

He laid her on the bed and stripped as she watched

him. And, great Zeus, was he magnificent. Flickerir candlelight played over the sheen of his muscled, ta body, a body more splendid than any of the marb statues that she had seen. It was beautiful, living fles! And his manhood was gloriously tumescent.

Her womb throbbed as she beheld him. She opene her arms. "Come into me."

"Not yet. There are places I've longed to touch an to kiss and to probe with my tongue. I'm going to tak my sweet time and do everything I've fantasized."

And he did.

She was wet from head to toe from his mouth an from the sweat of sexual excitement, screaming for r lease when he finally came into her.

He buried himself deep, and her back arched at th infinite pleasure he brought. He drew back, and sh flung herself upward to recapture him. They grapple like wrestlers, ferocious in their need to give and tak to cede and demand. They growled like animals; th bed heaved and the table rocked as their bodi slapped together in a frenzied, primitive contention

Her back bowed, her toes curled, and she sucked i a breath as deep as his shaft was buried. Like the run bling eruption of a dormant volcano, her climax cam ripping fire from her core and sending it spewing fort in a powerful series of convulsions that shook the be

He gave a strangled cry and stiffened, then pumpe powerfully into her.

For long moments they lay there, too spent to mov

"Darlin', I may be too old for this. You about ga me a heart attack. I feel like I've been sucked dry."

Welcome laughed. "Well, sweetie, I guess I'll ju have to find myself a younger man."

"Like hell you will. Lady, you're mine. I'll cut th balls off anybody who tries to take you from me."

"Wade?"

"Yes, darlin'?"

"What's that smell?"

"I don't smell anything. But then I haven't been able to smell so good since last season when Mazzio smashed my nose all to hell again. What's it smell like?"

"Like something burning."

He chuckled. "I told you that we would probably set the mattress on fire when we made love, and, babe—"

"Wade! Something's burning."

He raised up and looked around. "Holy shit! The mattress *is* on fire. Get up." He bounded from the bed and dragged her with him. "I'll get the fire extinguisher!"

Smoke billowed up from the bed beside the table where the candles had been. "The candles!"

He dashed for the deck, and she grabbed the ice bucket just as the smoke alarm went off. She took out the bottle of champagne and tossed the melted ice on the smoldering area.

Wade ran in with a fire extinguisher and covered the mattress with chemical foam. On his heels were J.J. and Solo. Shark and the captain weren't too far behind. Half the crew poured into the room.

Welcome grabbed her caftan and pulled it over her head; Wade snatched up his pants and put them on. Welcome's caftan was wrong-side-out, but she was covered.

"What happened?"

"Are you all right?"

Solo arched one brow and looked pointedly at the ruined bed. "Looks like you were having a hot time."

Shark snickered.

The captain cleared his throat and turned off the alarm.

The crew members smirked.

Welcome, who never blushed, blushed.

Wade didn't say a word.

J.J. said, "Okay, folks, everything is under control. Let's go back to our rooms." When everyone filed out, he hung back and said, "It does look like you were having a hot time."

Welcome threw the ice bucket at him.

He slammed the door just before it would have connected with his head. She could hear him laughing outside.

She and Wade looked at each other.

A little smile twitched one corner of his mouth.

One twitched a corner of hers.

The twitches grew heartier, and they both burst into laughter.

"I'll say one thing," Wade said, "life around you is never dull. I don't think I'll ever forget this night."

She fell laughing into his arms. "Me either."

"Dear God, how I love you, woman." He held her close for the longest time, savoring the sensations, remembering the wild lovemaking.

He felt her suddenly stiffen in his arms. "Oh, no!" she said.

"What's wrong, darlin'?"

"We forgot something very important."

"What's that?"

"The condoms."

"Uh-oh. Sorry about that. I just damned well got carried away. Maybe it's a safe time of the month."

She counted the days on her fingers. The blood drained from her face.

Twenty-seven

Lead me, Zeus, and you, Fate, wherever you have assigned me.

Cleanthes
c. 330-232 B.C.

Welcome was stunned by the news. She had dreaded going to the police station and making her statement. Although she knew that she would be given the VIP treatment because of her own name and that of Theo Dalaras, albeit she'd never met the man, the notion was still scary. One never knew what to expect of the law enforcement agencies of foreign countries. She knew that many were either corrupt or unbelievably severe in their dealings, even with foreigners. Over the years, she'd heard some real horror stories of people languishing in jail for what seemed to be minor infractions of the law.

Her infraction wasn't minor. She had failed to report a murder. Well, she had reported it . . . sort of, but the police might not count her anonymous call or the other one that was supposed to have been made by a man who was actually sound asleep in California.

She hadn't slept well, even in Wade's cabin and snuggled in his arms.

"Darlin'," he'd said, "why are you being such a wiggle-worm?"

"I can't get to sleep."

"Still embarrassed about the mattress fire?"

"That, too. Remind me to speak to the captain about repairs."

"Don't worry your pretty head about it for one minute. I'll tend to everything." He kissed her shoulder. "Now go to sleep."

She'd tried, but she was wide awake. "Wade?"

His only response was a soft snore.

What if she was brought up on charges?

Would they put her in jail?

Oh, God.

Why had she ever agreed to deliver that bracelet for Philip? She could kick herself.

Never, *never* was she going to do a favor for him again.

When the *Ionna* docked that morning, Welcome had said a tearful good-bye to Takis and Niki and hugged them both twice. "If I'm not able to see Spyros and your grandmother before I leave, please give them my gifts along with my very best wishes. Tell them that I'll be back before long, and we'll break plates together."

Two men, who may or may not have been Egyptian, had been waiting at the dock. One helped Takis and Niki to a taxi; the other escorted the rest of them to a van, a different color and make from the one they had taken to Delphi.

They had taken their accustomed places. J.J. drove with Shark in the front, Welcome and Wade were in the middle seat, and Solo was in the back with the luggage and equipment that they would need for the day. J.J.'s men took charge of the rest of their bags.

Although she tried to give the appearance of being cool about it, Welcome had stewed and fretted all the way to the station. By the time she arrived, she almost marched inside and stuck out her wrists for the handcuffs.

The Greek police couldn't have been nicer.

Wade, Shark, and Solo had waited in the lobby while J.J. accompanied Welcome to one of the big cheese's offices. The man—Welcome forgot his name—was incredibly polite, not to mention darned good-looking. He was apologetic that she had been subjected to such atrocious incidents in his country.

"Alas," he said in perfect English with a slight British accent, "your statement is no longer needed. Andreas Chroni has committed suicide. He hanged himself in his cell last night."

Welcome was stunned. For a moment she didn't feel anything, then she felt remarkable relief. Callous of her perhaps, but she felt it nonetheless.

She would have asked a dozen questions, but J.J. quickly extolled the hospitality of Greece and its people, thanked the man politely for his courtesy, shook his hand, and ushered her from the office before she could say a word.

J.J. motioned for the waiting group to follow, and they hurried to the van.

"That was quick," Wade said.

"J.J., why were you in such a hurry?" Welcome asked. "Aren't you curious about Chroni?"

"Not a bit. Chroni hanged himself in his jail cell last night," J.J. told the others.

"I see," Solo said.

"See what?" Welcome asked, befuddled.

"Well," Shark drawled, "I don't know how it is in Greece, but in a lot of places, the police don't cotton to being questioned too close when somebody commits suicide in their cell."

"You mean—"

"There are always questions about the integrity of security or . . ." Solo shrugged.

"The possibility that they were helped along a little?" Welcome said.

"Sure," Solo said. "Either by the jailers being deliberately lax or—"

"Or by somebody slapping the horse's flank, so to speak."

"That's about it," J.J. said. "But of course we know that nothing like that happened here."

"Certainly not," Solo added.

Welcome shuddered. "But don't ask."

"And nobody will miss the son-of-a-bitch," Wade said. "What's next on the agenda?"

Welcome glanced at her suit. "Since I'm all decked out in my going-to-the-police-station togs, maybe we could do a few quick shots in the up-scale shopping area. Wade, I imagine that this is going to be boring for you and Shark. Why don't we drop you off at the hotel?"

"No," Wade said emphatically. "Where you go, I go, and where I go, Shark goes."

"That's right," Shark said.

"But if Chroni is dead, I don't have anything to worry about anymore. Which reminds me, J.J., with him out of the picture, we don't have to be in such a hurry to leave Greece. We can stay an extra few—"

"Forget it, *mon ami*. You're booked on a flight to Cairo this evening."

While Welcome and Solo were shooting some pictures in the city's swankiest pedestrian mall, Wade found a kiosk that was a combination newsstand/tobacconist and spotted an American news magazine. While he was paying for it, he noticed a pay phone and decided to check his messages at the hotel. Barney was probably royally pissed-off by now.

He was. His agent had left several messages which all boiled down to: *Call immediately!* Wade glanced at his watch, then shrugged and made the call.

"Barney? Wade."

"Do you know what time it is?"

"Yep. Ten o'clock in the morning here. Must be about midnight there."

"Are you still in Athens? Where in the hell have you been? I've been trying to get in touch with you at the hotel for the past three days."

"I've been busy. What's up, Barney?"

"We've got a honey of a deal on the table, that's what's up."

When Barney outlined the Vulcan's offer, Wade whistled softly. "That's better than I hoped for."

"Me, too, but I didn't tell them that. I don't know if you heard, but Olmstead was in a motorcycle accident. Crushed his ankle and broke his passing arm in three places. Looks pretty serious for his career. Your backup being out of commission is probably the reason for the big offer. The only catch is that they want the papers signed by day after tomorrow, so get your ass on a plane and get back to L.A. *now.*"

"Can't do it. I'm going to spend a few days in Cairo."

"*Cairo?* In *Egypt?* What the fuck for? I'm talking megabucks here, Morgan. I don't think I can put the front office off for a few days. Get on a plane now."

"I'll be back next week for sure," Wade said.

"Next *week?*" he yelled. "Next *week?* Are you outta your fucking mind?"

"Calm down. Remember your blood pressure, Barney. I'll see you in a few days."

He hung up quickly. Barney always got more emotional with every zero after the dollar sign. But Barney was right: it was one sweet deal. Wade grinned. It would never do for the Vulcans to know that he would have signed for a hell of a lot less.

They decided on lunch in one of the nicest restaurants in town, and the manager was delighted to have them photograph the elegant interior.

After several shots, they were seated at tables by the window. J.J., Solo, and Shark discreetly opted to sit together and allow Wade and Welcome to dine privately. Their small table had a breathtaking view of the Acropolis with the sun glinting off the Parthenon and the various other temple ruins.

Wade laid his hand over hers, and they gazed out the window together.

"When I look at that hill, sometimes I can almost see the way it used to be," Welcome said quietly. "The flashes last only a millisecond, but I can see—"

"The roof intact on the Parthenon, and the other buildings whole and smooth—"

"And the gigantic statue of Athena standing guard over the city—"

"The light striking her gold shield and making it gleam so brightly that it could be seen from the sea," he finished.

"You, too?" she whispered.

He blinked a couple of times and frowned. "Me too what?"

"Boy, you sure have a short memory. What we were just talking about. About being able to see the Acropolis in its former glory. About the colossal statue of Athena that used to stand there."

He continued to look puzzled. "I don't know what you're talking about. I'm lost. What statue?"

"Never mind." She opened her menu and began studying it.

"No, don't brush this off. I'm sorry, but I was thinking about something else, something my agent said, and I don't remember what we were discussing. Sorry, sugar." He kissed her hand.

Was it possible that he really didn't know what he had said? Maybe so. Maybe his comments were completely unconscious. "Wade, do parts of Athens seem very familiar to you? I mean like someplace that you might have visited as a child, but the memories are very hazy."

"Now that you mention it, yeah. Like the stadium at Delphi."

"And do I seem very familiar?"

"Very familiar." He grinned, leaned close, and whispered something extremely intimate.

She swatted his hand and laughed. "I don't mean that. Seriously, does it seem as if you and I were never strangers?"

"Seriously? I feel as if I've known you forever and waited my whole life for you to appear. How do you feel?"

She hesitated a moment. "The same."

A waiter appeared, and they ordered. When another had poured complimentary wine from the manager and left, she said, "Have you ever heard much about the New Age beliefs?"

"Living in California? Are you kidding?" He laughed. "All that goofy stuff starts in California. One week the latest fad is chanting in a bathtub of orange blossoms, buttermilk, and alfalfa oil, the next week it's something else. Why?"

"I was just wondering if you had ever thought much about reincarnation or such things."

"Not much. I have enough trouble trying to make

it through this life without worrying about another one. Is that something you believe in?"

"I've considered it from time to time, figuring that the idea explained lots of things to me that traditional Western philosophies couldn't. And after Meri's experiences when she first met Ram, the notion was reinforced."

"Meri is your Egyptian friend?"

Welcome smiled. "She's Texan, but she and her husband, who is Egyptian, live in Egypt part of the time. They keep a suite at the Horus Hotel in Giza and have a home in Luxor, as well as an apartment at the Dakota in New York and another in Dallas."

"They get around a lot."

"A fair amount. But they have memories of spending other lifetimes together. The moment they saw each other, it was Katie, bar the door. Instant attraction. There's more, but it's long and complicated and really not my business to tell, but the point is that they remember being lovers before. They are . . . well, I guess you could say that they are soul mates."

He took a sip of his wine, then set the glass down and turned the stem round and round in his fingers. "Do you think that we've been lovers before?" he asked quietly.

"I don't know, but—" She stopped, unwilling to hedge any longer. "Yes, yes I do. I'm sure of it. And it was here in Athens, in Greece. Do you think that's ridiculous?"

"No, darlin', I don't. I know that something very unusual is going on between us, something more than being attracted to one another. I don't pretend to know what it is, but it's powerful. Did I ever tell you why Shark and I are here?"

"No," Welcome said. "I assumed that you were on vacation."

Wade shook his head. He paused while their lunch was served, then told her of the unusual urge that brought him to Athens.

"It's a little scary, isn't it?" Welcome said. "That events and unconscious urges have brought us together here, now."

"It's a lot to think about, that's for sure. I wonder about the timing. Why here? Why now?"

"I don't know," she said, "but I've read some about such things. I think it has to do with karma."

"Karma? I guess I've heard the term, but I don't really know what it means."

"The way that I understand it, karma is sort of like unfinished business. Some sources say that it's the same principle as action/reaction or reaping what you sow, and it all has to do with learning and growth. Supposedly we come back with the same groups of people at different times to enjoy the good things we've created in another life or to right the wrongs—something like that."

"Sounds complicated," Wade said. "I'll have to think about it some."

After lunch, Welcome changed into casual clothes in the ladies' room, and they went to photograph her as she visited Hadrian's Arch, the Temple of Zeus, and made a quick excursion by Mitropoleos, the cathedral of Athens, and through the bazaar. They stopped for a rest at a small café near the flea market, and Welcome changed clothes again.

She chose her outfit deliberately and slipped a cape about her. As soon as everyone had finished their drinks, she led the group to the Roman Agora and the Tower of the Winds. As a tourist attraction, the place rated below many others that she would have to forego, but personally, returning there, especially with Wade, was critical.

When she reached the agora, she was grateful for the balmy afternoon as she shrugged off her cape and handed it to Shark. She wore sandals and a gauzy dress reminiscent of the costumes of ancient Greece . . . and very similar to those she'd seen at the National Museum. She posed laughing beside a tall pillar, the one with the nick in it.

Slowly, she swept her gaze to Wade.

He stood as still as a marble Apollo. His eyes appeared glazed, and his expression was a mixture of consternation and bemusement.

After several shots in the area, Welcome signaled a wrap to Solo. Very quietly she approached Wade, who appeared not to have moved. She laughed and touched his shoulder.

"Astrid," he said, smiling as he reached for her.

"No," she said, "not Astrid."

He frowned. "What are you talking about?"

"My name isn't Astrid."

"Well, hell, I know that."

"But that's what you called me."

"I didn't."

"You did," she said. "Something unusual happened to you as you stood here, didn't it?"

"No, nothing unusual. I just watched you and got horny like I always do. Wonder what the others would say if you and I went back to the hotel for an hour or so?"

She glanced at her watch. "They would say that you ought to keep your pants zipped for a while yet. Time is getting away from us, and I still want a *few* shots of Plaka at least. I'm saving the Acropolis for last. Come on, we need to hurry." She slipped her arm around his waist as they walked. "Are you and Shark still planning to go to Cairo with me?"

"Yep. Where you go, I go. Where I go, Shark goes."

After another quick costume change for Welcome, they were able to capture some of the color of Plaka: the interesting streets and the characters that roamed them, the restorations of old homes arrayed in their vivid shades, the shops and the tavernas. Although many places were closed for siesta, most were not. Athens was getting away from the old custom, especially in Plaka and other tourist areas.

Thankfully, Welcome was able to squeeze in ten minutes to spend with Spyros and his family, and she made sure that there were lots of shots of the taverna, including several at an outside table with Spyros himself serving her and with the Taverna Katrakis sign evident in the background.

"I'll make sure that you get a prominent place in the brochure," Welcome told Spyros.

"What brochure?" the old man asked.

"The family of my best friend has purchased one of the large hotels here and will be totally renovating it very soon. She and I have a company that is producing a very nice little booklet that will entice tourists to come to Greece and stay in their hotel while they see the sights and visit interesting places."

"And Taverna Katrakis is one of those interesting places they should visit?"

"Most definitely." She kissed his leathery cheek. "The best taverna in Plaka . . . *and* the only one that serves chicken-fried steak."

He simply beamed.

How she hated to tell them good-bye. Maybe she

had known these people before as well. They had become very dear to her very quickly.

J.J. tapped his watch.

"I know. I know," Welcome said, tearing herself
away.

They had only half an hour to spend at the Acropolis, forty-five minutes if they cut it very close. Thank
goodness that all they had to do when they finished
the shoot was to speed to the airport and board the
plane. J.J.'s men were taking care of collecting everybody's luggage and checking it through.

The sun was riding low when they climbed the steps
of the Acropolis toward the summit of the site where
so many people had walked through the ages. The
breeze seemed to carry faint echoes of prayers, of rejoicing, of anguished cries. Of—

The thought fled, and chill bumps rippled over her
skin.

History seemed to permeate the stones of the rocky
hill and imbue the very air with unseen emanations,
the lingering effects of the layers of emotional events
that had transpired here. Welcome's chest swelled in
wonderment when she thought of the greats who had
walked this path: Plato, Aristotle, Socrates, Pericles,
Phidias—

She stumbled as a pain ripped through her chest.

Wade caught her arm. "Darlin', what's wrong?"

With the sound of his voice, a heavy curtain in her
mind drew back momentarily, then closed abruptly.
She shook from his grip and glared at him.

"You *bastard!*"

Twenty-eight

It is not possible to step twice into the same river.

Heraclitus
c. 540-480 B.C.

Wade figured that his mouth must have dropped open when Welcome tossed that bomb. Talk about coming out of left field. "What did I do?" he asked, totally baffled.

"I don't remember. I need to sit down. My knees are wobbly."

He helped her to a stone seat. "Shark, bring some of that bottled water over here." To Welcome he said, "You need to rest. Why don't we forget this? You've tried to cram a week's work into a few hours, and you're exhausted."

She took a swig of the bottled water, closed her eyes, and breathed deeply. "Just give me a couple of minutes. I'll be fine. We *have* to have shots of this area. Who could do a brochure of Athens and leave out the Parthenon and the Acropolis? Such an idea is ludicrous," she said sharply. She shoved the bottle into his hand and started away in a huff.

"Whoa, tiger," Wade said, catching her by the arm. "You want to tell me what's going on? I get the distinct

feeling that you're royally pissed at me, and I don'
have any idea why. Fill me in."

"How can I fill you in when I'm as befuddled as you
are? Even I don't know what's going on. I don't know
anything any more. It's as if I suddenly woke up and
all the rules had changed while I slept."

"Then let's take it slowly," Wade said, still holding
onto her. "Are you angry with me?"

"Why would I be—" She stopped and took another
deep breath. "Yes."

"Why?"

"I don't know. And I don't have time to figure it ou
now." She pulled away. "Solo, let's get some shots o
this area, then head for the Parthenon. We'll want a
panoramic view from up here, too. We need to get the
museum and the Erechtheum. Oh, and the Temple o
Nike. God, half an hour isn't long enough. J.J.—"

"No way," J.J. said. "In exactly thirty-nine minute
we're going to be in the van and on our way to the
airport. If you don't get all the pictures you need, you
can hire someone to come back later and fill in the
holes."

Welcome tossed her fiery hair, jutted her jaw in tha
cute way she had of doing, and started barking ou
orders. In thirty seconds she had them all hopping like
crickets on a hot griddle.

Hands in his pockets and a grin on his face, he stood
watching her. Damn, he thought, she was some kind
of woman. He might not know what was going on in
her head half the time, but he wouldn't trade her fo
a dozen of any other woman he could think of.

He was going to marry her. Soon.

He knew that she had her heart set on living on he
ranch in Texas, but maybe he could convince her to
table that idea for a while. He needed to be in L.A.

at least during the season. Maybe they could spend part of the year in Texas.

But he'd been approached to do a couple of TV shows out in California, and he was anxious to try his hand at acting. No, Texas would have to wait. He would explain to her that L.A. was where the action was. And besides, he had a fantastic house. She would love it.

By some miracle the whole bunch was in the van and rolling at the time J.J. had appointed.

"I needed more time," Welcome groused, tucking her trademark red hair into a jaunty cashmere beret. "Half a day at least."

"Sorry, *mon amie*," J.J. said, "but we're barely going to make the flight as it is."

"Ohmygod!" Welcome cried, sitting up suddenly. "The bracelet!"

"What bracelet?" Wade asked.

"*The* bracelet. J.J., we have to go back to the hotel. I can't leave without that bracelet, and it's in the safe at the GB."

"What bracelet?" Wade asked again.

"It's, uh, a piece of my jewelry. Very valuable. *Extremely* valuable. J.J., turn around."

"Forget the bracelet," J.J. said. "I'll have one of my men pick it up later."

"But—"

Solo touched her shoulder. "Leave it. You know that it's secure where it is. I can return and retrieve it for you if you would like."

"Must be *some* bracelet," Wade said. "Diamond?"

"Gold," Welcome said. "Okay, Solo. I suppose you're right. We can call Philip—" She quickly clamped her mouth shut.

"Who's Philip?" Wade asked.

"He, uh, he's—"

"He's at the GB," Solo supplied glibly. "The assistant manager I believe."

"Yes, I can call him at the airport and explain the situation," Welcome said.

"Or I can call if you like," J.J. said, a trace of amusement in his voice.

"Thank you, no. I'll handle it personally." She sat back and slipped on the large tortoiseshell glasses that served as the rest of her disguise.

Chuckling, J.J. picked up the small radio unit beside him and spoke briefly and quietly. "We are coming up on the airport," he said, all business. "Four of my men are there. One will take the van; two others will escort us to a VIP area near where we'll be boarding; the fourth will take Welcome's bag and the photographic equipment to be checked through customs and loaded on the plane. One of the men will lead the way; Solo and I will be directly behind him with Welcome between us; the other man will follow us. Wade and Shark, you bring up the rear. Keep tight. Here we are."

He pulled into a space near a door, tucked his ponytail under a black Greek fisherman hat, and turned up his jacket collar just as two men stepped forward and opened the van doors. "Let's move," J.J. said.

Everything went off without a hitch.

Inside the elegantly appointed VIP lounge, Solo nodded to J.J. "Nice job."

"Thank you. We try."

"I need to make that phone call," Welcome said quietly to J.J. and Solo.

"Feel free," J.J. said, gesturing to a phone on a nearby desk.

"Isn't there one that's a little more private?" she

whispered from the side of her mouth, cutting her eyes to the side to indicate the others in the room.

"Try the ladies' room, but make it quick. We board in five minutes."

"Good idea." She smiled sweetly at Wade who was approaching. "Excuse me for a moment."

Thank God there *was* a phone there.

And thank God she got through to Philip fairly quickly.

"Are you still in the hospital, sweetie?"

"I'm still here. And bloody bored, I can tell you."

"You should have been with us," she said. "Things have been very lively. They caught the bad guy—who, by the way, ran with a *very* tough crowd—and tossed him in the slammer, but he hanged himself last night. Even so, J.J. and Solo are insisting that I leave Greece for Cairo. We're at the airport now, but I forgot and left my jewelry in the safe at the GB. They wouldn't let me go back for it. Solo offered to pick it up later. What shall I do?"

"Leave it by all means. Is Solo going to Cairo with you?"

"Yes."

"Tell her to call Wayne Baldridge, a friend of mine at the Embassy. He would love to take her to lunch."

"Will do. I—"

Solo stuck her head in the door. "Time to go."

"I have to run, Philip. We're boarding."

"Fine, love. Thanks. And I'm sorry about the flowers this time. I'll make—"

"Gotta go, sweetie," she interrupted as Solo gestured urgently. "Talk to you later."

Their group was the last to board, and they had the first-class section to themselves. Welcome slid into a window seat, and Wade took the aisle seat beside her before J.J. or Solo decided to extend their watchdog duties to the plane.

"I've never been to Egypt," Wade said.

"Then you're in for a treat," Welcome told him. She took off the ugly glasses and stuck them in her purse. "Everybody should see the pyramids. How long can you stay?"

"A couple of days at the most. I need to get back to L.A. and tend to some business. You been here often?"

"A few times, mostly since Meri and Ram have been married. We try to get together as often as we can, usually in Paris or in Cairo. Now I suppose we'll be meeting in Dallas or in Athens."

"Athens? Do you think that's safe?"

She laughed and patted his thigh. "Athens, *Texas*, sweetie. At the ranch."

He almost said something about living arrangements then, but he decided that the timing wasn't right.

She took off the hat she wore and shook her head. Her mass of flaming curls fell in a wild riot over her shoulders. Massaging her scalp, she said, "I could sure use a tall bourbon and branch water right now."

They ordered drinks from the stewardess and drank them while Welcome told him about several places that he and Shark had to see in Egypt. When the last of her bourbon and water was gone, she yawned and stretched.

"Tired?" he asked.

She nodded. "I didn't get much sleep last night as you recall, and today was a killer. Mind tossing me a pillow and a blanket from the overhead? I think I'm going to take a snooze."

"No problem."

When he stood to open the compartment, one of

J.J.'s men who had been sitting ahead of them came back and stood next to Wade. "Excuse me, Mr. Morgan, but you had these messages at your hotel." The swarthy man handed Wade several slips of paper.

"Thanks." Wade stuffed the messages in his jacket pocket and collected the pillow and blanket for Welcome. He didn't have to read them; he knew damned well who they were from.

Barney would just have to stew a while longer. Wade was determined to spend at least a couple of more days with Welcome before he went home. Contrary to what his agent thought, the Vulcans could wait a few days; the offer would hold. With Olmstead out and all of the major pro quarterbacks already signed, actually Wade was in a position of strength for a change. Barney was smart enough to know that, too. Barney just needed to make noises and feed his ulcer to feel important.

Wade leaned back, stretched out in his seat, and watched Welcome as she drifted off to sleep.

God, she was gorgeous.

And sexy.

And bright.

And fun. And vibrant. And unpretentious. He could go on about her outstanding attributes all day long.

Welcome was choice in every way.

She was as easy to talk to as any of his buddies. Easier in some ways—when she was making sense. He cut her some slack in that department. She'd been under a hell of a lot of stress, enough to make anybody a little goofy.

He didn't know if he could buy that business about reincarnation and karma, but he knew that he was crazy about her. And if it wasn't fate or karma that brought them together, he knew that he was damned lucky to have found her. What if he hadn't followed his urge to go to Greece? He wouldn't have met her.

And, Holy Mary, she might have died!

A sick feeling gripped his gut and tied it into a thousand knots. Sudden panic kicked up his heartbeat.

Be cool, he told himself. He *had* found her; she was alive and well and would stay that way as long as he drew a breath. From now on, her happiness and her safety were his number one priority.

Cairo

Culture shock hit Wade the minute he got off the plane. While Greece had been different from the U.S., this was another world. If Athens was organized chaos, this was simply chaos. A babble of languages, a babble of people, fretful children, a conglomeration of odors from bodies that smelled strange, odd clothes.

"Man," Shark said, "and I thought LAX was a zoo."

Welcome laughed. "You'll get used to it. Thank your lucky stars that J.J. and his men are with us."

"Why?" Shark asked.

"Because they're recognized among the airport officials for one thing, and because they know where to spread the *baksheesh* for another."

"*Baksheesh?*"

She rubbed her thumb over the pads of her fingers. "A polite translation would be a gift or a tip, a monetary consideration for services."

"A bribe," Wade said.

She grinned. "You got it. It's a common practice here. See if this crowd doesn't part for us like the Red Sea for Moses."

It did.

They were whisked outside to a white limo waiting

at the curb. Even though night had fallen, Wade noted that the air still held the day's heat, and it felt dry and twenty degrees warmer than Athens had been. And the place smelled different, too. Alien, yet vaguely familiar. He couldn't quite put his finger on it, but something reminded him of his boyhood and of the powdered snuff his grandpa used to dip. Snuff spat upon bone-dry dirt stirred to dust behind a mule-pulled plow.

It smelled of poverty.

Welcome, Solo, Wade, and Shark got into the back of the limousine; J.J. sat up front by the driver.

The limo shot out of the airport and drove like a bat out of hell, honking loudly and barely slowing as it sped through red lights at various intersections.

"I hope somebody got our bags," Shark said as he held on to the strap. "I'd hate to know that I died in a strange country without any clean underwear."

J.J. laughed. "Sometimes it seems like Egyptians adhere to the kamikaze school of driving, but don't worry. Our luggage is in the car behind us, and Ahmed is an excellent driver."

"Doesn't a red light mean stop in Egypt like it does everywhere else?"

"Sure it does," J.J. said, "but nobody pays any attention. If it looks fairly clear, you just honk loudly and run it. And if you have a big car and are in a hurry, you just honk and floorboard it."

"And play chicken."

"That's about it."

"Look," Solo said as they honked and passed a slow moving wagon pulled by a mule. "That's a gutsy fellow to be in this traffic."

"He's a garbage collector," J.J. explained. "We have many like him over the city."

"Seems rather primitive in such modern surroundings. He's hardly in the same league with the New York Department of Sanitation."

"No, but he and his cohorts aren't likely to go on strike, and the price is right. They pick up the city's garbage for free."

"For free?" Shark said. "How come?"

"Then what they collect belongs to them. They're allowed to keep whatever they find. Whole families live on the dumps and survive by scavenging."

"Man," Shark said, sitting back and shaking his head. "That's hard to believe."

"Egypt is a very poor country. They don't have the oil that their Arab neighbors do. They have a little strip of farming land along the Nile, and tourism."

"With so much poverty, what about the crime rate here?" Solo asked. "It must be sky high."

"Actually, it's very low. The greatest concern in that area is the occasional extremist incident. But such are rare."

"Exactly where in Cairo are we going?" Wade said.

"To the Horus Hotel," Welcome told him, "which, strictly speaking is in Giza, not Cairo, but I doubt if you'll know when we leave Cairo. They sort of run together. Giza is where the pyramids are located."

"And the hotel is owned by—"

"The Gabrey family. Ram is the only son and manages most of the family business now that his father has retired to travel with Charlotte. Ram's mother is Charlie Clark, the mystery writer."

"Charlie Clark?" Solo said. "You're kidding. She's my favorite author. But I never knew that she was Egyptian."

Welcome laughed. "She's not. She's a fellow Texan. Zaki, Ram's father is Egyptian. Well, half Egyptian. I think his grandmother was a Scot."

"Are we going to finally get to meet this Ram guy?"

Wade asked. "I was beginning to think that he was a figment of somebody's imagination."

"Oh, he's real all right."

"There it is," Welcome said as the hotel came into view. Lit by the grounds lights and others discreetly placed among the fronds of the palm trees lining the drive, the Horus Hotel was impressive. A tasteful combination of ancient temple style and Moorish architecture, it blended with the surroundings and complemented the older Mena House Hotel which was nearby.

As soon as they pulled to a stop, a bevy of attendants in long, striped *galabiyahs* hurried to open doors and assist them inside to the lobby.

"Man, oh, man," Shark said, gaping at the tall domed ceiling, the wall paintings, the general opulence of the hotel and its furnishings.

"This place is something else," Wade said.

"Thank you," a deep voice said.

Wade turned to the speaker. He was a big man, tall and dark, with black hair and mustache, but the first thing that jumped out at you was his light blue eyes. Even Wade noticed what a good-looking devil he was when he flashed a broad, white-toothed smile and held out his arms to Welcome.

She squealed like a teenager and threw herself into the pretty-boy's arms. Wade's fists clenched, and when she kissed the guy, he wanted to flatten the bastard.

"Where's Meri?" Welcome asked him.

"She's been pacing a hole in the floor right here until about two minutes ago. She had to go to the bathroom, a frequent occurrence these days."

"*Welcome!*" a woman cried as she ran toward them.

Welcome opened her arms and the two hugged like long-lost sisters and began chattering a mile a minute.

Watching them, the man laughed, then turned to the others, "You'll have to excuse my wife for a moment, but if I know those two, they won't come up for air for a while. I'm Ram Gabry. Welcome to the Horus."

J.J. made the introductions, and Wade noticed that Ram had a firm handshake to go with his air of self-confidence. But after the group had talked for a few minutes, Wade had to admit that he kind of liked the fellow, especially after he said, "Damn, but that was a fine play you made in the last few seconds of the Super Bowl. I was on the edge of my chair. Meri thought I had slipped a gear when I started yelling at the TV."

"I nearly slipped one myself when I turned to hand off to Frederick and he wasn't there," Wade said.

"You managed the situation brilliantly. I read that you hadn't signed with the Vulcans yet. Planning to retire?"

Wade smiled and shrugged. "We're negotiating."

Ram chuckled. "I see. Heard about Olmstead. I imagine that you're glad you delayed signing."

"Right."

Ram turned to engage the others in conversation, asking them about Greece. Wade decided that Ram was a hell of a nice guy, and Meri was a jewel, he discovered when she and Welcome finally ran down enough for Meri to meet the newcomers.

"Sorry," Meri said, "but Welcome is like my sister and my best friend rolled into one, and we haven't seen each other in over three months. For us, that's an eternity. I know you must be tired. And hungry too, if the food on the plane was the usual fare."

"You got that right," Shark said.

Solo laughed and said, "Shark is always hungry."

"Come along," Meri said, "and we'll show you to

your rooms. We've put you in the guest suites on the same floor with us. Take some time to rest, shower and change if you like, or come as you are to supper at our place. Oh, it's so good to have you all here." She grinned and squeezed Welcome's hand as she winked at Wade. "He's a hunk, sugar," she whispered to Welcome in a loud voice. "Better grab him before I do."

"Like hell," Ram said, his gracious smile dying as he moved possessively beside his wife.

Meri lifted one eyebrow. "That's a one."

"Sorry, *sukkar.*" Ram laughed and kissed her nose. "This way to the elevators. Your bags should already be in your rooms."

They were on the top floor of the hotel. The accommodations were unbelievably sumptuous: the carpet was ankle deep; the couches were like pillows, the beds perfect; the bathroom looked like something out of the *Arabian Nights* complete with whirlpool.

There was just one problem, Wade thought.

He was alone.

Each of them had been given a private suite.

He'd wanted to share one with Welcome, and when Meri was pointing out rooms, he'd almost spoken up. In fact, he had his mouth open when Welcome must have read his mind and given a small shake of her head. Not wanting to embarrass her in front of her friends, he kept mum.

Dammit, he ached to have her in his arms again.

Maybe after supper, he thought as he shed his jacket. He felt something in his pocket and remembered the messages from the GB. He quickly sorted through them.

They were all from Barney, each more urgently worded than the previous one. The last one, which had probably been left only a few minutes before J.J.'s man had checked them out of the hotel and picked up the messages, made Wade chuckle.

Forget going to Cairo! Get on a fucking plane to L.A. now! Now was underlined four times. The hotel operator's ears were bound to have been red. He wondered if Barney had to spell any of the words for her. *Damn that jerk!* he thought when he realized that their destination was written on the message slip.

No, I'm the jerk, he told himself. Why had he even mentioned Cairo to Barney? It's a good thing that Chroni was dead or Wade would be nervous.

Not that it was likely that the killer could have had access to Wade's message slips in any case, but they'd been so damned careful, he wouldn't want to be the cause of a dangerous leak. But Chroni was dead; they were in Giza, not Cairo; and the chance of somebody locating Welcome here among millions of people was reaching.

Wade crumpled the message slips into a wad, tossed them in the trash, and headed for the shower.

Twenty-nine

At one time through love all things come together into one, at another time through strife's hatred they are borne each of them apart.

Empedocles
c. 490-430 B.C.

"Ahhhh," Welcome said as she lay back in the tub filled with bubbles and wiggled her toes. "That feels wonderful."

"You must be exhausted," Meri said, handing her a glass of orange juice. "Sure you don't want wine? Just because I can't have any doesn't mean that you can't."

"No, thanks. Orange juice is perfect, Mommy."

Meri laughed. "Isn't it wonderful? That I am going to be a mommy, I mean. Ram is so excited. And do you know what I dreamed last night? I dreamed that you and I were pushing strollers together. In mine was a dark-haired little boy, and in yours was a red-haired little girl about the same age. Isn't that a hoot? Wouldn't it be fantastic if it were really true?"

"Bite your tongue, sweetie."

"Don't you want to have children?"

"Someday, sure. But don't you think I'd better have a husband first? I know that nowadays that doesn't matter to lots of people, but I'm a little conventional about having kids and raising them properly."

"From what I saw," Meri said as she sat down and propped her feet on the side of the tub, "Wade Morgan would slip a ring on your finger in nothing flat."

"Think so?"

"I know so. The man's besotted. He looks at you as if he could eat you with a spoon. And you're not exactly immune to him either I gather. How far have things progressed?"

"Pretty far." Welcome told Meri about the events of the past few days, downplaying the scary stuff and focusing on her meeting Wade and the strange incidents connecting them. By the time she finished, the water was cold and Meri was wide-eyed.

"Holy cow, Welcome! I'm glad that I insisted that Ram send J.J. and some men. You've been through the wringer."

"But Chroni's dead, and I came out fine. Except for the mess with Wade. Now I better understand what you went through when you first met Ram. This thing with Wade is a lot more complicated than any relationship I've ever had before. We've progressed further in mere days than Eduard and I did in years."

"Looks like you and Wade have as strong a connection as Ram and I do. But I suspect that you have a few things to work out, too. Any idea why you're sometimes angry with him for no reason?"

"None. I've got to get out of the tub, I'm turning to a prune. And I'll bet Shark is about ready to eat table legs by now."

"He's cute," Meri said, "but don't worry. We ordered lots of hors d'oeuvres and Ram will entertain him. I like Solo too, from the little I've talked with her. Is she a good photographer? How did you find her?"

"Philip found her for me. I've seen some of her work; it's excellent. I only hope that these photographs turn out well, especially today's. You wouldn't believe the pace J.J. kept us to."

The doorbell rang.

Meri hopped up from the vanity chair. "I'll get it while you get dressed."

Welcome had dried off and was in a robe when Meri stuck her head in. "It's Solo. She wants to talk to you. I'm going to take this bag of film she shot back to our suite. Come on down when you're ready."

Welcome was surprised when she walked into the sitting room. Instead of her usual jeans, Solo was dressed in a little black number that looked like an Ungaro. "You look fabulous," she told the petite blonde, who was considerably taller in her high heels.

"Thanks," Solo said, a sudden grin spoiling her sophisticated appearance. "I came to deliver the film and to say good-bye."

"Good-bye? Surely you can stay a few days and see Cairo."

"Sorry. I wish that I could, but duty calls. I phoned Wayne Baldridge, and I'm having dinner with him tonight. I suspect that I'll be flying back to Athens early in the morning to wrap up things there. Then I'll be going back to the States. Do you have that letter for the manager of the GB?"

Welcome retrieved the envelope from the desk and handed it to her. "Thanks for everything, Solo. I hope that we can get together again. I think that we could become good friends. My address at the ranch is in the envelope, too. Maybe you can stop by sometime on your way to Port Neches."

Solo laughed. "I rarely get to Port Neches, but I'll make it a point to stop by the ranch one of these days."

They clasped hands warmly, and Solo left.

* * *

After dinner, long after dinner, Shark had dozed off in an easy chair, and Wade's eyelids were getting heavier and heavier. Ram stood, smiled, and said to Wade, "I think these women may be up all night. How about we turn in and leave it to them?"

Wade had been trying to wait Welcome out, hoping that she would spend the night in his bed, but he was flagging fast. And after his host made such a proposal, what could he do?

"I think you're right," Wade said, thumping Shark's foot and waking him.

"I'm getting tired myself," Welcome said. "We won't be much longer."

Meri kissed Ram's cheek. "Sorry, sweetheart. I'll be along in a minute."

After the men left, Meri giggled and said, "Wade wanted you to come with him. I swear that when you look at each other, the air positively sizzles. But I'm surprised that you picked a professional football player, especially one so well known. I thought that you wanted to retire from the limelight and live the quiet life."

Welcome sighed. "I do. That's why my head tells me to cool it with him."

"And what does your heart tell you?"

"That nobody has ever made me feel the way he does."

"Not even Eduard?"

"Good Lord, no. Eduard is too *civilized* to make love like a wild man."

Meri smiled. "Gone that far already, has it?"

"Yep." She rose. "And probably will again. Very soon." She grinned. "The chemistry is unbelievable, but I don't see anything permanent coming of this.

Don't start planning a wedding, sweetie. It's not going to happen."

In Welcome's bedroom, the covers had been turned back and a huge bouquet of her favorite yellow roses sat on the dresser. Humming, she bent to smell the buds, then hurriedly changed into a sexy negligee and touched an extra drop of perfume between her breasts.

She opened her side of the connecting door, fluffed her hair, then tapped "shave and a haircut" on the other panel.

When Wade tentatively opened the door, she put her hand on her hip and smiled provocatively. "Hi there, big boy. How about some company?"

Before she could draw another breath, he pulled her into his arms and kissed her as if there were no tomorrow.

She went wild.

He went wild.

Clothes easily shed flew every whichaway. The rest stayed on or were shoved aside or ripped away if they interfered with his destination.

Amid feral sounds and urgent touching, he lifted her onto the dresser's edge, stepped between her legs, and buried himself into her hot wetness. She locked her ankles around his waist and urged him to take her harder, deeper.

Their joining was savage, mindless. They both climaxed quickly, cries wrung from them as they breached the wall and convulsed.

Panting and sweaty, they were still after the last shuddering spasm died.

"Goddammit!" Wade ground out.

"What's wrong?"

"Honey, did I hurt you? I can't believe that I went after you like a boar in rutting season. And on the goddamn dresser. Hell, the bed is only four yards away."

She laughed and laid her forehead on his damp shoulder. "We do tend to get a bit vigorous, don't we? But I'm as bad as you are. Maybe we can try the bed next time." She peered around his shoulder. "There aren't any candles around, are there?"

"I hope to hell not. I'd hate to burn Ram's hotel down." He finished ripping off the shirt that hung on one arm, wiped his face with it, and tossed it aside. "I need another shower. Join me?"

"Will you wash my back?"

"Darlin', I'll wash every single part of you before I'm through."

Welcome was almost asleep when she jerked straight up in bed. "Oh, no!"

"Honey, what's wrong?" Wade asked.

"Guess what we forgot again?"

After a couple of seconds, the answer dawned. "Condoms. Babe, I'm sorry."

She fell back onto the bed. "It's too late to worry now; it's done. But this is the last time it can happen, Wade. I mean it. You'd better keep your fingers crossed and pray."

He smiled and pulled her into his arms. "I will, darlin'. I'll pray real hard."

And he did. Nothing he would like better than having her carry his child. Would he rather have a boy or a girl first? Didn't matter as long as he had their mother.

* * *

Welcome awoke first. Wade was on his back, sound asleep, his legs spread and his arms outflung. She had been sleeping with her head on his shoulder, her fingers threaded through his soft chest hair, and her leg looped over his. He couldn't have been comfortable with her all over him; his shoulder was probably numb. She raised her head and started to ease her leg away.

"Where you going?" he grumbled, hugging her back against him.

"I must be heavy."

"Nope, light as angel wings. The Raider line is heavy."

"I need to get up anyway. I want to show you something."

"Something better than you showed me in the shower last night?"

She grinned and gave his tummy a playful slap. It was rock hard.

So was something lower.

"I can't believe you," she said.

"Me either. But since I've met you, I stay horny all the time. If it doesn't get better by the time football season rolls around, I'm going to have to have a custom-made jockstrap for my uniform."

"Give me a break!" she said, laughing. "Come on, get up. I want to show you."

He pulled her astride him and gazed up at her with an expression that melted her bones. "I'd rather look at you." His hands followed the curves of her hips and thighs, then cupped her breasts.

Tugging slightly, he urged her to move toward him until he could take a nipple into his mouth.

One thing led to another, and they made slow, sweet love that sent her reeling with its gentle intensity.

"I love you, sweetheart," he whispered. "I love you so much."

Echoing words almost came from her mouth, but she stopped them. "I'm pretty fond of you too," she said, as a compromise, then smiled brightly. "Now do you want to see what I want to show you?"

"Sure."

She opened the heavy draperies, thrust out her arm, and said, *"Ta ta!"*

"Gorgeous! Fantastic! I love that little mole by your belly button."

"Not me, you dolt!" She laughed. "Look out the window."

"Wow." He rose and joined her at the window that framed the pyramids of Giza. Hugging her to his side, he peered at the three great wonders. "They hardly seem real."

"They're real all right. We have to get dressed. Breakfast is in fifteen minutes, then Meri and Ram are going to take you, Shark, and me on a sightseeing tour." She tiptoed to kiss his cheek. "You're scratchy. You need to shave. Rap on the door when you're ready, and we'll go down to the coffee shop."

"Let's skip breakfast." His arms tightened around her.

"Not on your life. I'm starving." She scooted away and grabbed her rumpled negligee on her way through the connecting door. She closed the door firmly behind her and headed to her bedroom for another shower.

That's when it struck her.

They had forgotten again.

Damn!

Double damn!

A few minutes later, she was stepping out of the shower when she heard the phone. How long had it been ringing? Wrapping a big towel around her, she dripped water as she hurried across the big bathroom to the extension and snatched it up with a wet hand.

"Hello."

Silence.

"Hello. Hello."

Still nothing. She'd missed the call.

Or had she?

A tiny little niggle of apprehension tightened her stomach.

She was still gun-shy from the events in Athens. Relax, she told herself. Probably Meri calling, reminding her of the time. No telling how long it had been ringing while she had the water running full blast.

No big deal. Chroni was dead. None of his cohorts could possibly know where she was.

Welcome dressed quickly in khaki slacks and a blue cotton sweater and pulled on a light windbreaker in case of an early morning chill outside. She hung a thin string purse over one shoulder, and as she started to stick her keys in her jacket pocket, she snagged a fingernail.

"Damn!"

The minute she reached for an emery board in her makeup case, she remembered. She was out of emery boards and had forgotten to pick up any more. Rats!

When she stuck her head through the connecting door and called to Wade, he said, "Give me about another five minutes."

"I'm going on down; I need to buy some emery boards. See you in the coffee shop."

Downstairs in the hotel gift shop a few minutes later, Welcome took an emery board from the package immediately to repair her nail. She was slipping the file back into the sack when she spotted a magnificent silk negligee displayed nearby. It was sexy as all get out and looked just her size. "I'd like to try that on," she told the saleswoman.

She left her jacket and the paper sack with her purchase on the counter and went into the dressing room.

The negligee was perfect. It would knock Wade's socks off.

"Would you hold this for me, please?" Welcome asked when she came out. "Or better yet, I'm in suite 514. Would you have someone deliver it there later?"

"You are a guest of the Gabreys'? Certainly, I will see to it."

"Buying out the store?" Wade asked as he stepped beside her.

Caught red-handed. She almost blushed. "Not quite. Ready for breakfast?" she asked, hustling him from the shop.

They met Meri, Ram, and Shark inside and enjoyed an American-style feast, complete with pancakes and maple syrup. Shark was in hog heaven.

"Man, oh, man," Shark said as he lay on the chaise by the pool later that day. "Those mothers are something else. Never thought I'd see the day when D'Angelo Thomas would climb around in anything like that."

"They're bigger than I imagined," Wade said.

"I've never heard of anybody who isn't awed by the size of the pyramids," Welcome said. She opened her tote and found a tube of sun block. "You'd better put some of this on. Even though it's late, and we're under umbrellas, the Egyptian sun is fierce. I learned my lesson the hard way."

They had spent the morning at Giza, riding camels to the pyramids and climbing inside the largest one until they reached the King's Chamber. An archeologist who was a friend of Ram's gave them a guided tour of the Sphinx and the surrounding temple areas.

After lunch they had gone to the Cairo museum to see the displays there, primarily the Tut collection. Ram and Meri had a full evening planned, so they had returned to the hotel to rest. Ram had insisted that Meri nap, so Welcome, Wade, and Shark decided to hang around the pool, sip cool drinks, and do a few laps.

The sun block tube made a loud burp as Wade squirted it on his belly. Shark rose up and frowned pointedly at Wade.

"The tube's empty," Wade said.

"I have more in my room," Welcome told him. "I'll run upstairs and get it."

"Want me to go?"

"Nope. Enjoy your Stella beer and doze. I know exactly where it is. I'll be back in a shake." She slipped on a robe and hurried into the hotel.

He didn't argue much. Fact was, he could use a few more z's. He hadn't had a decent night's sleep in awhile. "I need to get something from my room too," he heard Shark say. Wade mumbled a reply as his big toe twitched twice, and he could feel himself drifting off.

Welcome got on the elevator and inserted the key for the top floor, which was accessible only to the Gabrey family and their guests. She had misplaced her keys earlier. Sure that she'd put them in her jacket pocket, she was afraid that they had fallen out during their jaunt, but after she searched her suite, she'd found them on the bathroom counter and breathed a sigh of relief. After her broken nail incident, she must have laid them on the counter instead of putting them in her pocket.

The fact was, Welcome was still jumpy.

As soon as the elevator door opened, she hurried down the hall to her room and unlocked the door. She had started toward the armoire in her bedroom for the spare tube of sun block when she stopped abruptly.

The roses.

Her bouquet of roses had been mangled. Yellow petals had been ripped from the stems and crushed on her bed; the vase was smashed.

Lipstick letters slashed across her dresser mirror the words: DIE BITCH.

Her fist stifled a scream. She started to shake all over. Dear God, was the person who did this still in her room?

She was about to turn and flee when someone grabbed her from behind.

Thirty

Those whom God wishes to destroy, he first makes mad.

Euripides
c. 485-406 B.C.

"Bitch! *Salope!*" The words hissed against her ear dripped with venom. "Die, bitch!"

Strong hands closed around her throat, and Welcome screamed.

She wasn't going down easy.

Biting and kicking and scratching, she fought the assailant behind her with everything that was in her. The constriction tightened, and she gasped for breath, clawing at the attacker's hands. Her thoughts cried Wade's name over and over.

Her field of vision burst red, then blue-black, and she knew she was losing.

Abruptly, the hands left her throat, and she heard Wade's voice. "Run, dammit, run." Through blurry eyes, she saw Wade struggling to act as a barrier between her and the enraged intruder behind him. "Run, darlin'. Hurry. Get help."

She staggered through the suite, crashing into tables as she went, trying to scream but able to do no more than utter a pathetic bleat. At last she made it to the door and flung it open.

"Help! Help!" she croaked, fearing that she would collapse at any minute.

"Welcome! What's—"

"Shark. Oh, thank God, Shark. Help Wade. Man tried to . . . to strangle me. In my room. Hurry!"

Shark took off, and holding on to a hall table, she sank to her knees, coughing, gasping. She heard shouting and a scuffle, but she was too weak to move another step.

In a few minutes she saw Shark dragging a prone man by the pants legs from her room. The man was unconscious . . . or dead. Either way he was going to have one hell of a nose burn from the carpet. Shark wasn't gentle as he pulled her attacker into the hall and dropped his legs with a *thunk* just as the elevator door opened.

Wade charged out of the elevator, wild-eyed and bellowing her name like Stanley Kowalski.

"I'm here," she rasped. "Pipe down. You're giving me a headache with all your yelling."

He knelt beside her. "My God! Are you hurt?"

"Of course I'm hurt. Somebody tried to strangle me." Suddenly it hit her. She looked from Wade to the elevator to Shark who stood with his foot on the back of her assailant. "How'd you get in the elevator?"

"The usual way. Let me see your throat. Dammit, I'm going to kill that sonofabitch with my bare hands." He jumped up and strode to where Shark stood.

"You ought to wait till he comes to good before you kill him," Shark said.

The man on the floor groaned and stirred just as Ram came from his suite. "Is something going on out here?"

Shark pointed to the man under his size fourteen.

"This piece of shit just tried to choke Welcome in her room. And somebody—him, I guess—tore up her flowers and wrote stuff on the mirror with lipstick."

"Just like in Athens," Wade said. "Bastard." He kicked the prostrate man in the ribs and went back to Welcome. "Get a doctor up here for her." Gathering her in his arms, he strode to a nearby couch and sat down with her in his lap. "Shhh, darlin'."

Ram picked up a phone in the hall and spoke briefly. "Security will be right here," he said. "And a doctor." He stripped a tie-back cord from a drapery and tossed it to Shark. "Tie him up."

While Shark tied the man's hands, Ram took a handful of the moaning man's hair and lifted his head to see his face. "My God! It's Eduard Moreau."

Welcome stiffened, then sat up. *"Eduard?* You can't be serious," she croaked.

" 'Fraid so," Ram said.

"I didn't think the little putz had it in him."

"Who's Eduard Moreau?" Wade asked.

The elevator opened and a half-dozen men poured into the hall to take charge of the prisoner who had roused and was cursing loudly. As the security men dragged Eduard toward the elevator, Welcome stood and walked toward him. Wade stayed by her side.

"Why, Eduard?" she rasped. "Why did you do this?"

Eduard's dark eyes blazed. "Is he the one?" His contemptuous gaze raked Wade. "Is this . . . this crude American, this *foutu satyre,* the one you preferred over me?"

"What do you mean? I only met Wade a few days ago."

"Lying bitch. I offer you my name, my fortune. I defy my family for you, and you fling my love in my face. You prefer this . . . this football player. *Merde!"*

He sneered and spat on the floor. "God damn you both."

"Take the bastard downstairs," Ram said, "and turn him over to the police. I'll be there directly."

The security men dragged him away cursing Welcome alternately in English and in French.

Her knees sagged, and Wade caught her to him.

"Dear God," she whispered. "He's completely mad."

Groggy from the shot the doctor had given her, Welcome was installed in Wade's bed, an ice bag on her throat and two bottles of medicine on the nightstand. Meri and Shark sat in nearby chairs looking worried. Wade paced and looked worried. Ram was still downstairs speaking with the police.

"I—I don't understand," Welcome rasped, her voice still hoarse.

Meri patted her hand. "Neither do I, but Ram will get it all sorted out. You go to sleep now. Rest."

"Exactly who is Eduard Moreau?" Wade asked.

Welcome meant to answer Wade's question, but she couldn't gather the energy to speak.

When Welcome awoke, Wade lay beside her. Sound asleep atop the covers, he still wore his swimsuit and a knit shirt. Because the room was dim from the heavy draperies, she couldn't tell if it was night or day, so she glanced at the red numbers of the digital clock. Seven-thirty. She must have been asleep for two or three hours.

Wade stirred and raised his head. "How do you feel?"

"Kind of muzzy-headed. Thirsty." Her voice still sounded raspy.

He jumped up. "Here, I'll get you some water." He poured a glass from a bottle on the table.

She winced as she swallowed.

"Throat still sore?" he asked.

"Yes. But I'm starved. I'm glad I awoke in time for dinner."

Wade smiled. "Sorry, sugar, but you woke in time for breakfast. You slept through dinner. It's morning. Want me to order some food for you?"

She nodded and tried to get up, noting that she wore only the bottom of her bikini. Her knees were rubbery, and she sat back down on the side of the bed. "What did that doctor give me?"

"I don't know but you went out like a light. Need some help?"

"No, I can make it. Just give me a minute."

She rose and took a few steps, then swayed. Wade lunged and grabbed her. She waved him away, determined to make it to the bathroom under her own power. It wasn't easy, but she made it.

When she saw herself in the mirror, she was shocked. Not only did her mop of hair look like a wild woman's, but her throat was darkly bruised.

"That bastard!" she muttered. Never in a million years would she have suspected Eduard of doing something like he did. Had he been behind the harassment and attempts on her life in Athens? But what about Chroni? A dozen questions swirled in her head. She shook them off and washed her face.

A few minutes later, with her hair tied up and wearing a caftan, Welcome was having breakfast in bed. Wade was having his own breakfast with Shark at a nearby table, and Ram and Meri sat in chairs beside the bed. Swallowing was difficult, but Welcome managed to eat most of a poached egg and a bowl of oatmeal.

When Welcome winced after a bite, Meri said, "Oh you poor baby," and looked so distraught that Welcome tried her darnedest not to show any discomfort.

Welcome put her spoon down, patted her lips with the napkin, and said, "Okay, I've finished. Now, Ram, will you tell me about Eduard?" Meri had refused to let Ram say a word until she had finished her breakfast.

"Moreau should have kept quiet, but according to my men who went to the police station with him, he raved like a madman and spilled his guts. From what I've been able to piece together with J.J. and others, Eduard was furious that you had turned down his proposal and were leaving Paris. He was convinced that there was another man, and he followed you. I get the impression that he tried to kill you in Paris after he saw you with a man at a café."

"My God, the car that almost hit me! But it was only Philip Van Horn that he saw me talking to. Surely he didn't think—"

"Apparently he did," Ram said.

"Do you suppose that it was Eduard who ran down Philip?"

Ram shrugged. "That I don't know. But Eduard followed you to Athens, stalked you."

"But I don't understand," Welcome said. "I thought Chroni— Then who tried to kill me?"

"Both of them. Two men were after you. It was Eduard who sent the roses and made at least some of the harassing phone calls. From his handiwork here, we can assume that he's the one who destroyed the flowers and wrote on your mirror in Athens as well."

Puzzled, Welcome said, "Wrote on my mirror?"

Wade cleared his throat. "We didn't mention that to you. Shark saw it when he checked your room."

"How did Eduard know that I was here?"

"We're not sure," Ram said. "Perhaps he assumed

that you would come here after you left Athens. We found a key to the elevator and to your room on him. Somehow he copied your keys at some time or another."

"That's what happened to them," Welcome said. She explained about missing them after she went to the gift shop. "Who shot at me in Athens?" she asked.

"We're not sure, but probably it was Moreau. Chroni preferred to use a knife."

Welcome shuddered. "Thank God Eduard is a lousy shot. And thank God for Wade and Shark yesterday afternoon. In another few seconds I would have been a goner if Wade hadn't pulled him off me."

"Darlin', much as I'd like to take credit for rescuing you, I can't. It was Shark who punched out the guy."

"I know that," she said. "I saw him drag Eduard out of my room. But I meant before that. I was almost unconscious when you pulled him away and told me to run and get help. When I opened the door to my room, that's when I saw Shark."

There was an awkward silence.

Finally Wade said, "Honey, I was sound asleep down by the pool. An attendant woke me up because I was raising such a ruckus. Having a nightmare, I guess. All I know is that I woke up knowing you were in trouble and beat it upstairs as fast as I could. When I got there, it was all over."

"I remember seeing you get off the elevator, but . . ."

"When I got there," Shark said, looking up from his plate, "wasn't nobody in your room but that Frenchy."

"But—"

Meri patted Welcome's hand. "Don't worry about it. With all the trauma that you've been through, I'm not surprised that things seem confused."

"Meri," Welcome said sharply, "please don't patronize me. I know damned well what I heard and what I saw. I couldn't have gotten loose from Eduard without help. I tried."

There was another painful silence.

Meri looked hurt and was trying not to.

"Oh hell, Meri, I'm sorry I was cross." Welcome held out her arms to her best friend, and they hugged. "Now everybody out. I want to get dressed."

"Get dressed?" Wade said. "What for?"

"Because we're going to Memphis this morning."

"Memphis?" Shark asked. "They got a Memphis in Egypt, too?"

"Memphis is out," Wade said. "You need to rest."

"I agree," Meri said. "Don't you, Ram?"

Welcome glared at Ram, and he chuckled. "I wouldn't touch that one with a ten-foot pole."

"Been to Memphis, Tennessee, and to Memphis, Florida," Shark said.

"Memphis, Florida?" Meri said. "I've never heard of it."

"Just south of Tampa. Wouldn't mind going to Memphis, Egypt, myself," Shark said, grinning devilishly.

"Thank you, Shark," Welcome said. "Maybe you and I can go alone."

"Like hell."

They spent the morning sightseeing at both Memphis and Sakkara on the condition that they return to the hotel for lunch and siesta.

Truthfully, Welcome was glad to see her bed again. She'd have sooner been staked on a fire ant bed than to admit it, but trudging over rocky ground in the hot sun had taken its toll on her.

Meri had clucked over her like a mother hen, and Wade was almost as bad, she thought as she went into the bathroom in her suite. She untied the scarf that hid her bruises and splashed water on her face.

After repairing her makeup, she retied the scarf and started for Meri and Ram's suite where a private lunch was being served in their huge dining room. But her big bed looked awfully inviting. She glanced at her watch and saw that she had ten minutes to spare.

She would rest for just a couple of minutes.

Wade stuck his head in again. She was still asleep. Quietly, he eased away and went through the connecting door to his suite. Bad as he hated to, he needed to call Barney and let him know that he wouldn't be on the plane to L.A. in the morning. Armoring himself for the tirade, he dialed Barney's home number.

A voice mumbled, "Hello."

"Barney, Wade. Aren't you up yet?"

"Up? It's five fucking o'clock in the morning. Who gets up at five fucking o'clock in the morning? Where the hell are you?"

"In Cairo."

Barney let loose with a string of invectives. "I told you to forget Cairo. If you don't get your ass back here right now, you can forget signing with the Vulcans. Word's out they're talking with Jimmy Joe Webster."

"I thought the Dolphins had Webster sewed up."

"He may come unraveled if the price is right. He hasn't signed with anybody yet. You need to be here *now*, Wade. My best guess is that if you haven't signed in the next twenty-four hours, by Monday, Jimmy Joe's wife will be calling Bekins, and you can kiss your football career good-bye."

Wade's stomach knotted, and sweat popped out on his upper lip. He had a feeling that this time Barney was telling the truth.

Thirty-one

Love distills desire upon the eyes,
love brings bewitching grace into the heart . . .
I pray that love may never come to me with murderous
    intent,
in rhythms measureless and wild.

Euripides
c. 485-406 B.C.

When Welcome jolted awake, she sat up and glanced at the clock. Dear God, she'd slept for two hours.

"You missed lunch," Wade said, smiling as he looked up from the magazine in his lap. He was stretched out in an easy chair across the room. "It was real good."

"I hope there's some left. I'm hungry."

"Yep. Meri fixed a tray for you with explicit instructions. I'm to microwave the soup for two minutes and take the other stuff out of the refrigerator. Ready to eat?"

"You bet. I think being around Shark has increased my appetite."

While Wade fixed her lunch, Welcome retired to the bathroom to freshen up. When she returned, her lunch was waiting in the sitting room.

"Sorry I zonked out," she said.

He smiled. "You're entitled."

"How does going to the bazaar this afternoon sound to you? It's a great place to visit, and they have everything under the sun for sale there, but the place is a horrendous maze. Even Meri still gets lost sometimes, but Ram can guide us around. I know that Shark would love—"

"Darlin', could we skip the bazaar?"

"Well, sure. I suppose so. But if you're concerned about me, don't be. I feel great. My throat is much better."

"That's not the reason. I mean, of course I'm concerned about you, but I'd rather spend some time alone with you. I know you want to be with your friends, but Shark and I have to leave for L.A. first thing in the morning. Business. I tried to put it off, but I can't. I have to go."

Welcome felt as if she'd been punched in the stomach. She knew that he would have to leave soon; he'd told her that. But she found that she wasn't prepared for their affair to end so soon. "You can't stay for one more day?"

He shook his head. "Sorry."

Her appetite fled, and she laid down her spoon. She wanted to cry.

"Baby, don't look at me like that. It tears my heart out. It's not as if we were never going to see each other again. I'm just going to L.A. for a couple of days to sign my contract and take care of a few—"

"What contract?"

"My new three-year contract with the Vulcans."

"You're signing for *three* years?"

He grinned. "Yep. And the terms make me one of the highest paid quarterbacks in the game. Not bad for an old horse like me."

"What happens if you don't sign?"

"Then I'm out. I guess that I'd have to take that TV

offer. Don't worry, sugar. I'd be able to support you in style either way."

"What TV offer?" she demanded.

"I have a couple of options. One is an acting role on a proposed series for NBC, the other is with FOX sports. Both of them are sweet deals. How do you think you'd like being married to a big TV star?" he asked with a cocky grin.

"Not worth a damn."

He laughed. "You don't have to worry about it for three years at least. I'm going to sign with the Vulcans."

"That's worse," she mumbled. "Wade, if you continue to play football or do anything on TV, you'll have to live in a fishbowl for the rest of your life."

He shrugged. "Comes with the territory. I've gotten used to it."

The more he talked, the more Welcome realized that there could be nothing permanent between them. She was so weary of living under public scrutiny that the idea of continuing that kind of life totally repulsed her.

Not even for Wade could she consider it. She couldn't. It was eroding her soul.

Their time together in Greece and here were a fantasy. A lovely fantasy away from the reality of his fame. But she'd learned from others exactly how popular he was in the States. A life with him would mean having to endure women throwing themselves at him. They wouldn't be able to go to a restaurant without people gawking or hounding him for autographs, and she would have to always be "on." Their personal life would be tabloid news.

No. No way. She was walking away from her own life like that; she wasn't going to take up his. Nor was she going to start bawling like a kid about it.

C'est la guerre.

She pasted a bright smile on her face. "Then we'll just have to make the most of our last day together."

"You make it sound like a final farewell. Darlin', I'm not going off to war or saying good-bye forever. I'm just going to L.A. for a couple of days. Believe me, I wouldn't go if I didn't have to. I can come back if you're going to stay here in Egypt for a while, or you can come to California."

She evaded the issue by saying, "But it will be our last day together . . . for a while. What would you like to do?"

He chuckled and gave her a pointed look.

"Besides that? We can't spend the entire time in bed."

"Can't we?"

An idea struck her. Welcome smiled and dialed Meri's suite. After she spoke briefly and quietly on the phone, she hung the "Do Not Disturb" sign on the door. Wade unplugged the phone.

She picked up a cluster of grapes from her tray, kissed his chin, took his hand, and said, "Come with me."

"Where are we going?"

"How long since you've had a truly decadent bath?"

"Truly decadent? I can't remember ever having one."

She smiled. "Then it's time you did."

She opened a door across the sitting room from the one that connected to his suite and led him into a small foyer. She opened another door and led him into another world.

Ram had recreated for Meri the luxurious lotus pool bath from their home in Luxor. But instead of being in a secluded spot alongside the Nile, this one was atop the hotel and one entire wall was a special kind of privacy glass. They could look out at a panorama of the Sphinx and the pyramids in the desert or glance upward to see a canopy of stars from the skylighted dome at night.

The air of the garden room was redolent with the fragrance of scented oils and exotic flowers, a mysterious mixture of spices and a hint of luscious rare fruit. Urns of papyrus reeds and small trees surrounded the small pool lined with colorful mosaic tiles in Moorish patterns. Lotus blossoms floated on the water.

"Ho-ly moly," Wade said, taking in the huge vibrant murals on the walls that depicted life in ancient Egypt. "This place is something else."

"Isn't it? It's ours for as long as we want it."

"That's a big bathtub," Wade said, eyeing the lotus pool.

She laughed. "That's not the bathtub. This is the bathtub." She pulled him past a blossoming tree to where a waterfall splashed into a smaller pool sectioned off from the other by a mosaic wall.

"Looks like a spa to me."

"Ram calls it a bathtub." She laid the grape cluster on a ledge by the cascading water.

"This is part of his and Meri's private quarters?"

"Um-hmm. But they've gone out with Shark." Her eyes captured his, and she slowly began to unbutton her blouse.

Wade began to slowly unbuttoned his shirt.

Blouse and shirt dropped to the floor.

She took off her sandals.

He took off his loafers.

With their gazes still locked, she unzipped her slacks; he unzipped his. The noise ripped through the quiet room.

Off came two pairs of slacks.

She unclasped her bra and tossed it aside.

He grinned. "You got me."

Laughing, she looked at his feet. "You might try your socks."

"Good idea." Off came the socks. He hooked his thumbs in his shorts and glanced up. Her panties were already gone.

She smiled. "I won."

"I didn't know that it was a contest."

"We're playing follow the leader. Want to play again?" She turned and went down the stone and tile steps into the water. She sat on a ledge so that the gently bubbling water rippled over the top swell of her breasts.

Wade ripped off his shorts and quickly followed to sit beside her.

Fragrant with the faint scent of lotus, citrus, and sandlewood oils, the warm water lapped sensuously against their skin and covered them with a dewy sheen that sparkled in the afternoon sun like diamond dust. Filtered sunlight from the skylight cast leafy patterns on the water and glinted off their hair, catching the gold in his and turning hers into crackling fire.

He reached for her, and she playfully slapped his hands. "I'm the leader, remember?"

She picked up the cluster of grapes, plucked one, and offered it to him. He nipped it from her fingers. She laughed and fed him another, moving closer to straddle his lap. When she fed him a third grape, he bit it in half and the juice ran down her fingers.

The scent triggered an array of sudden intense emotions that sucked her breath and froze her movements. A love for this man, so deep and so profound that it defied definition, sprang forth and engulfed her senses.

For a moment they were suspended in time. Through the corridors of the ages, she could hear his laughter—his, but not his; she could see his face—his, but not his. She could feel his love like a palpable thing, always the same—boundless, vital, eternal.

"We have done this before," she whispered.

"I know." He licked the juice from her hand and sucked her fingertips. "Oh, God, how I love you," he moaned, the words rising from the depths of his soul. He pulled her as close to him as possible and trailed kisses over her face. "I think I must have always loved you. Always. Where have you been for so long?"

"Waiting for you," she murmured against his mouth. She could taste the grapes as his tongue touched hers, and the sweetness was as heady as fine aged wine.

He took a grape, crushed it, and rubbed the juice over her throat. "I would heal these awful bruises to your tender skin." He kissed and licked her neck, his lips and tongue as gentle as the stroke of swan's down. "And slay the bastard who put them there."

" 'Twas not the first time. Where were you then?"

"You mean the sonofabitch hurt you before?"

The viciousness of his tone jarred Welcome from her state of semi-reverie. "Before?"

Anger had hardened the rugged planes of his face. "Had Eduard ever hurt you before yesterday?"

She shook her head. "He never so much as raised his voice to me. I was shocked at his behavior. But I don't want to talk about that now. I never want to think about him again." She kissed the furrows of his brow, popped a grape in his mouth, and teased the tiny scar on his chin with her tongue.

He plucked another, crushed it, and rubbed the juice on her nipples. She had never felt or watched anything so sensual as when he licked away the vestiges of the fruit while his fingers worked wonderful magic beneath the bubbling water.

"Like that?" he murmured when she moaned and moved against his hand.

"Mmmmm. But there's something I would like better."

"Me, too."

He eased into her slowly, then stood and laid her back so that her head and body floated atop the water to the point where they joined. The warm, scented water bubbled and brushed against her skin; the cooler air kissed her nipples and belly; his eyes devoured her. With their hands interlocked and their gazes linked, he began to thrust.

Sunlight bathed his muscled body, glinted off the water droplets, and turned him into a golden Poseidon rising from the sea. She twined her legs around him and moved in rhythmic counterpoint to his thrusts.

Thought fled. She was plunged into pure sensation. Water. Fire.

Fragrant, sensual, moving water.

Blazing, burning, consuming fire.

She flung herself into the fire and burst into a kaleidoscope of sparkling color, floating on the ethers, pulsating to the music of the planets as they turned on their axes.

When the heat was spent, she came into his arms and clung to him. How could she ever let this man go?

"Stay with me," she whispered. "Don't leave me. Please. Please."

He groaned. "Oh, darlin', don't. You break my heart. I have to go."

She sighed. "I know."

It was her heart that broke.

Thirty-two

*Knowledge must come through action; you can have
no test which is not fanciful, save by trial.*

Sophocles
c. 495-405 B.C.

They laughed and talked and loved for hours, stop
ping only to order food from room service. Scores of
times, Wade had told her that he loved her. Only once
had he wrung the whispered words from her.

Sometime in the wee hours they had snatched a
brief period of sleep. Wade had awakened her at dawn
with murmured words of love and kisses to her belly.
When she stroked his hair, he'd raised his head and
looked at her with such tenderness that the words
slipped out before she could stop them.

He stopped dead still. "What did you say?"

"You heard me."

"Say it again."

"I love you."

"Thank God," he said, laying his cheek in the hol
low beneath her breast bone. "I thought maybe this
was a one-way thing."

"No." She threaded her fingers through his wavy
hair, lifted her hand slowly, and let the springy strands
slip away. Over and over she repeated the action, sa

voring the thickness and texture, aching to close her fingers and clutch a handful of his hair. She wanted to shake him and scream at him and demand that he stay with her.

An exhortation deep inside prevented her from telling him plainly that he must choose—between her and the lifestyle he chased after. Before she had doubted her own motives, wondering if this was a test of her love, wondering if her selfishness would keep them apart. Now she knew that wasn't the case.

This was a decision that he must make, a critical judgment for him—and not just because of their relationship. It was something bigger, more profound. She didn't understand all of the ramifications, but she knew how very crucial this time was. Just as she knew that the choice was his to make, and it must be made freely.

"What style of furniture do you prefer?" Wade asked.

She laughed. "Where did that come from?"

"I was just thinking about my house. I don't know much about furniture styles—a decorator handled it—but it's kind of modern and maybe too masculine for your taste. But after we're married, you can toss everything out and start over if it doesn't suit you. Hell, we can buy a whole new house if you want to."

Her hand stilled against his hair. "And where would this house be?"

"In California, of course. Maybe we could move to Malibu. You like the—"

With two fingers to his lips, she halted his words. "Wade, I haven't said that I would marry you, or live with you in California. Don't make that assumption."

He sat up, took her chin, and kissed her gently. "Sorry, sugar. I forgot that women like things a little more romantic. I wish that I had a big diamond ring and violins playing right now, but I don't. I can only say: I love you with all my heart. Will you marry me?" He smiled brightly, waiting for her answer.

"No."

"*No?* Shit! I screwed it up, didn't I? You wanted th‹
ring and candlelight and all that. Next time I'll do i
right, honey. I'll—"

The phone rang.

"Shit! Who the hell is that?" Wade snatched up th‹
receiver and barked, "This better be good." After a fev
seconds, he said, "Right. I'll meet you outside in twent
minutes." After he hung up, he turned to Welcome
"Time got away from me. That was Shark. We have t‹
leave for the airport in twenty minutes to catch our fligh
home. You stay in bed and snooze. I have to pack an‹
jump in the shower." He kissed her, then rose.

Welcome threw back the covers as well. "I couldn"
go back to sleep now. You shower. I'll pack for you
Pick out what you'll be wearing home."

After he went into the bathroom, she rose an‹
pulled on her caftan. Taking his luggage from th‹
closet, she began to pack his things. His scent clun‹
to every article of clothing she touched, and her throa
began to ache with building tears as she remembered
that he wore this shirt the first time she saw him ir
the taverna, this one in Delphi, that one the first nigh
that they made love aboard the *Ionna*.

When she was done, she went into the bathroom
Dressed in his shoes and pants, he was bare-cheste‹
except for a towel around his neck as he shaved. Sh‹
lifted herself onto the counter to sit and watch him
He winked into the mirror and continued to rake awa
foam and beard, then slosh his razor in the sink. Th‹
last row of soap disappeared, and he wiped his face
then splashed on after-shave.

Welcome would never forget that aroma. Forever sh‹
would think of his arms, his body, his lovemaking wher
she smelled it. The blended fragrance of the after-shav‹
and his distinctive male scent was imprinted on her soul

Clasping her knees to her chin, her eyes devoure‹

er last glimpses of him as he tucked in his shirt and brushed his hair. He was so handsome, so dear.

As soon as he zipped his shaving kit, she picked it up and hugged it against her. Struggling with tears, she said quietly, "I don't want you to leave me."

"Aw, honey." He took her shoulders and kissed her. "I wish I didn't have to go either."

When one of the tears that she'd fought so valiantly against, escaped and trickled down her cheek, he winced as if he'd been knifed in the gut.

Dear God, she hated being such a weenie!

She turned away quickly and went to stow the shaving kit in the space she'd left for it. Be damned if she was going to cry over a man who preferred a football and screaming fans to her!

Clamping her teeth together, she zipped his garment bag and set it by the door beside his other small piece of luggage. When she returned, he was at the dresser fastening his watch. He scooped up loose change and other small objects to put into his pockets, pulled on his sport coat, and tucked his wallet inside.

He heaved a big sigh. "I guess that it's time."

She nodded.

He put his arm around her waist and together they walked to the door. "Honey," he said, taking her hand, "I may not have the diamond engagement ring or the violins, but I have this. It means a lot to me." He took off his big Super Bowl ring and laid it on her palm. "Maybe until I can manage something better, we can at least go steady." He grinned.

She didn't appreciate the humor. Looking down at the gaudy thing she held, the modern day version of a laurel leaf crown, her heart hardened. "I don't think so." She glanced up and gazed deeply into his haunting eyes. "The road forks here."

"What are you talking about?"

Laying her hand against his cheek, she said, "It's

very simple. Life is about choices, and we've come t‹
a fork in the road. You're taking one path, and I'ɾ
taking another. Good-bye, love."

He clutched her to him. "Don't talk like that, daɾ
lin'. I don't know what you're getting at half of th
time, but talk like that scares the hell out of me. Jus
let me go schmooze with the front office boys and sigɾ
this contract, and I'll be back. I swear to God, I wiʜ
Two or three days, four at the most. We'll take one c
those romantic cruises up the Nile you were telling m‹
about. Or we'll go back to Hydra. Yeah, we'll go bac
to Hydra." He kissed her fiercely.

As she kissed him one last time, she slipped his riɾ
in his coat pocket.

There was a knock at the door.

"That'll be Shark," Wade said.

She nodded.

"Thank Meri and Ram again for us."

She nodded a second time, refusing to beg him onc
more to stay. Instead, she forced a smile and said gaiʜ
"See you in the funny papers, sugarplum."

A quick kiss, and he was gone.

Leaning her forehead against the closed door, sh
stood in the thunderous silence for an eternity of mc
ments, trying to control her emotions, trying to draʋ
a breath past the constriction in her chest.

She understood it all now, for she had dreamt iɾ
those few hours that they had slept. The love and th
pain of a lifetime over two thousand years ago were a
fresh as this morning's roses. He had made his choic
then; he had made the same choice again.

He had missed his opportunity. He had abandone‹
her for adulation and a laurel leaf crown.

The ache in her heart was almost beyond endurance
She grieved for herself, and she grieved for him.

But she would not die of it this time.

Welcome Venable was made of stronger stuff.

Thirty-three

Every advantage in the past is judged in the light of the final issue.

Demosthenes
c. 384-322 B.C.

Welcome and Meri sat at the huge dining table in the Gabrey's suite with stacks of proof sheets scattered over its surface.

"Some of these are outstanding," Meri said.

"I'm surprised that they turned out so well, especially those at the Acropolis. The way J.J. had us running around, we hardly had time to do more than take a few snapshots."

"Well, Solo did a great job. She's an excellent photographer."

A door slammed. "Meri!" Ram called.

"We're in the dining room, Ram."

When he came in and made a bee line for Meri, touching her shoulder and kissing her cheek with such tremendous and obvious love, a potent and unreasonable resentment flashed over Welcome. She was immediately ashamed of her envy, but her shame didn't diminish the feeling.

Ram Gabrey would no more have abandoned Meri than he would have sprouted wings and flown to China.

Hurt and anger snarled inside her, clawing at he stomach until it burned with bitter bile. Granted sh was hurt and angry with Wade, but she was just as a gry with herself. She'd known better than to hook u with someone like him, but hardheaded, she hadn listened. Now she had no one to blame but herself.

Meri touched Welcome's arm. "Isn't that right?"

"Sorry, my mind wandered. What did you say?"

"I was telling Ram that I thought that the Gree photos were great, and that we have plenty for th brochure. I can get started on it next week."

"Oh. Right."

"I have a bit of news," Ram said. "I understand fro J.J. that a woman was found dead at the GB in Ather yesterday. Strangled."

Welcome shuddered. "Who was she?"

"The hotel operator. She was found in a supp closet on the sixth floor. A maid had last seen th woman with a man who was described as resemblin Eduard Moreau. The same man, who disappeare from Athens shortly afterward, also had a room on th same floor as yours."

"The poor woman." Welcome shuddered agair hugging herself and rubbing her arms. "Dear God, t think that he might have been so close all that tim Are they sure that it was Eduard?"

"Fairly certain. He used an alias, of course, but th Athens police are checking his fingerprints now."

"I'm still shocked that Eduard did the things tha he did. He truly must be insane."

"Obsessed is more like it. Most stalkers are. A batter of attorneys and several representatives from th French embassy have been trying to secure his r lease," Ram said.

Meri's eyes widened. "Surely they're not going to l him go!"

Ram grinned. "Not likely. My family and the chief of police have been friends for a very long time. In fact, I believe that my father is his distant cousin."

"Thanks, Ram," Welcome said.

"Don't mention it. With his attempt on your life here, and now this new development in Athens, Moreau will be locked away for a very long time. When you two tire of your pictures, I'll take you to lunch at the Automobile Club." He kissed the top of Meri's head and left.

"You're very happy, aren't you, Meri?"

"Extremely. But you're not very happy, are you?"

Welcome shook her head. "No, my friend, I've got a bad case of the miseries."

"Wade?"

"Yep."

"Want to talk about it?"

With no more prodding than that, the whole story spilled out of Welcome. "While I know that this latest episode seems even more strange than the others, it makes sense."

"He blew it, didn't he?"

"He blew it big time."

"But you still love him?"

"Of course I love him," Welcome said. "But my love isn't enough, wasn't enough."

"Have you considered biting the bullet and going to California for a while? He can't keep playing football forever. For a quarterback, he's already considered an old man at thirty-seven."

"Of course I've thought about it. I've made myself sick thinking about it, but I can't do it for several reasons. I long for privacy, for a quiet, ordinary life. I couldn't have that if I became part of Wade's world, and sooner or later I'd grow to resent it and blame him. Too, and maybe even more important, the debt, the lesson, the karma if you want to call it that, is his, not mine. He made the vow, and he broke it. The atonement must be his."

"Have you talked to Wade about this?"

"No. I didn't want to influence his decision. If he gave up his career because of my forcing him to, he would end up as bitter and resentful as I would have. He's so hell-bent on following the same proud path that it hasn't even occurred to him that he's on the wrong road. It's best that it ends now."

Meri hugged her. "I'm so sorry. You deserve all the happiness in the world. Tell you what," Meri said, suddenly brightening, "let's go eat about a gallon of prawns at the Automobile Club, then we'll come back here and paint each other's toenails, just like old times."

Welcome laughed. "You're on."

Although Meri and Ram tried to keep lunch light and gay, Welcome could see that, with her lousy mood, it was a struggle. She just couldn't hold up her end of things. When they returned to the Horus, Welcome decided that it was time to go on home to Texas.

Despite Meri's urging otherwise, she booked an evening flight to Dallas.

The time had come to lick her wounds and get on with her new life.

Wade was deeply troubled. He didn't know the cause of his distress, but he felt it clear to his bones. Shifting and twisting, he tried to get comfortable in his big first-class seat, but he couldn't.

Something was wrong. Bad wrong. But he didn't know what. His first thought was Welcome, but she'd been fine when he'd left her a few hours ago.

Somewhere over the Atlantic, Wade had finally

drifted off to sleep thinking of Welcome, hoping to dream of her.

He wandered through the mist, calling her name, trying to detect her essence, but he couldn't find her traces. Frantic, he intensified his search, and when he discerned a faint glimmer very far away, he commenced in that direction.

An old man, dressed in a long gray robe and carrying a staff, barred his path. He tried to go around the old man, but he raised his staff and made it impossible to pass.

"Who are you?" he demanded of the graybeard. "Why do you hinder my endeavors?"

"I am called Kairos," the old one said, "and I come not to hinder but to facilitate your greater journey."

"Then facilitate my journey by stepping aside."

"Not until I have my say," Kairos replied. "If you do not heed me now, we will not meet again for another two and a half millennia. She will be lost to you until then. Or perhaps forever, for she moves swiftly along her narrow path."

Panic filled him. "Lost to me?"

Kairos nodded.

Grabbing a handful of the old man's robe, he snarled, "You lie. We are pledged for eternity. We made vows."

"You broke those vows. Only her great love for you has brought me here a second time to give you another opportunity."

"You speak in riddles, old man."

"Come. See." Kairos turned and raised his staff. The mist parted, and a glade was revealed. In the midst of the glade was a crystal clear pool. "Look," the aged one said, dipping the crook of his staff in the water.

The water undulated, then stilled.

A scene slowly formed on the surface.

Astrid and Marco knelt before the temple flame, their gazes locked, their fingers intertwined. "I promise to love you for-ever," she said, "and to watch over you so long as I am able."

"And I you. I vow by all that is holy to stay always by your side and be your protector. No harm shall come to you while I draw human breath. I swear."

She poured wine upon the altar, and he set upon it a dish of olives and figs. The love between them was so powerful that the flame leapt to the ceiling with fuel from it, warming the depths of his soul and brightening the stars overhead.

"Do you remember this?" Kairos asked.

"I do," he whispered. "How could I forget so profound a love?"

"Look." Kairos touched his staff to the water again. The scene disappeared. In its place came not one but two displays. One of Astrid, one of Marco.

He watched as Marco competed in the games, watched as he became victorious, felt the triumph and the joy as the crown of leaves was placed on his head and citizens raised him to their shoulders. He reexperienced the wonderful exuberance of laughing and drinking with his companions and basking in his glory.

He glanced to the scene beside it. Astrid, while he celebrated and caroused, lived the life of a slave. Day after day, she drudged for the household of Phidias. He could feel her body's weariness of the work, of the tedium, experience her loneliness and her despair. He could feel too her hope, the hope that soon he would fulfill his promise and come for her.

Shame filled him. "I didn't know."

"Look," Kairos said, forcing his attention back to the pool.

Astrid was outside the portal listening to Phidias and a foreigner speaking. He felt her apprehension grow as she lis-tened, fearing that she would be sold and sent to someplace far away from Marco. He watched as she ran to the stadium and tried to gain entrance. He felt the heat of the sun on her tender skin as she waited all day on the stone, the heart-

*wrenching despair when she cried out Marco's name as men
carried him laughing and victorious to the temple.*

*The frivolous kiss he threw to her when she was in such
dire need, shamed him farther still.* "Oh, God," *he groaned
turning away from the piercing pain in her breast.*

"Look!" *Kairos demanded.*

His gaze went again to the pool.

*Astrid fell to her knees before Phidias, begging that she not
be sold and sent away. Her cries went unheeded. And while
Marco, short miles distant, drank wine with his companions
and laughed at the entertainment provided to the victors of
the Athens games, Astrid's wrists were bound and she was
dragged weeping to the foreigner's vessel.*

*While Marco trained to throw the javelin and joked with
his fellow athletes, she was carried to a distant land, her
heart breaking, her hope perishing.*

*When the death of her anguish hit him, he fell to his knees
and clutched his chest.* "I cannot endure it."

" *'Tis not the worst of it. Look!*"

*While he ran races and relished the feel of the wind against
his body, the foreigner offered Astrid silks and jewels to grant
her favors. She refused and ran away to hide among the
bushes in his fine garden, her chin trembling, her hands shaking.*

*Over and over the foreigner tried to entice her; over and
over she refused, crying out in her mind for Marco. His pa-
tience wearing thin and obsessed with his determination to
have her, the new master had her brought before him. He
demanded that she disrobe and lie with him on his cushioned
couch.*

"I cannot," *she said.* "I am promised to another."

"You are a slave," *the man sneered.* "Slaves can make no
such promises." *He pulled her against him, and when she
tried to resist, the foreigner struck her across the face.*

A roar of rage came from him, and he reached to strangle

the beast who dared harm Astrid, but his arm met only water. The scene shattered with the agitation of the pool.

"That time has passed," Kairos said. "You cannot attack painful memories as if they were flesh and blood. We are not finished here. Look again."

"I cannot endure her torment," he said.

"She endured it. Because of you, she endured it."

"Explain yourself, old man. Was it my fault that she was a slave? I did not sell her to that foreign monster. That was Phidias's doing."

Kairos appeared disgusted. "It was your doing. You did not keep your vow. Phidias would have bestowed her freedom a year before had you but petitioned him. The foreigner would never have laid eyes on her and become obsessed with her beauty and her spirit."

"But the year before I was training for Olympia."

"Ah, yes. Olympia. The games. You were victorious there. Look. See what you lost." Again Kairos dipped his staff into the crystal pool.

Horrified, he watched as the foreigner beat Astrid unmercifully and ravished her again and again. She screamed and begged and called Marco's name as she wept.

Falling to his knees, he cried out, "No more. Merciful God, no more."

"Look!" Kairos demanded.

Despairing to the depths of her soul, Astrid sobbed and gathered the remnants of her clothing about her. Bleeding and bruised, she dragged herself outside the house and hobbled to the crest of a cliff overlooking the sea. Gazing toward Athens, she cried his name to the wind, then jumped.

Her body crashed on the jagged rocks below.

"Noooo!" He could only beat his fists against his thighs and stare in shock at the scene before him. Astrid, his Astrid lay dead, and his heart felt as if it had been ripped from his chest and trod upon. As the wind and the sea washed over her, the sounds of children weeping echoed among the stones.

"Who weeps?"

"The children who would have been born to you," Kairos replied. *"They wait in vain again."*

"Not true, old man. Welcome and I will be married soon. They can come to us then."

The ancient one shook his head. *"She refused your offer. Did you not hear her? Did you not listen?"*

Stunned, he stared at Kairos. *"But she loves me. She told me so."*

"Aye. Yet loving you, she will not marry you while you pursue the path you follow, the path that caused her destruction when last you shared a lifetime. The suffering was too harsh, her atonement too intense."

"Her atonement? I do not understand."

"Taking one's life brings consequences, but we will not speak of those here. You owe her much. Would you have her for your own and rectify the wrongs you have wrought?"

"Yes! Yes! I'll do anything. I love her with all my heart and soul."

"Then you must choose."

"Choose? Explain yourself."

"You must choose. Games and glory . . . or her."

"But that is madness. Why choose when I can have both?"

"Once you could have had both, but no longer. Your moment of opportunity slips away swiftly. See the future if you do not choose wisely." He dipped his staff into the pool once again.

The water shimmered, then gave up two more parallel images. One was the smoldering wreckage of an airplane. The other was of Welcome standing before an altar with a tall, dark-haired man. She was beautiful, radiant in her bridal gown; the man looked at her with eyes full of adoration.

He cried out his anguish. *"No! She loves me. Me."*

"He waits to take your place in her heart. Hear me, son. I am Kairos. I will not linger long. Choose.

"Choose."

"Welcome! I choose Welcome!"

Wade jolted awake with Shark shaking him.

"Man, what's got into you? You been carrying on something awful. Folks are staring."

"Oh, my God! We've got to get off this plane. Now. I have to go back to Egypt, to Welcome."

Wade started to rise, but Shark pulled him back down into his seat. "You nuts? You can't get off this plane now. We're thousands of feet up in the air and over the middle of the ocean."

Wade sank back to his seat. His insides felt like a bucket of bees had been dumped in there, and his hands shook.

"It was Moreau!" Wade said. "Damn that bastard! I'll kill him for what he did to Astrid."

"Man, you talking crazy. Who's Astrid?"

"Welcome."

"That her real name? Astrid?"

"No."

"Man, you ain't makin' a lick of sense."

Wade raked his fingers through his hair. "I had a dream . . . a vision . . . maybe it was a nightmare."

"Must have been a ballbuster."

"You don't know the half of it." He dry-washed his face with his hands. "I'm going back, Shark. As soon as this plane lands in New York, I'm getting on the next available flight back to Cairo."

"But what about your contract with the Vulcans?"

"I'm not going to sign the contract. I'm retiring, Shark. Hell, I was getting too old for the game anyhow. If I have to choose between Welcome and busting my ass trying to win another Super Bowl ring, it's no contest. I'd rather have my woman and a couple of kids. I love her, Shark. More than anything in the world."

He nodded. "Figured you did. Barney's gonna have

a shit fit when he hears you're not going to be in L.A. to sign."

"He'll survive." Wade settled back into his seat and relaxed, feeling as if a two-ton weight had been lifted from his shoulders. "You going back with me?"

"Where you go, I go."

"From now on, where Welcome goes, I go. It might be to a ranch in Texas. You game?"

Shark shrugged and settled back in his seat too. "Always liked horses."

"Me, too."

"Wade, exactly what does *kairos* mean?"

"Where'd you hear that?"

"You were yelling it before I woke you up."

"It was the old guy's name in my dream. I don't know what it means."

"Excuse me," said a voice across the aisle. "Pardon me for eavesdropping, but I couldn't help but overhear your question. I can tell you the meaning of *kairos*."

Wade rose up and looked across at the speaker. An old gray-haired gent in a priest's collar nodded to him.

"*Kairos* is a Greek word. It means: the opportune and decisive moment, the exact time when conditions are right for accomplishing a crucial action. The moment of truth, so to speak."

Wade felt the hair on the back of his neck stand up as he watched the old priest and listened to him speak. Not only did his words have special meaning, but also something about him seemed familiar. *Very* familiar. "Thank you, sir."

The elderly man smiled and winked. "You're very welcome, my son. Good luck."

Thirty-four

One word
Frees us of all the weight and pain of life:
That word is love.

Sophocles
c. 495-405 B.C.

"*Gone?*" Wade said, raking his fingers through his already disheveled hair.

Meri Gabrey looked pained. "I'm afraid she is. Welcome left last night."

"But she can't be *gone*. I brought her these flowers." He held up a gigantic bouquet of mixed blossoms in a cellophane wrapper. "You can't imagine what we've been through to get here. And God knows where our luggage is. We got off the plane in New York and tried to catch the first flight back, but it wasn't due to leave for six hours, and it was already overbooked. We put our names on the standby list, and I took a cab into Manhattan to try to find Welcome an engagement ring. Damned if I wasn't nearly mugged by a gang of kids wearing Vulcan jackets and earrings on their lips. I had to show them my driver's license to prove who I was."

"Good Lord," she said. "Come in you two and sit down. You look exhausted. Let me fix you a drink."

"If it's all the same," Shark said, "I'd rather have a sandwich and walk around a little. We been sittin' a long time. We got here by way of Switzerland."

"We made it on that overbooked flight," Wade said, "but I had to pay two college kids a thousand bucks apiece to let me buy them a ticket on the next available flight to Cairo and give us their coach seats. I also promised them a free room at the Horus for a week. I hope to God that you have one available. Am I running off at the mouth? We haven't had much sleep. I sat next to a woman with two little kids, and one of them was teething or something. Poor kid cried a lot. And he threw up on me twice."

Shark wrinkled his nose. "You ain't telling me nothin' new. I been sittin' next to you."

Laughing Meri held up her hands. "Hold it. Why don't I give you your old rooms back. You can clean up, order some food, and get some rest. Then we can straighten things out."

"I'll vote for that," Shark said.

"Can't," Wade said. "I have to go after Welcome." He frowned. "Where did she go?"

"To Texas," Meri said.

Wade heaved a big sigh. "Then I've got to catch a plane to Texas."

"You won't be able to leave for hours. Shower, eat, rest. I'll make your reservations for Dallas."

"A shower and a shave would feel good," Wade said, rubbing his scratchy chin, "but I don't even have a razor or any clean clothes."

"Told you we shouldn't have checked everything through," Shark said.

"Don't worry about it," Meri said. "I'll call down to the gift shop. By the time you've eaten, everything you need will be delivered."

She walked out into the hallway with them just as

the elevator door opened and Ram stepped out with a mustachioed man in a tux who was carrying a violin case.

"I found this gentleman downstairs," Ram explained to Wade. "He said that he was hired to play for you."

Wade slapped his head. "Oh, God, I forgot about him." He handed Meri the big bunch of flowers, and dug out his wallet. He fished out a twenty and handed it to the violinist. "Sorry, the occasion is canceled."

"Somebody want to let me in on what's going on around here?" Ram asked.

Meri laughed. "I'll explain later. Wade and Shark are pooped."

"You got that right," Shark said. "And hungry."

Shark ate a cheeseburger with one hand and drove with the other as they headed the rented Lincoln down highway 175 toward Athens, Texas. "Man, that tastes good," he said, chomping down on another bite. "Don't know about you, but I was gettin' pretty tired of cucumbers and yogurt and stuff wrapped in leaves. Think I missed mayonnaise and mustard 'bout as much as I missed anything. Say, you not eatin' your fries."

"Too nervous. You eat them." Wade pulled the ring box from Tiffany's out of his pocket and opened it. "You think she'll like it?"

"I think the same thing I thought the last eighteen times you asked me. Rock like that? What's not to like?"

"You don't think it's too gaudy do you? She's a classy lady."

"No, I think it's just right. It's— What was it that saleslady at the jewelry store told you?"

"Elegant but tasteful."

"That's what I think too," Shark said. "Elegant but tasteful. You gonna drink the rest of that milkshake?"

"No. Here." He handed Shark his nearly full cup. "We have to turn up ahead. Do you remember the directions?"

"Like they was tattooed on my eyelids. We don't turn for another twenty miles. You gonna wear the hinge on that box out you don't keep it in your pocket."

"I'm nervous."

"I could tell."

Welcome spread the rust-colored flokati rug in front of the stone fireplace. Perfect. Just perfect. She knew that it would be. She only wished that it were cool enough to have a fire. But this time of year in Texas was almost summer. Even the nights were warm.

She went into the kitchen and poured a glass of lemonade from the pitcher in the fridge. Thelma had left the lemonade along with a chocolate cake and a jar full of oatmeal cookies when she left just after noon. Thelma and Paul Willis were the couple who looked after the ranch, and if Thelma kept feeding Welcome the way she had so far, in no time she would be a butterball.

Thelma and Paul had been good about keeping up the house and the barn and, with the help of a high school boy, looking after the few head of horses and cattle they kept. But if Welcome intended to make the place a real working ranch again, she would have to buy more stock and get more help.

But not for a while.

She was going to take a long time and do nothing. Just kick back and do nothing.

She walked through the house, touching a vase here and a book there, remembering the times when her

parents were around. Remembering a warmth and love
so strong that it permeated the walls and the old pine
floors and made her mother's potted plants grow fuller
than any of her neighbor's.

And laughter. There was always laughter. Sometimes
gentle chuckles. Sometimes loud guffaws. But always
laughter. She ran her thumb along the mouthpiece of
one of her father's favorite pipes and felt the nicks his
teeth had made on the stem.

The old house seemed very quiet now.

A little bit . . . lonely.

Her thoughts strayed to Wade, and she wondered—

Here, now! Enough of that, gal, she told herself. Wade
Morgan had made his choice, and as much as it had
hurt her, she was determined not to look back. She'd
made hers as well.

She took her lemonade and wandered out to the
front porch. She sat down on one end of the old
wooden swing, gave a little push, and stretched her
feet out, as much as the length of the slats would allow.
Her mother's roses along the walk to the gate were
already in bud. Before long, they would be blooming
yellow and pink. The yellows had always been her favorites, and not even Eduard's twisted behavior with
the flowers would ruin them for her.

A gentle wind rustled the oak tree at the end of the
porch and set a hanging basket of ivy to swinging. Bees
droned around the last few clusters of wisteria left on
the vines that climbed the arbor. A lizard sat on the
rail, blending with the weathered gray of the cedar
and waited for a bug to saunter by.

It was very peaceful.

Very quiet.

Too quiet.

Almost lonely.

No, not lonely. She was not lonely. She would not

think about Wade Morgan. Not about his sexy smile or his gorgeous gray-green eyes or his wonderful hands on her—

She would get a cat.

Or maybe a dog.

Maybe both.

Maybe two of each.

Thelma probably knew someone who had a kitten or a puppy that they wanted to sell or give away. Maybe that handsome new vet that Thelma kept gushing about all morning would know of a nice pet that needed a good home.

She would call him tomorrow.

A plume of dust coming up the road caught her attention, and she squinted into the sun, holding up her hand to shade her eyes as she tried to make out what was coming.

A car.

A big car. And obviously headed her way. Callers already?

As the big silver vehicle stopped outside the gate, Welcome stood, set her glass on the porch rail, and rearranged her T-shirt over the top of her jeans wondering—

Wade!

Her heart almost flew from her chest when he jumped from the passenger seat and strode up the walk with his hand around the neck of a champagne bottle.

Grinning from ear to ear, he took the steps two at a time and grabbed her in a hug that almost broke her ribs. "What are you doing here?" she asked when she found her breath. "I—I thought you were in California."

"Not hardly. I've been everywhere but there. I've been to Egypt and back again since I saw you last."

"But why?"

"It's a long story that I'll tell you later, but I wa looking for you."

"Why?"

He set the bottle of Dom Perignon on the porch rail beside her lemonade and pulled a box from hi pocket. "To give you this. I had a violin player booked in Cairo, but you were already gone. Meri didn't ca you, did she?"

Welcome shook her head.

"Good. I wanted to surprise you."

She smiled. "I'm surprised. What's in the box?"

He opened it. The most exquisite diamond that she had ever seen winked at her from its Tiffany box. He took the ring out and lifted her left hand. With eye filled to overflowing with love, he captured her gaze and said, "Welcome, somebody could probably say prettier words, but nobody could ever love you an more than I do. Will you marry me?"

Her throat tightened, and it was all she could man age to choke out his name. "I—I can't."

"Why the hell not? Don't you love me?"

She didn't know whether to laugh or to cry. "I trie to explain—"

"Oh, hell, I didn't tell you, did I? I'm not signing another contract with the Vulcans. I called Barney and told him that I was retiring. I told him to nix the TV stuff, too. From now on I'm gonna be just plain ole Wade Morgan, gentleman rancher. Welcome, love, i you'll marry me, I vow by all that is holy to stay alway by your side and be your protector. No harm shal come to you while I draw human breath. I swear."

Shocked by his words, her eyes widened, and she searched his face. "You know."

"I know. I had a dream on the way home from Cair the first time. Scared the bejesus out of me. I got of the plane in New York to go back to you." He pulled her close and kissed her gently. "I am so sorry, love, for what I did all those ages ago. So sorry. Blame it on my selfishness and my ignorance. Can you ever forgive me?"

"Of course."

"And will you marry me?"

She smiled. "I will."

He slipped the diamond on her finger. It was a perfect fit. "You like the ring?"

"I love it." She held out her hand. "Elegant but tasteful."

He grinned. "That's what I thought too." He lifted her chin and kissed her with every bit of the love that was in him. When they finally came up for air, he said, "Want some champagne?"

"I'd love some." She peered toward the car parked by the gate. "Is that Shark in the car?"

"Yeah. He didn't want to intrude."

"Tell him to come on in. There's a whole chocolate cake in the kitchen. It's a big house, I imagine that we can find a private spot."

By the time they emerged from Welcome's bedroom, the champagne was gone, the chocolate cake was mere crumbs, and a karmic slate was wiped clean.

Epilogue

Evening star, you bring all things which the bright dawn has scattered: you bring the sheep, you bring the goat, you bring the child back to its mother.

Sappho
c. 612

Athens, Texas, late January

"Olmstead, you idiot!" Wade yelled at the television set. "Did you see that? Shark, did you see that?"

"I saw. I'm going to the kitchen and get another piece of pie. Anybody want anything while I'm up?"

"Not me," Wade said.

"Me either," Welcome said, scooping a handful of popcorn from the bowl she balanced on her very large belly. They were watching the Vulcans and the Rams in the Super Bowl. The Vulcans were down by one touchdown. "What did Olmstead do that was so dumb?"

"He had a receiver wide open. Wide open. And he let himself get sacked."

"Does it bother you that you're not there to play in the big game today?" Welcome asked.

"Nope. Not a bit. I'm glad that Olmstead's injuries weren't as serious as first reported and that he's able to play for the Vulcans. And if my watching the game on TV disturbs you, all you have to do is say the word, and I'll turn it off."

"In the middle of the fourth quarter?" Welcome laughed.

"In a heartbeat." Wade hooked his arm around her neck and kissed her. "Scoring with you is a lot more fun." Patting her tummy, he said, "You and this daughter of mine mean everything to me."

"Are you disappointed that we're not having a boy first?"

"No way. Boy or girl, this child is very welcome."

"Nope, I'm Very Welcome. She's Kairos."

Wade laughed from pure joy. "That she is." He brushed his lips against Welcome's.

She stiffened and sucked in a sudden breath.

"Honey, what's wrong?"

"I think that I may have had a contraction."

"Ohmygod! I'll get the car. Shark!"

"Wait, wait, Wade. Not yet. I have to be sure. It may just be a gas bubble."

"Is this the first one you've felt?" Wade's hand was splayed across her tummy.

"No. I felt a couple of little twinges before the half and a couple more afterward, but I didn't think it was anything."

"Maybe I should call the doctor."

"Why you gonna call the doctor?" Shark asked as he walked back in with his pie.

"Welcome may be in labor."

"How far apart are the contractions?" Shark asked.

"We didn't time them," Wade said. "Honey, tell me when you feel the next one, and I'll time them."

"Noooow."

"Ohmygod. Darlin', did that hurt?"

"Just a little."

For the next half hour, nobody in the house paid any attention to the Super Bowl game except the cat who liked to watch the pictures move on the television screen.

Just about the time that the two-minute warning whistle blew, Shark went to get the car while Wade called the doctor. They were on their way to the hospital when the last score was made.

Wade didn't give a damn about the game or the Vulcans. In the end, he had won everything.

May the gods grant you all things which your heart desires, and may they give you a husband and a home and gracious concord, for there is nothing greater and better than this—when a husband and wife keep a household in oneness of mind, a great woe to their enemies and joy to their friends, and win high renown.

Homer
c. 700 B.C.

Dear Reader,

Greece is one of the most exciting places that I've ever visited. How grand it was to be able to look out a hotel window and see pictures from a history book come to life! How awesome it was to walk up the steps of the Acropolis or among the wild flowers at Delphi and think of all the generations of people who had walked those paths before. I wondered about those people and about how it would have been to have lived in the heyday of the classical period. Unfortunately, I discovered that for all their architectural and artistic genius, for all their philosophical acumen, the classic Greek masters were male chauvinist pigs who much preferred each other's company to that of lowly women. Fie!

Yet Greece has greater appeal than merely its rich history. An energy permeates the air there, and the later the evening grows, the more vibrant the energy becomes. I challenge anyone to walk through Plaka, choose a lively taverna, and not want to shout, "Opa!" and break a few plates.

The food is fantastic. Nowhere else in the world is grilled lamb or pistachio ice cream so delicious. And the Greek men! Be still, my heart! I've never seen so many gorgeous men per square foot in my life. The Greek men are charming hunks, but I found them still a bit too chauvinistic for my taste. So when Welcome's story began to take shape in my mind, I gave her an all-American hero—with a Greek past.

I hope you enjoyed this love story that spanned the ages as well as seeing some old friends from *Dream of Me*. I also hope that some of you, who occasionally feel as if your mates choose Sunday afternoon football over you, got a chuckle over the choice that Wade was forced to make.

Phidias, the sculptor mentioned in the story, was a real person and active in designing many of the structures which still stand on the Acropolis today. He was well known as the sculptor of a magnificent Zeus at Olympia and a masterpiece of Athena, but so far as I know, he didn't have a slave named Astrid who posed for the latter, nor one named Marco that he encouraged in the games. Those Greek games, the precursors of the Olympics, were very real, though, and in classical Greece the athletes and the fans were as avid as the Dallas Cowboys and their following are today. But *no women were allowed*—not even cheerleaders.

I drew information for *Angel Hours* from many sources, including some that are only available for distribution in Greece, but I found Zenfell's *Athens*, an Insight City Guide, and Frommer's *Athens* particularly helpful. Chapter quotations were courtesy of Bartlett's.

If you ever have an opportunity to visit Greece—go. Perhaps I'll see you there, and we'll have a drink at an outdoor café on Syntagma Square and speculate about living there in ages past, about knowing Plato or Phidias or a man like Marco.

Addio!

Jan Hudson